The Power of Clothing & Personal Packaging

CHANGE YOUR MIND, CHANGE YOUR CLOTHES, CHANGE YOUR LIFE

Dawn Thibodeaux

Every day that you wake up is a blessing; a new opportunity. It is,
literally, a new dawn. Today.
Your Brighter Future Begins Today!
DawnToday

TABLE OF CONTENTS

Note from the Author

For all of the women who have been overlooked, unheard, and pre-judged, I see you. I hear you. To those who are just over it - the whole clothing thing - you just want help. I see you, too. Please know that you, simply being you, is enough. You were created perfectly, and wonderfully, and your life has meaning and purpose. You are not a mistake. All of the experiences, both shared and those known to only you, are what makes you unique and you are deserving of THE VERY BEST.

Now, let's stack the odds in your favor and let the outside reflect the brilliance that's on the inside. How? By harnessing the transformative Power of Clothing. Did you know that you only have seven seconds to make a first impression? Yes, it's unfair, materialistic, and it's shallow - but it's true and it's scientifically proven.

As you read the words I've written here, you'll discover how to make your seven seconds count. And you'll finally get "let in" on the secret of how to leverage The Power Of Clothing to help you accomplish those business, career, and relationship dreams and goals and live the magnificent life that you really want and deserve!

So, get ready to be entertained and inspired—and if you apply what you learn, get ready for your life to change for the better.

Your fan and supporter,

Dawn

Summary

What you wear and the way you package yourself will either help or hurt your chances of getting what you want (and deserve) in your life. Whether that's in your career, your relationships, or your self-esteem, the impact can make a world of difference and have a life-changing impact.

In this book, you will discover the secret of how to harness the little-understood Power of Clothing™ (POC) and the Power of Personal Packaging (PPP) and learn to leverage the two critical pieces to create the life you want.

The book is written from the vantage point of Quinn, the Vice President of People and Culture (Human Resources) at a major wealth management firm in Chicago. You will come to understand who she is, where she is, and why she is the perfect person to share firsthand experiences about the lives of the characters in this book.

We start where it all ends, at the chic, upscale Bellemore restaurant in Chicago, IL.

Who could have known that within twenty-four months their lives would be permanently changed?

Preface

For as long as I can remember, I've had a passion for fashion and compassion for the underdog—the unseen and the unheard.

Now, after thirty-five years of helping women see their worth, helping them with their wardrobes, and accomplishing what seemed impossible, an idea hit me—and it appeared to come right out of thin air. But I know who the creator is. And I know that this was an idea that was divinely inspired by Him.

I decided I would write a book that weaved together my knowledge with the lessons I had learned through styling more than twenty thousand personal clients, who taught me just as much as I ever taught them.

It would also reveal the enlightening and invaluable experiences from watching my grandmother, Flossie-Irene, and her sister, my great-aunt Ceora, as they left to attend after-five events, to which they wore sequins and pearls, and hosted their own private soirees where every woman arrived with perfectly polished shoes, freshly styled hair, and a handbag that matched her shoes.

I saw firsthand what happens when a woman is fully empowered to be who she was meant to be. Although in their generation, and in their circles, many didn't make it to the boardroom, you would never have known this by looking at them. Why? Because of the way they packaged themselves. When they entered a room, people noticed and they wanted to hear what they had to say.

As I sat down and began to type, the names and descriptions of the lives of each character poured from my head and onto the screen of my laptop as if they were women who I had known all of my life.

Since they represented me, my grandmother, my great-aunt, and the thousands of women who I had worked with in person or online, I guess I *did* know them.

I knew their frustrations. I knew their insecurities. I knew about their lack of confidence which kept them from achieving and being seen.

Beautiful, strong, tenacious women who had failed in the past, but who had the courage to try again, and again, until they eventually succeeded.

If you love to learn, be entertained, and root for the underdog, this book is for you.

The culmination of decades of generational training, over twenty thousand clients styled both in person and online, and a divinely inspired idea come together to present to you, "The Power of Clothing and Personal Packaging."

Enjoy.

Beginning with the End in Mind

Seated at a table at what has come to be their favorite restaurant, Brandi, Charlotte, and Darby are here at Bellemore to celebrate their one-year anniversary as a team.

Who would have known that over the last twenty-four months their lives would be sent into a deep dive, and that getting off the roller-coaster before the next big drop would land them in a partnership so lucrative that they ended up on the cover of *American Business* magazine?

For any of this to make sense, I'll have to back up a bit. Let me tell you a little about the women who are arriving at Bellemore.

At five-foot-ten, Brandi is striking. Her long brown hair is styled just so, and after some changes on her end, she is now the epitome of classic and understated style.

Her clothes fit like they were custom-made, and each outfit indicates that quality is of the utmost importance. Her style says she means business, but she is also approachable, successful, and humble.

This hadn't always been the case. For far too long her clothes had told a different story—one that she wasn't aware of. She attributed the positive change to her new-found knowledge and exposure to the Power of Clothing and Personal Packaging.

Next to arrive are Charlotte and Darby. There is a similar sense of boldness when they enter a room. Whether any of these women are alone or in a group, they attract the attention of other patrons who wonder who they are and what they do. What people know without asking is that success is part of whatever it is.

As the three of them greet one another, the final partner of the firm, Dawn, enters with a warm and inviting smile. Exuding the same self-confidence and sense of purpose that she had helped each of them find, her style is a walking advertisement of everything she'd instilled in them. You see, just eighteen months before, they were all attendees at one of her group training sessions.

Everything that people see in Brandi, Charlotte, and Darby is apparent in Dawn. They aren't cookie cutters of one another, but there is something to be said for the resoluteness they share.

Tonight is special. They are celebrating the one-year anniversary of forming their company. As regulars at this decidedly sexy restaurant in downtown Chicago, they had come to know the staff well.

"Who could have known that you would all be business partners, colleagues, and friends? Does it still surprise you?" a member of the restaurant's team asked.

"Well, the way I remember it," Dawn chimed in, "is that after the three of you completed your time with me, you decided to have dinner here, at Bellemore, as a sort of celebration. I am often here at the end of a group session and it just so happened that I was here that night, too. The three of you spotted me, waved me over, and announced that you were starting a company!" Unanimous laughter erupted at the thought of how erratic this must have sounded by the way they presented it.

Would you like to avoid one of the common, but stealthy, clothing mistakes that could quietly ruin your life and destroy your career? Then meet Brandi...

Brandi

NAME: Brandi Michele St. James

DOB: 17 April 1985, Michigan, USA

EDUCATION: B.A. Accounting, Howard University; MBA - Accounting, Stanford University

HEIGHT: 5'10

WEIGHT: 180

ETHNICITY: Black

PARENTS: Darwin & Patricia Jackson

MARITAL STATUS: Married, SPOUSE: Jared St. James (14 years)

CHILDREN: Landon (M) Age 11, Harper (F) Age 7

It was a typical morning in the St. James household. Everything seemed familiar to them now after living in this house for thirteen months. They transferred here, to the Chicagoland area, after having lived on the east coast for three years. Before that, she and her husband, Jared, and their two school-aged children, Landon and Harper, had lived in Atlanta. This was where she and her husband settled after attending a Historically Black College where they'd met almost two decades before. Her husband's job promotion prompted the move east, and they had been excited to take on the challenge, even with young children.

But when an opportunity for a promotion was presented to Brandi, it meant a change not only for her, but for the entire family. The kids were settled in their schools, her husband liked his job, and they were comfortable with their large salaries, church groups, and community involvement.

Her acceptance of this job and new position would mean a dramatic increase in pay. It would also mean that the portfolio of high-profile clients at this powerhouse investment and venture capital firm would put her on the road to success and partnership in this industry.

Like many other wealth management companies, this one was referred to as "the firm." The term, in its purest form, simply describes a business that seeks to make a profit through the sale of goods and services, and this one was leading the pack! Its reputation preceded it, and being in the Chicagoland area meant that the family wouldn't sacrifice the unique blend of big city life and suburbia that they had come to love.

Making the potential move even more enticing, rumor had it that the firm was in talks to add a new partner. Gaining this spot would be a highlight of Brandi's career for more than one reason; she would become the first woman to hold this position and she would also be the first person of color on the partnership team. With all of this in mind while pondering the move, they decided to go for it and now they were settling in.

They had a beautiful new home that was double the size of the last one. It had an indoor basketball court that her son was thrilled about, an outdoor tennis court, and a state-of-the-art workout room with floor-to-ceiling mirrors and hardwood floors at one end that her daughter used regularly to practice dance. The kitchen had every modern convenience, and they found the cleaning service that came highly recommended to rival that of the one they had to leave behind.

Brandi's favorite room in the house was the custom closet just off the primary bedroom. It had been expertly crafted into a masterpiece. Due to scheduling conflicts, the closing procedures for the purchase of this home happened without the two parties ever meeting in person. Despite this, she was amazed that the previous owner had such similar taste and vision when it came to storing, displaying, and enjoying her wardrobe and accessories.

The California Closets company, or something very similar, had clearly been tasked with designing and installing built-in shelves in this closet that was the size of a small bedroom. There were places to display handbags and shoes, and lights had been installed to make them look as if each piece was in a boutique. A few minor tweaks may be needed down the road, but for the most part, it was like this closet had been built for her.

With Brandi's new schedule, her time would be in high demand with little downtime to speak of. She and her family were accustomed to a busy schedule, but this was going to require more hands on deck to keep the St. James' family ship moving. So, before moving to what was now their home, they secured a house manager/nanny to help with school pickups, driving the kids to their various lessons and practices, and oversight of all aspects needed to be sure that things would run smoothly.

They joined a church, enrolled the kids in school, transferred to a local chapter of Jack and Jill, and they filled in any gaps by connecting with their various sorority sisters and fraternity brothers. Adding to their already full plates, both of their companies hosted a variety of charitable events that kept them busy. She was grateful that her husband was able to make a lateral move without missing a beat.

This morning started out just like any other. As a partner-hopeful at the multi-billion-dollar firm that had moved her here, she was often one of the first to arrive at the office. Before leaving home, she got in a good workout and made time to see her children before she left for the day.

She vacillated between a forty-five-minute ride on the Peloton in the home gym or a thirty-minute workout with the Lululemon workout Mirror that she had installed in a spot just outside of the walk-in closet. She decided to go with the Mirror to save time.

Today was going to be interesting. The firm had been in a restless state of uncertainty while they waited for a response from the Security Exchange Commission (SEC). Recently, charges had been brought against them, and because they were a financial institution, the governing body was the SEC.

Members of the SEC team had been called in to investigate. Situations like this could be like a rabbit trail of searching, taking crazy dips and turns along the way, and this case did not disappoint.

After months of their digging and prodding, inquiring and fact-finding, the team would now learn what would be required to rectify any issues raised, and hopefully remain in business.

Large financial institutions are often a target of legal issues, so Brandi was familiar with the examination process, but this level of probing was a breed of its own and new to each member of this team. Getting the investigator's long-awaited findings, expectations, and next steps into their hands would bring a state of calm after the storm, even if the cumulation meant months of work ahead.

She knew that today called for a power outfit, and even though she always dressed as if she owned the place, today was different. As she continued her workout she was thinking through outfit possibilities. One of her new blouses came to mind, but she immediately frowned when she remembered the looks she had gotten when she wore a similar top. Just the other day, she walked by the clear plexiglass quad of cubicles where the executive administrative assistants often congregated. She was used to the attention they gave her, but this time she thought she heard a giggle. And was that snickering she had heard? They couldn't have been laughing *at* her. They wouldn't dare. She imagined that it was pure admiration of the designer-clad closet that she had curated over the years.

With the steady incline of her career and income came an increasingly large number of pieces to choose from. She had amassed quite a few sales associates (or "S. A.'s" as they are often referred to) as a result of her moving and now frequent travel for work. So, when she was presented with the latest and greatest in retail goods, her most common response was, "Yes!"

She had sales associates at every major department store in four major cities and a few out of the country so the Yeses came even more frequently these days.

There was no doubt in her mind that she was the best dressed in the office; the entire building for that matter! So, she just chalked up the smiles and laughter to admiration, fascination, and maybe even a little jealousy.

These were the stories that she made up in her mind, and unfortunately she couldn't shake the fact that this was happening more often.

But, there were far more important things to think about today. Unfortunately, she couldn't shake the fact that this was happening more often. Something had to be going on. She would have to deal with that later.

As she finished up her last set of squats, her daughter walked in and broke her away from her thoughts. "Good morning, Harper! Did you rest well? What's exciting about today for the smart, kind, and talented daughter of mine?"

She stopped to give her a hug, and as soon as she did, her daughter squealed, "Whoa! You're all sweaty, Mommy!" When Brandi laughed and leaned in for another hug, her daughter ran away, giggling down the hall.

Without missing a beat, Brandi was able to jump right back into her thoughts about what she would wear today. She finished her workout and walked over to her closet to pull the items together. She chose a classic black pencil skirt that fit, at least in her own mind, to a "T," but some would say it was at least half of a size too small. At five-foot-ten, she was built like a beautiful blend of Serena Williams and Beyoncé, with no shortage of beautiful and bountiful curves.

After grabbing the hanger with the skirt, she chose an AKRIS camisole and a floral Alexander McQueen blazer that for anyone else would have been reserved for date night. The red roses on the blazer would tie in with the red bottoms she removed from the shoe wall. The black Valentino tote was her bag of choice for the day, and she pulled it out of its protective felt bag before putting everything in the valet area of the closet. She hung the pieces on a pull-out rod and placed the shoes beneath them, put the bag on the tufted cushion, and then walked over to the built-in counter height island that was in the center of the room.

Pulling on the handle of one of the smooth-gliding, soft-close drawers in the island, she smiled as she thought of the previous owner; how this room had been designed by someone else but was so perfect for her.

She reached into the drawer and removed several Chanel necklaces. "Why wear one when you can wear three?!" she said out loud to no one but herself. She grabbed the rest of the jewelry: a statement ring, earrings, and her Chanel watch before moving to the other side of the island where she chose a pair of Dior sunglasses.

With everything ready, she headed to the shower, got ready, and then stopped to greet both of the kids and her husband in the breakfast room where they were enjoying a fresh and healthy breakfast. She grabbed her shot of wheatgrass juice, a prepared green juice, and a bottle of VOSS water from the glass-front beverage fridge while she asked her son, "What does my bright, confident, and talented son have on the agenda for today?" While he answered, she walked over to the built-in Sub-Zero refrigerator with doors that matched the cabinets, camouflaging its existence in the kitchen.

Pulling out her pre-made salad that the new vegan delivery service had dropped off, she added it to her pile and then placed everything in her Dagne Dover cooler and Empreinte Leather OnTheGo Louis Vuitton Tote. She made her way back over to the table where she kissed each of them goodbye between their bites of handcrafted granola, fruit, and yogurt before heading out of the door for the day.

She walked into the garage and placed all the bags on the passenger seat of her Porsche Cayenne. The shiny black finish of her turbo model glistened as she pulled out of the six-car garage. She settled into the Cohiba brown leather seats and left her Winnetka neighborhood as the sunshine filtered through the mature trees. She guided the car onto Interstate 94 toward downtown, exiting on Wacker Drive to face what was sure to be a metamorphic day.

Would you like to feel like you can take on the world and look amazing, no matter what life throws at you? Then meet Charlotte and walk with her as she uncovers old tapes that she has been subconsciously playing in the background of her mind. The messages were ruining her chances for a new life, but she's quickly learning that it doesn't have to stay that way.

Charlotte

NAME: Charlotte Elizabeth Whitlock

DOB: 12 May 1983, Dayton, Ohio, USA

EDUCATION: B.S. Political Science, Ohio State University; 2.75 years of J.D. Studies, University of Chicago

HEIGHT: 5'7"

WEIGHT: 135

ETHNICITY: White

PARENTS: Dale & Marjorie Hanson

MARITAL STATUS: Divorced (Former spouse—Charles Whitlock)

CHILDREN: Connor (11), Chandler (9), Clark (7)

Briskly walking into the kitchen with full stride and purpose, juggling the seasoned Coach briefcase in one hand while buttoning the last few buttons on her navy twin set with the other, Charlotte was met with a messy counter filled with field-trip permission slips, immunization update request forms, and book orders—all of which needed to be signed.

"You guys! Are you kidding me right now? I've told you, Mommy is starting a new job today and I can't be late. Why didn't you pull these out for me to sign on Friday afternoon when I asked you what papers you had for me?"

"We did. We gave you important stuff like the birthday party invitations. This was just the rest of it," her daughter, Chandler, replied.

Rolling her eyes and letting out an audible small groan, Charlotte gathered the papers together into a pile and started signing—frantically, without reading them. "Hurry, Connor, let's get going. Finish your cereal. Do you have your soccer cleats, Chandler?"

Walking toward the table in an attempt to help speed things along with clean-up, Charlotte saw her youngest, Clark, reach for a bagel. Her sixth sense, the one that all moms have, kicked in, and like a slow-motion sports playback, she could see what was about to happen.

Clark, oblivious as to how this scene was about to play out, had his arm just one inch too close to the container of juice. He pulled his first-grade-sized hand back toward him while grabbing the bagel, and SPLASH! The orange juice spilled across the table and splattered onto the floor. The kids jumped back and away from the table, started yelling, and chaos ensued. Charlotte grabbed the roll of paper towels and instructed all three children to put everything into the sink. A swipe with the paper towels and a quick pass over the chairs and the floor, and everyone headed out of the door. *I will have to deal with the sticky residue later*, she thought to herself.

Connor, her oldest, was now in the sixth grade and had announced he wanted to ride the school bus to the nearby junior high instead of riding with his mom and siblings. "No one gets dropped off by their mom, Mom!" She'd already agreed, so when they walked out of the door, Connor headed to the bus stop while the other two jumped into the family van.

"Buckle up!" Charlotte said as the automatic doors slid closed.

When they arrived at the school and the van was parked in the carpool drop-off line, the kids jumped out and everyone said goodbye. Charlotte noticed that a bit of juice had splattered onto her khaki skirt.

"Great. Just great! It's my first day and I am walking into a Fortune 500 company—that just happens to be one of the most prestigious firms in America—with a stain on my skirt."

She had no idea what the other people in the building looked like or what they would be wearing because her initial interview was held via Zoom during the height of the COVID-19 pandemic. When things began to open up and people started meeting in person again, she had a second interview, in person, but at a smaller, off-site location. Her first day on the job was going to be her first time at the firm's head-quarters.

After a twenty-minute drive, she approached the building that was located on one of the busiest streets in downtown Chicago. The van's navigation system instructed her to "Turn left," then "Make a sharp right into the ramp," before it finally announced, "You have arrived. Twenty-Four North Wacker Drive." She had received a visitor's passcode for the digital access box located outside of the parking garage. After she entered the code, the doors slowly folded open on both sides, and she drove down the slight incline into the underground parking garage.

As she entered, her palms began to sweat. She drove down the first aisle she came to and noticed that just ahead on her right was a black car that was stopped outside of a parking spot. She slowed down, and as she approached, she wondered why the car hadn't pulled into the spot. She surprised herself when she realized that she knew the brand name of the car. It was a black Porsche Cayenne, and from her vantage point, the spot seemed to be marked PRIVATE/PARTNER PARKING.

She wasn't really into cars, but she knew this one because Connor had mentioned it during one of the last times he had ridden to school with the family. They'd pulled into the carpool line and this same kind of car was parked in front of them.

Connor excitedly said, "Mom, look! That's Eric's nanny's new car! Isn't it cool? We should ditch the van and get one of those!" He went on and on about it while they were waiting for their turn to pull up to the drop-off spot and didn't relent until she acknowledged the "coolness" of the car. He was just as big of a car buff as his dad. Charlotte audibly acknowledged his excitement, giving no hint of the fact that in her mind, she was rolling her eyes with irritation at the reminder.

She watched this car sit just outside of the parking spot. The brake lights released and then it drove away to park in a nearby spot. She could see that the driver was a woman and that she must have changed her mind. *Hmmm. That's odd*, she thought. *I wonder what that was about? I wonder why that woman didn't park in her spot. She's obviously someone pretty important in that kind of car. I wonder who she is. I wonder what she's wearing…*

Her thoughts ran away until she caught herself a few seconds later and said out loud to herself, "Come on, Charlie, get it together! You've had three kids and made it through twelve years married to the biggest jerk this side of the Mississippi. You've got this! Stay focused. Don't get intimidated by the fancy car or the woman in it!"

She pulled into a spot near the elevator, and just as she put the van into park, she saw the woman from the black Porsche in her rearview mirror walking toward an elevator marked 'Private.'

"You have got to be kidding me!" she said out loud in her van. "How can she walk in those things?!" She recognized the shoes' red bottoms from an episode of *The Real Housewives* and the designer bags from her friend Astrid's collection in grad school. She had always admired Astrid and the way that she carried herself. Even as a student, she was always so put together.

I wonder who that woman IS, Charlotte thought. *A guest? The CEO? A partner? No, she didn't take the parking spot, so she's not a partner. Oh, well.* She shrugged her shoulders before returning to her futile attempts to get the stain out of her skirt until it was time to go in.

As she sat in her van, still fifteen minutes ahead of schedule because traffic had been on her side, she thought back to her first corporate job. She thought about buying and wearing the expensive Hugo Boss suit for the interview, which made her think of her frugal and conservative Lutheran mother's reaction to its price and how she had made it a point to make her feel ridiculous for spending that kind of money.

"What on Earth will people think?!" she'd said to Charlotte in a fluster.

Charlotte had looked at the suit in her closet when she was getting her clothes out for her first day. When she held it up, she was impressed that her years as a runner had kept her in shape, and even after three kids and a cheating spouse she could still fit in it, and she looked good! But she decided that she wouldn't wear it. Hearing the words of her mother playing in the back of her mind, she was convinced that she needed to choose a "responsible and mature" outfit. She had to make a good impression and let them know that she meant business, and she didn't want them to think that she thought too much of herself. She knew that she was overqualified for the position, but they didn't. She had removed some of her accomplishments from her resume and she didn't mention her internship at a similar firm, her J.D. coursework classes, or how far along she had gotten in her program studies.

She'd worn the sleeveless black funeral dress in her closet to her in-person interview and she'd paired it with a blazer, a pair of low-heeled pumps, and a pair of nylons. She had put the nylons on before saying out loud to herself, "Wait! No one wears nylons anymore... Ugh!" And then quickly removed them. Why was getting dressed such a chore?! "I have a closet full of clothes and nothing to wear!" And indeed, she did.

She had several sections in her walk-in closet: running clothes, athleisure, jeans and tees, and her old work clothes from twelve years ago that she pulled from on occasion, but she still always felt like she didn't have anything to wear when it was time to get ready to go someplace other than the carpool line, soccer practice, or piano lessons.

She decided on the navy twin set and a khaki skirt. Simple, clean, and classic. Unfortunately, now without the clean part, thanks to her kids and this morning's adventure in the kitchen.

And now it was time to enter the building.

Have you ever wished that you had the confidence and the power to become the best version of yourself? You know, the one who is only on your vision board at this point? Then meet Darby and follow along as she learns how her mindset has been holding her back without her even knowing it was happening. She discovers that there is so much more involved in making a change, and that it starts with something that she's overlooked for years.

Read on.

Darby

NAME: Darby-Skye Mishka Yadav

DOB: 17 April 1996, Patna, Bihar, India

EDUCATION: B.S. Biology, Minor – Finance, University of Chicago

HEIGHT: 5'4"

WEIGHT: 147

ETHNICITY: Indian

PARENTS: Darpan & Prisha Chopra

MARITAL STATUS: Single

CHILDREN: None

Hitting the snooze button for the third time, she dragged herself out of bed and hit the shower. There was no time to dry her long black hair, and quite frankly, she couldn't care less.

"Those girls are all so cliquey and clicky!" A term she started using after she watched the 2006 American comedy-drama film *The Devil Wears Prada* on Netflix. She had heard so much about the movie when it was first released, but her parents would never have okayed her seeing it at the time because she was barely a pre-teen, and she knew how the conversation would go.

In her parents' eyes, it was, "Junk TV!" her father would have said out loud, even though it was a movie. Darby rolled her eyes just thinking about it. Her mother would have said that her time would have been better spent on her religious studies or traditional rites of passage ceremonies. Her parents wanted to be sure that she stayed in touch with her culture and all its traditions. Knowing this was the case and that these were her parents' priorities, even as a child she'd learned that bringing up conversations like seeing a movie would lead to the land of nowhere, so she didn't bother.

When she graduated from college and had the time to binge-watch movies and television series, it was at the top of her list. She laughed every time the character Miranda Priestly, who was played by Meryl Streep, said without even a hint of a smile, "That's all," in her dismissive and unbothered tone. It reminded her of the no-nonsense approach to life that her parents shared. *They would love this!* she thought.

Despite her thoughts about the cliquey and clicky women she would soon see at the office, she continued to get ready for the day.

She prepared leftovers from the meal she enjoyed last night. She'd found an authentic Indian restaurant that was almost as good as her Nanu's (or "grandmother" in English). Placing her order in advance made it easy for her to pick it up before her FaceTime call with her long-distance boyfriend, Ashton, a medical student who was currently studying at Stanford.

Eating and catching up via FaceTime was their Sunday night ritual. It was their version of a date night and a way to stay connected while they were dating long distance. Last night's call started and ended later than usual, leaving Darby overly tired this morning.

Nevertheless, she packed what was left of the tikka masala, chana masala, and the small pieces of naan and placed each portion in a separate bento box along with reusable flatware. She filled her Hydro Flask with water, her Yeti with chai and oat milk, added a splash of cinnamon before closing it tightly, and then sat everything on the counter before heading back to her closet to find something to wear.

She pushed her saris a little to the right and smiled as she thought of her rite of passage ceremony. "I've got to remember to bring these dresses home with me the next time I head back to visit my parents. There just isn't room for these in the doll-sized closet of this shoebox apartment."

Touring the apartment for the first time after graduation, she was immediately won over by the original brick walls and strategically placed furniture that highlighted the features of the old building. The high ceilings and exposed beams were exactly the style of an apartment she always imagined that she would move into after graduation. She was so enamored that she didn't pay attention to the lack of storage space, not to mention the price.

It wasn't that there weren't other options. Her parents would have gladly welcomed her back home, but she wanted to stay in Chicago. There was never any shortage of people posting about wanting a roommate, and the idea of having another person to share the expenses with was great, but after all the shenanigans she watched her college roommate perform, she didn't dare risk it with another stranger.

That less-than-ideal experience combined with knowing that her parents' end goal was for her to practice medicine like they both did (which would mean going back to school right away) was all the fuel she needed to drive this independent move.

Even though she had majored in biology, she also got a minor in finance. Knowing that her parents' other goal was to follow tradition and have her marry into the family of her father's choosing, she did this as a way to action small steps toward her own goal.

At one point, she overheard a conversation. It was rumored that the family on her father's radar wasn't as progressive as some. They held tightly to tradition, which meant that while she may have the opportunity to work, the option and expectation would be to join their family business or she would be expected to stay home and raise a family.

While she loved her parents, her family, and her culture, there were some beliefs that she did not subscribe to, and having a father choose a husband for his daughter was one of them.

Having her own space to put her plans into action was on her agenda, so she chose this space, despite its flaws and space constraints, to call home.

With her parents as prime examples, she understood that people who had resources had options and could make meaningful changes that would impact the world. She also knew that being financially independent and successful in a different line of work would weigh heavily on her side when it came time to have the conversation about marriage with her parents.

So, when she learned about the mentorship program opening at the firm, she wanted in. It was her opportunity to make big changes in her finances, her personal life, her future, and the futures of other young women.

She wasn't sure what everyone did in the glass-enclosed offices on the executive-level floors of the building she worked in, but she was determined to find out. She had seen the spaces when she was interviewed, and again when she had to bring her Social Security card to the Human Resources/People and Culture Department on her first day. Today, she was going to be there again, so she had to choose her outfit wisely.

To be considered for placement in the mentorship program, she had submitted her resume and completed an online application. A notification had popped up that said she would also have to complete some sort of Personal Development Training. She found this new addition to the list of requirements a bit odd. She peeked at the name of the company hosting the training, and after visiting their website, she learned that the primary focus and signature talk was, "The Power of Clothing and Personal Packaging." "What in the world?" she said out loud, looked down at her clothes, and then second-guessed her outfit.

She had talked with Ashton, her boyfriend, about it on their call last night. "Can you believe this? I mean honestly, Ash, they barely even know that I'm there. It's like I'm invisible. Those women are like the girls in that movie I told you about."

"Oh, the one with Meryl Streep and Anne Hathaway?" he asked.

"Yes! The way these women dress, it's like they watched it and hope that the firm is going to get picked up for a sequel, a reality show, or a book!"

"I'm sure that you'll look great whatever you wear, babe. You're already in the company. You nailed your interview and landed that position right out of college. Whatever you've been wearing hasn't caused an issue, so what's the big deal now?"

"Well, from the brief bit I saw online about the company, it has everything to do with everything!" she said with exasperation.

The Reason

The C-Level floor was a sight to behold. It was light, bright, and full of glass. Nothing could be hidden. No secrets, no mistakes. Everything was available to be seen and on intentional display. So, it came as no surprise that something was amiss or had gone awry when the cluster of suits began to slam their hands on their thighs, rub their temples, and speak at a volume that echoed down the hall.

Although the words were indecipherable and the conversations were muffled, the consternation was clear. There was a problem, and heads were going to roll. The question was, whose heads, and how far were they going to go? As the day went on, it all became clear.

A complaint had been filed against the firm, which led to the investigation and subsequent discovery of additional legal issues, all of which had been hidden over the several decades they had been in business. If all of the terms of this first step toward compliance weren't met, the firm would be shut down immediately. Thousands of jobs would be lost, millions of customer accounts would be frozen, and billions of dollars would be due on-demand, not to mention the possibility of jail time, licenses revoked, and only God knew what else.

One of the conditions of remaining in business was that—effective immediately—all employees being considered for any kind of movement within the company would be required to attend (in person) and successfully complete a series of personal development courses. From the C-Suite to the mailroom, regardless of their position or title, and whether the move was to be horizontal or vertical, their attendance

DAWN THIBODEAUX

ɪnd proof of completion were mandatory.

Exacerbating the situation, the confines were tight as to who could facilitate the training.

The personal development training must be facilitated by an entity with no affiliation with the firm. No previous investments, no family connections, no past or present investments, counsel, ownership, partnership, or familial connections. No comrades, cohorts, or co-workers past or present would be approved.

Their host of attorneys shared that this was to appease the outcry from board members and shareholders who would likely be demanding some sort of immediate action.

The pressure was on Quinn, the VP of Human Resources/People and Culture Department to put these pieces together and develop a plan of action. She was now tasked with contracting a company to facilitate the training for its employees. In addition to the long list of prerequisites set in place, the company also had to have experience and exposure in development and working with people from a variety of backgrounds. Most importantly, the company had to have a proven track record of privacy and discretion.

Quinn was grateful to have kept the business cards she acquired at a recent industry event. It was a quarterly meeting where human resource professionals gathered to network, participate in informal training, and visit the booths of vendors who showcased up-and-coming tools and trends in the industry. It was her way of staying on top of the latest and the greatest while staying connected.

She remembered hearing about a company that specialized in coaching and personal development. She didn't recall the specifics, but her peer raved about how their employee satisfaction and retention had dramatically improved and that their return on investment soared beyond their projected numbers, so she took one of the cards when they were passed around. It wasn't unusual to have a few cards on hand from a recent event or connection when you attended one of these meetings. In fact, it was almost expected that you have something of value to share from time to time.

She hadn't had an opportunity to scan the growing pile of business cards into her computer and add them to her spreadsheet of resources. This low-level task was something that she had intended to delegate to an intern at a later date.

Glad that she had followed her instinct to hang onto this one, she shuffled through the large stack of cards to find it. Some cards had photos of buildings, while others had catchy slogans, but she remembered that this one stood out because it was a bit off-sized and it had "Tips and Tricks" as well as questions that piqued her interest like, "Do you know what message you are sending with the clothes you are wearing right now, and is it the message you intended to send? Find out more..." The card was like a wake-up call. On the backside, there was a photo of a woman, well dressed, and she looked so confident but happy and warm at the same time. "Found it!" Quinn said out loud even though no one was in her office at the time. DAWNTODAY, YOUR BRIGHTER FUTURE BEGINS TODAY. The tagline read, *Change your mind, Change your clothes, Change your life!*

There was a sticky note attached to the back of the card where she had written, *booking 12-18 months out.* She remembered writing it after a colleague mentioned that he had contacted them and this was the wait time to get a spot on their calendar. Now she was even more concerned, but decided to look into the company anyway.

Low on options, the urgency seemed to escalate by the hour. She looked at the website and decided that even with this short notice, it was worth a shot. She started an email inquiry and then decided that, because of the gravity, privacy, and time sensitivity of the situation, it warranted a phone call instead.

"Voice mail. Dang it!" she said out loud. She left a discrete and somewhat cryptic message and then decided that a break was in order, so she grabbed her bag and headed to lunch.

She started down the hall toward the elevators. Feeling the tension in the air, she heard what felt like a catcall from Mitch, the firm's CEO, "How are we coming on that contract, Quinny?!" Ugh! Why did this privileged man think that he had the right to call her by a nickname?! And why was he yelling at her like she was his child? He could be so unprofessional and entitled in his interactions, and no one said a word about it. He had only used this name for her on a few occasions and she intended to address it but hadn't and now, here it was again.

This kind of behavior was part of the problem that had gotten them into the hot water they were all now in. It was thanks to a few men who thought that their actions could continue to go unchecked, forever. They didn't realize that those days were ending, and fast!

Women were using their voices, demanding equal pay and a seat at the table, and the men who knew the value that women brought to the conversation were joining in solidarity. The backroom, under-the-table dealings that kept groups of people out of the conversation—and ultimately money-making investment opportunities—were now, for the first time in history, under scrutiny, and it could cost the company everything.

Quinn's back was to Mitch as he called out to her. She rolled her eyes and clenched her teeth before swinging around with a plastered smile, replying, "I'm on it!" And just like that, she pivoted and continued on her way.

When Quinn got back to her desk, she saw that she had a missed call.

"Dang!" Quinn said. "I missed them!" She listened to the voice mail and heard a kind and friendly voice on the other end.

"Hello, Quinn. I got your message and I can hear the sense of urgency in your voice. I'd love to see how I may be able to help. Give me a call when it's convenient for you. I'll be in meetings this afternoon, but I've alerted my assistant that you may be calling and that you will likely want to find a time for us to connect as soon as possible. Just let her know who you are and where you're calling from, and Piper will take care of everything."

Wonderful! Quinn thought as she let out an audible exhale.

She dialed back, and the assistant answered the phone right away. Quinn explained who she was and what the message had said for her to do. Piper put her on hold for a brief moment, then returned with two potential times within the next two days that they could meet with her in person and two options for meeting online.

Already impressed with the prompt reply, professionalism, and candor that was in play, Quinn was excited and decided to meet online.

Ordinarily, she would have preferred to meet in person, but somehow she already felt good about this. Maybe it was the pressure of having to move so quickly. Either way, she felt that meeting online would work, so they did.

During the video call, Quinn described the situation in as much detail as possible without crossing the line. Quinn continued and explained the need for the utmost sensitivity to the situation, privacy, and urgency, as well as the terms required by the board, shareholders, and executive team.

After sharing all the information directly with Dawn, and letting her know that they were aware of their standard booking time, she emphasized that the firm would exceed her current rates to compensate for any inconveniences, seen or unseen, because of this short notice. They scheduled a time to reconvene in forty-eight hours.

That evening, Quinn received a follow-up letter detailing what they had discussed and what DawnToday understood to be the task at hand.

At the close of their second meeting, which did in fact happen in just forty-eight hours, Quinn was hopeful.

When she had first spoken with Piper, she was told that they were booked twelve to eighteen months in advance, confirming what Quinn had on her Post-It note, but that she was sure that Dawn would be willing to speak with her.

After a few changes and additional requests, the two companies signed, and DawnToday was contracted to provide the required personal development training. This particular training was called The Power of Clothing (POC) and Personal Packaging (PPP), and the workshops would be presented to one hundred employees over the course of several weeks, one day per week.

Dawn and Piper made a point to share that the firm was not signed because of the amount they would be paying—which of course was substantial and got their attention. They were signed because they had been able to personally connect with their current contracted contacts. These companies were able to shift dates without consequence. They shared that ethics are important to them, and had these companies been unable to change their dates, they would have had to deny the firm's request, despite the considerable compensation.

The employees of the firm would be mixed in with individuals from other companies to give as much privacy and autonomy as possible. This was an attempt to keep onlookers—and the media—at bay. Reporters were already clamoring at the heels of anyone who was remotely connected to the firm for an inside scoop or a quote from a "source."

The employees who were being sent to the workshops would be told that they could expect to interact with business owners, hourly employees, and executives from a variety of companies for a unique and broad experience. The sessions would be conducted at the offices of DawnToday, just outside of downtown Chicago, not far from the firm.

Quinn reported back to her bosses and the other C-level execs that the sessions would begin in three weeks and explained the details. The team was pleased, but as usual, they had no idea of the feat she had just accomplished (or the fee they would be paying to do so on such short notice).

Quinn's added value went unnoticed again, but this time she took note. *Of course I got it done! I always do*, her thoughts began and then continued. *How would you all run this place without people like me?*

She walked back to her office and sat down in her chair with poise. Being on constant display in these glass-enclosed offices did have its drawbacks.

Knowing that people would be watching her every move to try to get a read as to what was going on behind the scenes, she spun the chair on its wheels away from her desk and faced the window. Her frame disappeared into the oversized leather chair that was made to accommodate someone twice her size. She liked the comfort she found when she sat here. It was like getting a big bear-hug. Not to mention, it made moments like these—when she wanted to hide her face and her reactions—possible. Now, she could privately flop into the back of the chair. She exhaled, surprised with herself that she had helped to jump this historic hurdle.

Despite all the twists, turns, and obstacles that were thrown her way, she had navigated this uncharted territory. Now, the firm was on a road to recovery, which meant that there was hope that she, and so many others, would have a job next quarter and beyond.

Letters were drafted to all the employees explaining in very broad brushstrokes what was to come, the importance of keeping this information in-house, and next steps. They did not share that the firm was on a sort of probation and under the scrutiny of the SEC, but rumors had already been leaked to local and national news outlets, so most employees were keenly aware.

The letter also explained that if they had applied for movement within the firm—which included any vertical moves, internships, understudies, or mentorship programs—they would receive an additional letter outlining a new policy.

Naturally, assumptions were made and conclusions drawn. It's simply what happens when change is presented and accompanied with limited information—the mind creates stories. People considered lots of possibilities, including worries that their applications had been voided or that there were now going to be fewer positions available.

Charlotte had been at the firm for a few months now, and even though she had not been in her current role for a year, she had been inspired to apply for a new position after listening to a podcast called DawnToday. She had heard some ladies talking about it in one of the company break rooms, and they were going on and on about how motivational it was and how much they enjoyed it. She took out her phone and typed the name into her notes app so that she wouldn't forget. She listened to it on the car ride home and was immediately hooked. Listening to this podcast became a sort of ritual, and she listened every morning on her way to work after dropping off her kids.

In the most recent episode, Dawn had shared that she had been encouraged by a series of comments by Cara Alwill like "...the only limitations women have are the ones we put on ourselves," and "Who says you have to pick a lane? Why? You can do more than one thing!"

Dawn referenced Cara a few times throughout the podcast and said that this woman's podcast and books had been the push that she needed to expand her company. The DawnToday podcast was just one of the pieces of her business that she had started as a result.

It was this kind of a ripple effect that Dawn often talked about, and now Charlotte was experiencing it firsthand. "You may think that when you throw a rock into the water that the ripples stop where you can see them, but the truth is that the impact goes on and on, far beyond what your eyes can see. It's the same with our interaction with others. There is an impact that lives on; some that you may never see." Cara encouraging Dawn caused her to take action, who in turn was now encouraging Charlotte. That was the ripple in action.

It was this courage that had pushed Charlotte to apply for a position that she saw posted while she was on her computer at work. She knew that she had the skill set, and with Dawn's (and Cara's) words in the back of her mind, she did something totally out of character. On a whim, she applied for the position. She now found herself eagerly awaiting the follow-up email that she and everyone else who had applied for an internal move was on the lookout to receive.

When Charlotte got her letter, she couldn't believe that the firm had actually contracted with DawnToday. Not only was she excited to have received the letter of invitation, but she was also stunned that the woman who had been in her van with her every morning recently was now connected with the firm.

Darby had applied to the firm's mentorship program several weeks before. She'd received a letter of acknowledgment but hadn't heard anything since then. She started to wonder if that meant that she hadn't made the cut. Now, she understood what the holdup had been, and she thought that maybe, just maybe, she was still in the running to become a participant in the program. She received her letter and couldn't wait to share the news with Ashton. She had been officially invited to attend this training. The invitation meant that she was a viable candidate for the mentorship program and that things were about to start changing.

Brandi, on the other hand, was irate at the fact that she was being required to participate in this off-site training even though she was one step away from becoming a partner.

For some reason, she assumed that she and the other executives were immune to this requirement. She had seen it happen time and again. The partners had a different set of rules. Nothing illegal, just different, and she was often privy to these "perks."

After her administrative assistant put the printed copy of the "Invitation to Attend" on her desk, she picked it up, thinking that it was a copy of what everyone had received. However, she noticed that this had been personalized for her, and she thought, *There's got to be some kind of mistake!*

Snatching the letter from her desk with one hand and pushing her leather chair forcefully away from her desk with the other, she stood and walked around her desk toward the door. Pulling the glass door open forcefully, she left her office and marched past her assistant's desk while simultaneously motioning in a way that said, "Follow me, now!"

Her assistant grabbed her iPad, and the two of them walked purposefully and expeditiously down the hall with their heels clicking against the marble floors the entire time until they reached Mitch's administrative assistant's desk. It wasn't an unusual sight to see an assistant walking feverishly behind their boss who was clearly on a mission, but the fervor and pace of these two caused heads to rise and eyes to leave their computer screens.

Brandi raised both corners of her mouth to form a fake smile as they approached but didn't pause to ask about availability as she continued toward Mitch's office. The two admins—hers and Mitch's—now standing side by side, met eyes with the knowing and universal eyebrow raise that meant, "Something's about to go down and it won't be pretty!" Their eyes widened with every click of Brandi's heels as she approached the acrylic door handle.

Seeing that Mitch was in his office alone was one perk of these all-glass offices. He was on the phone and saw Brandi approaching.

Brandi entered his office and started, "Mitch. A word."

"Yes, Brandi, of course," he said as he pressed the end call button on his cell phone. He had obviously told the person on the other end of the line that he needed to end the call when he saw Brandi and her assistant approaching. "What's going on now? Did you get a call from a reporter or one of the board members? Or, was it a follow-up call from an SEC investigator? That's all we need," he said with a concerned tone, running his fingers through his salt-and-pepper hair. Brandi was convinced that it was much heavier on the salt than the pepper these days—likely a result of the stress of the SEC situation. It happened to presidents all the time. They entered the office with just a touch of salt, enough to look mature and experienced, but by the time they left office four or eight years later you had to go on an expedition to find the pepper.

"No, Mitch. It's not any of that. What in the world is the meaning of this?!" she said while placing her personalized invitation on his desk. She slid it toward him, and he sat down, picked up the envelope, and read it. He flipped it over to see the other side and frowned as if he didn't have a clue. *Games! These guys and their constant, ridiculous games!* she thought. As she watched his performance, her eyes couldn't have rolled back in her head any further.

"There seems to be some sort of mistake. I'm being asked to attend this personal development situation, and that can't be right! How am I supposed to keep things running smoothly if I'm tied up with this, this, this WORKSHOP?!" Brandi blurted without apology, making her frustration impossible to ignore.

"The investigators from the SEC office said that this pertained to everyone from the CEO on down, Brandi."

"I'm not a manager, Mitch. I'm being considered for partner."

"Well, the guys and I felt that it would be best if you played along and went with the program. You know, to look like a team player. After all, everyone is watching and it's best that we don't seem to show any form of partiality. Don't worry about the accounts. I know that you women get emotional, but the guys and I are professionals, and we were doing this long before your time."

"EMOTIONAL?! BEFORE MY TIME?!" *Did he actually just say that?* she asked herself as she walked back to her office with even more fervor than she had just minutes before.

Blood boiling, Brandi knew that she couldn't "lose it," because all they needed was an inkling of emotion to use as an excuse to say that a woman couldn't handle this job as a partner. She knew this was unfair and unequal treatment.

Now, after all this time, they wanted to play by the rules? She was a rule-follower but knew without a doubt that she was being thrown in with everyone else. None of her male counterparts were being sent to this training. She was sure of it. It was a clear act of sexism. Again!

She knew that she had every right to address this latest comment, but with the partnership looming she was finding herself overlooking these types of comments more and more. She thought about going to discuss the issue with Quinn in human resources, but decided that in the long run, playing along with these games would pay off and she would be rewarded with her invitation and designation as a partner after years of hard work, sacrifice, and dedication. And she knew that like her, Quinn also had a full plate right now with everything going on, so she bit her tongue once again and did what she always did when she "took one for the team." She put on a smile and changed her attitude with the hopes that this wouldn't be as bad as she thought.

Quinn

NAME: Quinn Geraldine Chambers

DOB: October 20, 1971, Fort Wayne, Indiana

EDUCATION: B.A. Business Analytics & Information Management, Purdue University M.A. Organizational Leadership, University of Chicago

CURRENT EMPLOYER: The Firm

TITLE: VP of Human Resources/People & Culture

As the Vice President of Human Resources/People and Culture at the firm, I hold a unique vantage point. I am privy to what many are not. I am attending the sessions at DawnToday, not as an active participant but to represent the firm, circumvent any potential issues, and for on-site damage control. Though I am in the room, I will not be called upon to participate in group activities. For most, it will appear that I am a member of the DawnToday team since only the members of the executive team know who I am.

Follow along with me and I'll share what happens in the meetings!

—Quinn

Heading to the
First Meeting

QUINN

In addition to what you learned about me in my short bio, I was also going to be on site to make sure that there were no hiccups, slip-ups, or surprises, including reporters. While I trusted DawnToday, I had not had any prior interaction with the organization and certainly no firsthand experience as to how they conducted business or a situation as sensitive as this.

I was impressed with the interaction I'd had with DawnToday, to date, but with the firm being under such scrutiny right now I knew that I couldn't leave anything to chance. Given the circumstances, I was given a special pass to attend the registration and to visit any of the sessions, at will.

The team at DawnToday provided me with a schedule and included inside information about a few surprises, potentially sensitive topics, and a detailed explanation about why they facilitated and presented things in a particular sequence and style. It was all part of the contract I had received and reviewed on behalf of the firm. It was all new to me and like nothing I'd seen. I have to admit, I was intrigued.

At the time of the first meeting, things were already exceeding my expectations. When each participant entered the room, it was like every care they had was lifted from their shoulders and soon forgotten. There was a lightness in the air, and every sensory box was checked. The flower arrangements and balloon arches were pleasing to the eye, and the aroma was enchanting. The instrumental jazz music was upbeat, and all of the hosts were dressed to the nines in the company's signature color palette. Somehow, black and white on this team didn't make them look like waiters at a hotel ballroom event or members of a choir. It was classy, chic, and sophisticated; understated yet memorable at the same time.

The greeting committee was second to none. There wasn't a single person who walked through the doors and was left standing alone, wondering where to go or what the next step should be. In this welcoming environment, the participants were personally greeted and escorted alone or in a group no larger than three to one of the many high-top tables strategically and thoughtfully placed throughout the lobby for check-in.

This experience was already making an impression on everyone. The presentation eliminated that typically awkward configuration of a registration table. Take a trip down memory lane and you will likely find someone who can corroborate your experience signing in for camp, the first day of classes, or a local voting booth. The scene is the same across the board.

You approach a row of people seated at a folding table that is far too low and bend down to share your name with the person who may or may not make eye contact. They nervously scan an alphabetized list looking for the last name of someone who has a silent consonant! Heaven help you if you have a name like Tchopitoulas or Pterodactyl! You could hold up the line an extra five minutes while beads of sweat from embarrassment run down your back, the registrar's brow, or both.

In complete contrast to that kind of experience, these counter-height tables seemed to be custom-made with plenty of storage underneath. The tables had everything we needed, including hooks for our bags or coats so that we weren't standing uncomfortably with our hands full. With optional bar stools for seating while checking in, this felt more like an after-hours reception or an upscale brunch than a traditional conference "check-in-here" kind of line.

Gathered around a given table, participants were met with a warm hello. The greeter found each name on an iPad covered with a custom DawnToday case. Once that part of the check-in was completed, the greeter would then thank the individual(s) for coming and calmly walk away. Before leaving, the greeter introduced them to a check-in host who had approached at seemingly just the right time, undoubtedly after being alerted by the greeter.

The transition was seamless, and the greeter left to approach a new individual or group to repeat the process as the host took over. All of this was done without any sign of distraction or disinterest in the group that they were currently with. Nothing felt hurried or impetuous, and it wasn't long after this team member made her exit that our check-in host offered bottled water and began explaining the next steps. Everything was executed in a way that made us feel special for being there, and this was just the check-in!

The stylish people checking in the participants made them feel instantly seen and heard. There wasn't the predictable vibe of being herded like cattle through a convention hall line. There was something different about this event. Not to mention that anything that had our name on it only had our first initial. We had been told in an e-mail before the first meeting that check-in would be different and that our full names would not be used right away. The way they navigated this at check-in had been skillfully mastered and made it seamless for us, as participants.

Each participant received a name badge on a lanyard with a black or animal print strap (our choice, of course, which was made during the detailed onboarding previously completed online). There was also a small notebook that coordinated with the selected lanyard along with a 5x7 heavyweight postcard-style card with the word "Fuel" on the front. On the back was a description of the lunch we had also pre-selected during the online onboarding process. The nutritional facts, and instructions as to how lunch would be distributed were also printed on the back of the card.

In addition, participants also received an unexpected "swag bag" that contained a customized DawnToday pen in a faux leather pouch, an 8.5x11-inch discbound notebook with tabbed sections to be filled with meeting notes and handouts, a branded package of mints the size of a business card, and a small pack of blank business cards with formatted headings: Name, Phone, Email, and Social with a blank space to fill in each category. These cards were in a clear vellum pouch emblazoned with a small sentence that explained the contents and the words, "Just in case you forgot yours!" There was also a keepsake tin filled with clear Pereguina mints, and a custom Hydro Flask water bottle that had the tag line, "Your Brighter Future Begins Today!" on the back.

The bag was completed with a personal care kit. This 4x4x4 pouch contained a lint roller, safety pins, bobby pins, an extra-large hair binder, clear nail polish, a Tide To-Go pen, dental floss, Listerine Strips, and travel-sized containers of pain reliever, hand cream, aluminum-free deodorant, hair spray, and hand sanitizer.

Unlike most conference bags and paraphernalia, the contents were great but the bag itself was exceptional for a conference bag. It was a customized, heavyweight, black tote with wide faux-leather handles. "DawnToday" and the tagline, *Your Brighter Future Begins Today*, were monogrammed with black thread onto the black fabric in a way that was legible without looking like a word explosion.

At most events, the bag was made from paper, plastic, or a very thin fabric, and you had to hope the handles wouldn't break before you left for the day.

In addition to all the unwanted paraphernalia typically filling the bag like the extra handouts, sponsored advertisements, and the leftover bruised apple from lunch, there was likely a half bottle of water in the cheap plastic bottle you didn't finish because it made too much noise during the meeting. The cheap bags normally handed out at these events would break from the weight of all of this, and the contents would fall to the floor, leaving its owner to scramble while holding one handle.

Inevitably, these bags usually end up in the corner of a kitchen drawer or pantry, never to be touched until it's on the way to the local Goodwill or church basement sale.

Somehow, this branded bag wasn't bad. In fact, it was usable. Maybe it was the bag, maybe it was the contents. Perhaps it was the environment. Maybe it was all three. The contents were brand names that I recognized, and even Brandi had to admit when we spoke in passing the next day that she was impressed.

The soundtrack in the speakers was lively instead of the hum of convention center ceiling lights. Beverages were offered at Pinterest-worthy stations that would make even Barbara 'B' Smith, Martha Stewart, Gordon Ramsey, or Nadia Santini proud.

The conference room was filled with round tables set for ten, and the tables themselves were arranged in a circle. As we took our seats, we saw that tent cards had been placed in the center of the table with a smaller version of the same at each person's seat.

The instructions on the cards were to introduce ourselves to the person seated to our right without talking about where or what we did for work. Then, at the sound of the change of music, which we were told would be quite obvious and almost like musical chairs, we were supposed to learn something that we had in common with the person to our left, again without mentioning where or what we did for work. When the music changed for a second time, we were to begin working independently to complete the card. We would be guessing what we assumed the person on our right and on our left did for work. Just a simple guess. If we were daring, we could also guess where they lived, where they had gone to school, if they were single or married, what their hobbies were, etc. We were assured that we wouldn't be sharing these thoughts with anyone so we could let our imaginations run wild. Interesting.

This was already starting out differently than any other seminar that Charlotte had attended while she was in school or the one year she interned while she was studying for her J.D.

All the pomp and circumstance here reminded Darby of the lavish events that were common in her country of origin (India), but not often rivaled by any of the American events she had been exposed to. Her parents often had comments that were of shock and awe. "In a country so rich with resources and full of opportunity, it doesn't seem that showing it at events is a priority for Americans," they had said while attending American friends' weddings or receptions. They were impressed, however, with things like the Presidential Inauguration and Ball, White House State Dinners, most things involving international dignitaries, and a few of the reality television shows that they scrolled by while changing the channel. Those cast members, wardrobes, and homes seemed to have no shortage of ostentatious displays of opulence and creativity, and by that, they were impressed.

We heard the music soften and someone approached the center of the room, announcing that things would begin shortly and that we should wrap up our conversations in the next few minutes.

It was apparent by the smiles, body language, and comments I overheard that everyone was eager to see what would happen next. At this point, every expectation of what typically happened at a conference or a training seminar had been shattered like a crystal goblet falling to the floor.

Welcome

DAWN

"Hello! Thank you for joining us here at DawnToday, we are so glad to see you and we hope that you are feeling welcomed and ready to take on the next several weeks that we have together. I know that sometimes when an 'outsider' comes into an organization it can feel like somewhat of a disruption for some, a welcome break for others, and maybe a little bit of curiosity or even anxiety. This is just one of the reasons we think it is best that you attend these meetings outside of your regular day-to-day environment.

"My name is Dawn, and I am the founder of DawnToday. We are an organization that helps people understand the Power of Clothing and Personal Packaging, and by doing so you can have a brighter future, today!

"With every company that I work with, I dedicate time to understanding who has been recommended and referred to take part in the meetings. This set of circumstances for some of you is a bit outside of your wheelhouse, and you may be wondering why you're here. The background information from your People and Culture or Human Resource Departments has proven to be helpful, and the information you shared on the intake forms that you completed was invaluable. Thank you for completing them so that I can have a little bit of background about each of you; there's nothing like you speaking for and about yourself.

"Each of you has received the information about how we will be conducting things with regard to privacy and anonymity. As a reminder and for reinforcement's sake, please refrain from announcing, asking, probing, discussing, or sharing any titles or employers with those you interact with.

"We will be sure to let you know when it is the time to share these details. In our experience and for the purpose of these exercises, we believe it is best to hold this information back.

"Now, I am going to take a few minutes to share a little background with you. Our hope is that it will help you understand more about what we do here. While doing so, I will be weaving in concepts that you will come to know very well by the end of our time together."

QUINN

Dawn began by explaining that she had worked with and styled over 20,000 clients both in-person and online and had seen life-changing transformations happen right before her eyes.

As she continued to share, the words began to resonate with each of the participants in a different way. Her brown eyes were trusting, and somehow you felt as though she really did care about you, your success, and your goals.

She let us know there would be a broad-brush approach applied to some topics, while some would be discussed in greater detail. She explained that she did this to reinforce the information and to emphasize its importance. "I promise, I am not repeating myself unnecessarily and I believe that you will find the concepts interesting," she said before sharing more.

She began by talking about her journey into the field. "As a school-age child, I knew that I wanted a big life and I knew that I was destined for it. I remember seeing a late-night commercial that showed hungry children with big bellies. The commercial announcer was asking for donations of money, shared where to send it, and then showed the children again. It was then that I knew that I wanted to be someone with influence so that I could help people; but I wanted to bring the transformation personally. I did not want to send money into what seemed at the time to be oblivion, hoping that the recipient would get it. I wanted to be sure that it was getting into the hands of the people who needed it.

"Much later in life, I was consistently moved to tears while watching shows like *Extreme Home Makeover*, starring Ty Pennington. Anybody remember that show?" A few dozen hands raised around the room while smiling brightly.

She continued, "For those of you who are curious, this was before the days of Chip and Joanna Gaines' first show, *Fixer Upper*, also on HGTV. Ahh, now I see that I got more of you to connect." There was laughter across the room.

"I wanted to deliver this kind of transformational joy to people. This whole being-moved to-tears situation would also happen while watching short segments of *Oprah* or *The Ellen Show*. Seeing millions of dollars awarded to people from different walks of life for a variety of reasons would get me every time. I loved a good transformation moment and wanted to be on the giving end of these scenarios; bringing life-changing experiences to deserving people.

"I was moved in a similar manner when working with clients and I quickly learned that I was on to something. There was a change that happened when we found the right fit and style. When a client experienced this, something special happened. Their shoulders raised and straightened, they walked with a new pep in their step, they held their head higher, and sometimes tears would come to their eyes when they saw themselves in the mirror.

"As the number of people I worked with continued to grow and the results and reactions were so similar, I wondered what it was that caused that sparkle in their eyes when we found just the right piece. I knew that it was about more than just a shirt or a pair of jeans, the quality or type of fabric; more than a designer logo.

"It was around this time that I volunteered at a few organizations. At two of them, I helped women find clothing for upcoming job interviews or new positions that they had landed. At both organizations, the clothing the women had to choose from had all been donated and most of it was used. Please hear me loud and clear. There is nothing wrong with donations. But when you start digging into the back of your cabinet or closet for donations, be it for food or for clothing, it's likely that you are grabbing things that have no value to you.

"These are likely and most often clothes you no longer fit, and it's not because of weight loss or gain, but because someone decided to put that amazing cashmere turtleneck or dry clean only dress into the dryer, and now it is only good for a child's doll or the family dog!

"Why do we donate junk? Would you want it? Now, I'm not talking about extreme circumstances where an individual has no shoes or needs a warm coat. That is not the time to check the brand label. The issue at hand during times like these is safety—their life could be in danger without weather-appropriate clothing.

"On the contrary, what I am referring to is basic human decency; considering others to be equally as important as yourself. Have you ever stopped to think about how or why a person finds themselves in a situation that requires them to take on someone's unwanted goods out of necessity?

"It's trendy, good for the environment, and less expensive to go thrifting and hunting for vintage finds. Many people also choose thrifting as a way to do their part to fight against fast fashion, and to decrease the amount of clothing that ends up in landfills.

"But, when you find yourself falling between the emotional and economic cracks, and your confidence is decreasing by the day because of a lost job, medical bills that put you into a financial bind, or finding yourself upside down in a mortgage because the market took an unexpected turn, donated pieces may be the most viable option to acquire clothes or other necessities. Life happens, and when it does, sometimes it means we have to shift. For some, this also means they have to make a choice and change where they shop.

"Falling into the confidence gap or finding oneself in financial hardship shouldn't be a prescription for dirty, unwanted, discarded, and shrunken goods. To drive home the point, and you'll hear me say this more than once, I use an example of the way many people determine which cans of food they will donate by whether or not it is dented, dirty, or expired. I have been known to say repeatedly and with passion, 'Let's stop donating dusty, dented cans of pinto beans!'

"With these thoughts reeling in my mind while volunteering, I started thinking about all of the clients whom I wasn't able to serve because they didn't have the resources that my high-paying clients had. Some of the women at these organizations found themselves having to choose between a new white blouse or groceries for the week. They were hard-working and deserving, but they needed a hand. Not a handout, just a helping hand. They deserve more than someone's unwanted, stained, or broken hand-me-downs.

"So, I started this part of DawnToday, first. We operate a non-profit organization created to serve women who fall into the Confidence Gap, and/or who, as a working woman, find themselves in a socio-economic gap where they make just enough to be disqualified for outside financial support but don't have enough money to invest in themselves after their (and oftentimes their children's) basic needs have been met.

"Why that name? It's simple: Dawn = a new day, sunrise, brightness, a new beginning. Today = right now. Not later, not tomorrow, but today. It was simple, Dawn + Today = Your brighter future can begin today! The more I looked at the words and the definitions the more I saw the possibilities, and twelve years later, here we are.

"We have a consulting firm that educates people about the Power of Clothing and Personal Packaging through in-person seminars, like this, or through one of our online courses. We share free content on our YouTube channel and our podcast, so there really is something for anyone and everyone who wants to see a change in their life.

"Clearly, things have evolved, because we now have a non-profit and a for-profit side of the business, but it all started with a passion for helping people understand the Power of Clothing and Personal Packaging and how their lives, the lives of their children, communities, and their world could change and be brighter and full of hope, not tomorrow, but today.

"So often people are told it will be better tomorrow or just hold on; it gets better later but we want people to know that life can change now; today—DawnToday.

"How does all of this happen? We will break for lunch and answer that question, and more when we come back. But, before you go, take a quick look at this quote about personal packaging. Thank you for your time this morning, everyone. Enjoy your lunch!"

The lights dimmed briefly as screens silently lowered from the ceiling in different spots around the room. Some people opened their notebooks to copy the quote while others gathered their things to prepare to leave the room. After a few minutes, the lights were bright and we headed to lunch.

Lunch

QUINN

When it was time for lunch, tables were released by number. This was another effort to avoid the typical conference chaos. At those events, there was always a long line for the disappointingly dry sandwich with packets of mustard and mayo that never had quite enough inside, a bag of chips that was usually half-empty, and an apple—the kind you never seem to see at your local grocery store—that you had to question whether or not it had been washed, how long it had been around and where it had been before it landed in the box! Oh, and let's not forget the cookie wrapped in plastic wrap. Did someone get brownie points for covering all of the food groups; despite the condition or quality of the food?

But not at this event. Things were different here. We were released by table numbers. Three tables at a time to approached the clearly marked lines we stood in. These were meals we requested when we completed our paperwork online. When we checked in, the hosts reviewed our selections, confirmed any dietary restrictions, and asked if there were any necessary changes or modifications.

The lines that we approached were clearly marked: VEGAN (plants, seeds, and vegetables), VEGETARIAN (line-caught tuna sandwiches labeled, "Tasty, with a little visit from our friends from the sea"), GLUTEN-FREE (Mediterranean pasta salad with grain-free pasta), and CARNIVORE & MORE (which was a New York- Style Deli Club sandwich piled high with all of the fixings).

Although Brandi, Charlotte, and Darby were all seated at different tables, they ended up at the exact same spot in different lines, parallel to one another. Unaware of each other, they picked up their food and turned to leave the line while looking down at the beauty of the package they had just picked up. The distraction is what likely caused the collision and the potential for losing their respective meals.

"Oh, my goodness! I am so sorry!" Charlotte exclaimed to the other two women as they bumped into one another.

"No, it was just as much me. I am really hungry and I'm also curious to see what's inside!" Darby said.

Brandi nodded and agreed, holding up her box saying, "This is definitely not what I expected." They all smiled and after a minute of small talk agreed to grab a nearby table to join one another for lunch.

Their name tags had just their first initial. "Why do you think there is such a sense of mystery around our names and where we work? I'm Darby, by the way," she blurted out, clearly not concerned with following the rule about the sharing of names before the predetermined time. "What are your names?"

"My understanding is that it was to help us avoid drawing conclusions and making assumptions. It is supposed to help us take in all that Dawn is presenting in an unbiased way," Charlotte shared without divulging her name. "I guess there are some *higher-ups* from different companies who attend these large group sessions and they like to play their hand pretty close to their chest," Charlotte continued. "I get it. It would be pretty hard to have people who report to you watching you or trying to show off with the hopes of getting noticed. It really could convolute the whole purpose of being here." Charlotte shrugged her shoulders and looked down to open her box.

Trying to change the subject without them noticing, Brandi did just that and asked, "Which box did you choose? I am trying out a plant-based diet, so I got the vegan one." Darby noticed that the woman had avoided her question and Charlotte's statement faster than a squirrel running up a tree. She didn't say anything about it out loud, but it did seem a bit strange. Charlotte jumped in and answered her question, sharing that she had chosen the vegetarian box. Darby chimed in right behind her, holding up half of her sandwich, "It is the carnivore and more for me!" And they all laughed and enjoyed a short but shallow conversation over lunch.

"Well, it was nice meeting you both. I hope that you enjoy the rest of the sessions. I'm going to take a few minutes to check my messages before it's time to head back in. Have a nice day." Brandi stood up and said goodbye to Charlotte and Darby, completely unbothered about not knowing their names. She really couldn't have cared less. She was more concerned about how she may be able to still get out of this whole thing.

The other two ladies watched Brandi pick up a designer tote bag and walk away in a pair of sky-high heels with the red bottoms.

"She's got to be somebody!" Darby said quietly to Charlotte. "I get it, we aren't supposed to know so I didn't ask, but there's no way that woman is anybody's administrative assistant. I mean, did you see the clothes and the jewelry that woman was rocking? She's not fooling anybody. The average administrative assistant usually dresses kind of plain, you know what I mean? A lower-level position like that doesn't require all of the fancy stuff. No style is required. I mean, at least until a few levels up. You look like you understand. You're not dressed like that." *Foot-in-mouth!* Darby thought to herself.

Charlotte was a bit embarrassed that Darby had unknowingly described her current position as a low-level job. The fact that she didn't think much of what she was wearing stung a little—and she was surprised that it did. It made her glad to know that she had taken the steps to make a vertical move. Based on Darby's comments, she was clearly not the executive type and likely wouldn't be taken seriously for a position any higher based on what she was wearing. She knew that she had the qualifications, but apparently, she needed to float in and out of a room the way that woman just had.

It seemed like the entire room stopped mid-bite to watch when Brandi got up to leave. Heads turned and watched her walk away. "I mean, who dresses like that for a conference? She's not presenting, or is she? This isn't a cocktail party, for crying out loud! She really should dress more conservatively and stop trying to draw attention to herself." Then, she immediately sat stunned, thinking, *Wow! I sound just like my mom!*

These thoughts flashed through Charlotte's mind while she was still sitting, speechless, at the table with Darby.

Bathroom Scene

QUINN

A few minutes passed after Brandi's departure. Charlotte was no longer contemplating and assessing what she'd just experienced or ruminating about the woman's outfit and the attention she garnered. She was no longer thinking about the other young woman's comments or her own revelation of thinking like her own mother.

It was her turn to exchange pleasantries, excuse herself, and make her way to the ladies' room before the afternoon session.

Not unlike everything else she had encountered at this event, the powder room was a sight to behold. This was more of a lounge than your typical ladies' restroom. It was complete with a loveseat, chaise lounge, and a separate standing shower with a waterfall showerhead enclosed in glass and walls with oversized tiles. Plush white towels were in abundance, and all the necessary toiletries were available and beautifully displayed. Photos of stylish women were triple-matted, and the frames themselves had to be at least twenty-four inches on each side. They were stunning. Walking in was like stepping into a spa. Fresh scents, great lighting, motivating quotes, and a waterfall wall, again, engaged all of the senses. It was no wonder that Charlotte was able to get lost in her thoughts and lose track of time. She stood at the mirror after washing her hands, taking it all in.

CHARLOTTE

She was glad that these meetings were going to be once a week because it gave her another opportunity to meet people. It was refreshing to be outside of her suburban-mom circle. She did love the friendships that she'd made with the other moms in her neighborhood, her kids' schools, and all of the extracurricular activities the children participated in, not to mention the tennis club and volunteer organizations she was involved in herself. These were groups and people that she had spent the last ten years with. But being at the office, and now being introduced to this event, was different. This was stirring in her a part of who she was that she had silenced. She hadn't realized it had happened until this moment.

She was still a little shocked at how the judgmental thoughts and comments about the woman's outfit came so effortlessly to her mind. They sounded so much like her mother's. She shook her head in disbelief, trying to shake them off. It was like her mom's comments and opinions were no longer making visits but they decided to take up permanent residence in her mind. When had this happened?

She continued walking to the powder room to freshen up before the lunch break was over and the next session began. Despite the uninvited thoughts, she was really enjoying the conversations.

The excitement and motivation she got from her interactions at the registration table, during the group session, and over lunch reminded her of the intellectual stimulation and satisfaction she felt during her last year in attendance at law school when she was an intern. Back then, it seemed like the sky was the limit and everything was on track—until she met Charles. Her mind wandered and she recalled the path that brought her here...

She had worked hard and fast to complete her undergraduate degree early, and she did. She'd finished in three years and started law school right away. By twenty-two, she had an internship at a notable firm and was slated to be offered a position upon the completion of her last semester and successfully passing the two-day Illinois Bar Exam.

Day one would consist of three Illinois-drafted essay questions (thirty minutes each), one ninety-minute Multistate Performance Test (MPT), and six thirty-minute Multistate Essay Exam questions (MEE). Day two would be the Multistate Bar Exam (MBE) and a 200-question multiple choice exam. Knowing that this was in the not-too-distant future, she'd started studying in between her current classes.

While studying at the local coffee shop as she often did, she turned around after picking up her order from the barista's station. With her triple espresso in hand, she walked toward the table that she had set up. A copy of *Modern Constitutional Law*, *Strategies and Tactics for the MBE*, *The Multistate GOAT*, and *The Ultimate Guide to the MBE*, all in the most current editions sat stacked alongside her MacBook Air, iPad, and blue Hydro Flask. Her backpack and a hooded sweatshirt were draped over the seat back, and it was clear that she had every intention of being there for a long stretch of time.

"Ooh! Must be a long night ahead with a triple espresso in your hand this time of night," Charles said as she passed him on the way to her table. He had overheard her order announced by the barista. He was seated one table away but close enough to read her stack of books. She laughed and agreed that indeed it would be an intense few hours.

"I recognized the titles in your stack of books and I am convinced that you are a law student. I'm guessing, third-year? And from the location we're in, I'd also venture a guess that you're at the University of Chicago? How'd I do? Am I right?" he asked, and a conversation ensued.

Before Charlotte knew it, several marathon phone calls and quite a few dates had taken place, and now she was getting ready for another one. This time, she was going to brunch with Charles where she would meet his family for the first time. They hosted a monthly gathering at their home with family and friends, and without hesitation she agreed to join him.

At the time they met, they were both at the University of Chicago, but Charles was only there as a mentor. He'd finished his law degree a few years before and was fulfilling his company's "Do Good and Give Back" campaign. He'd already made partner, and each person on the team had committed to a number of pro bono hours in the community and the same number of student mentoring hours at their respective alma maters.

The more they talked, the more she learned about Charles. She was impressed that he was so driven and he had already completed the education and career track she was currently on. He shared how much he enjoyed his day-to-day and sometimes he would share the company's current caseload—not the specifics, but the kinds of cases and the energy and effort that was necessary to see them through.

Their conversations made studying more bearable. If anything, studying almost seemed a little easier because she was already able to see a glimmer of light at the end of the tunnel. She could see what life after school would be like, and it was exciting! The hours she spent as an intern were great, too, but hearing Charles talk was like a jolt of energy; a ray of sunshine on a cloudy day.

In all of their conversations, they never discussed much about his family, or hers for that matter. They spent hours discussing law and its endless iterations, its history, and its future, and she loved every minute of it. Finding someone who shared the same level of passion around the topic was an unexpected and welcomed gift.

Punctual as usual, another trait she loved, he picked her up for brunch in his vintage Porsche convertible. They drove the winding roads and she couldn't believe her eyes. She'd never heard of, let alone seen, this part of the state. The views were spectacular, and what you could see of the houses in the distance was breathtaking. Each one was tucked away in its own private oasis, and she instantly began to feel underdressed.

"Why didn't you tell me that you were rich?" she asked as the houses seemed to get larger and the neighborhoods more exclusive with every passing mile.

"I'm not rich. My parents are rich," he replied.

"That's exactly what rich people say!" she said as she rolled her eyes and grew increasingly more uncomfortable in her seat. She pulled down the visor to look in the mirror and check her now wind-blown hair. *Great!* she thought while doing her best to pull the pieces into place. *I'm going to meet what is likely the Kennedys and I look like I'm ready to coach a little league game on a hot summer day.*

The car slowed as they approached an iron gate and a uniformed security guard walked toward them. Once there, the guard smiled and said, "Nice to see you again, sir," obviously recognizing Charles and his extraordinary and unforgettable car. "Have a nice time!" he said, giving Charlotte a polite nod as he waved them through the gate.

The house seemed to be getting bigger by the minute. To say that it was huge would be an understatement. It was almost overwhelming. Set high on a hill overlooking the tree-lined roads, it looked like a house on the cover of *Coastal Living* magazine. It was an estate.

As they pulled into a parking spot on the wide, brick-paved road, she heard music playing in the distance and saw a crowd the size of a small church picnic.

"*This* is a casual Sunday brunch?! Who are you people?!" Charlotte said in her best impersonation of Sandra Bullock's character, Margaret. "How could you NOT bring this up with all of the times we have watched *The Proposal*?! Sandra asks Ryan Reynolds's character this EXACT question?!" Charles laughed as he got out of the car. He watched Charlotte take one last look in the small visor mirror and then back at him as he made his way to open her car door.

"You look great. Come on. I'll introduce you to everyone," he said with a huge smile.

"What have I gotten myself into?" Charlotte asked herself as she watched him make his way to her door.

As they walked on pavers across the yard toward the crowd, a beautiful woman with perfectly coiffed hair spotted them and excused herself from the conversation she was in. She set her glass down on a tray carried by a member of the attending waitstaff and gave him a polite smile. As she walked toward them, her smile grew wider with each step. Her perfect white teeth were rivaled only by her beautiful sun-kissed skin. Her exposed shoulders and legs were akin to the famously coined "J-Lo glow." She was sure that this woman with the long legs and amazing stature had to be a model. Charlotte imagined that this beautiful woman had to be at least five-foot-ten-inches tall. She seemed so excited to see Charles and she walked toward him with such confidence and purpose that it was clear that they had some sort of relationship.

"Is she a former girlfriend? Why was she here? What have I gotten myself into?" Charlotte said to no one but herself. She hoped that it had only been in her head, not her mouth!

Once the woman reached them, she hugged Charles tightly as he lifted her off her feet while Charlotte looked on.

"Well, it's about time! What took you so long?!" the woman asked as they broke their embrace. "And who is this?" she said looking at Charlotte with a smile and back again to Charles.

"Mia, meet Charlotte. Charlotte, this is my sister, Mia." Sister? Charlotte was instantly confused and she could feel her cheeks begin to flush. It was too late to hide her shock and surprise. Her ivory skin left no way to hide her feelings, and she could feel the heat in her cheeks and knew they were likely as red as a beet.

Mia's skin was a deep brown, and her smile was electric. Just as she was searching for words to hopefully cover for the face of confusion she was likely making, a man grabbed Charles from behind. An arm wrapped around his neck and the man spoke loud enough to make heads turn. "We thought you'd never get here, man! What's up!? Have you seen Dad yet? He's in a mood and I could sure use your help distracting him from the fact that my grades came in, and let's just say, he wasn't thrilled."

Watching and listening, Charlotte's eyes darted like she was watching a tennis match. She thought, *Did he just say, 'Dad'?*

She was taking it all in, mind swirling, and Charlotte was eager to hear this story later, but it was Mia who said, "You're being rude, you two. Clark, this is Charles' friend, Charlotte. Charlotte, this is our younger brother, Clark."

"Hey, Charlie! I'm Clark. Way to go, man, you brought a female Charlie to meet the family. It's just like you to do something corny like that." And he nudged Charles in the arm before extending a hand out to Charlotte. Perplexed, Charlotte looked at their faces and tried to act normal. Clark was full of energy. He didn't look old enough to be in a post graduate program but was he young enough to still be in high school? Her list of questions was growing, fast!

"Nice to meet you, Clark," Charlotte said. Clearly, she was curious, but she assumed that they were a blended family. Since she hadn't yet met their parents, she wasn't able to put the whole story together, but she was excited to get to know them. They seemed so genuine and downright fun.

"Okay, enough, Clark. You're going to give her a bad impression before she even meets Mom and Dad. He really isn't that bad," Charles explained. "Let's head that way, Charlotte. I want to introduce you to my parents." They started making their way through the crowd, stopping to say hi and introducing Charlotte to different people along the way.

The family seemed to continue to grow with every introduction. It was incredible. Charles' parents were wonderful people who had three biological children and then adopted three more—Charles, Mia, and Clark.

She learned that everyone called him Charlie, and that afternoon, after they had heard Clark say it, everyone (including Charlie's parents) called her Charlie, too!

George and Nina were delightful. George was a retired circuit court judge whose influence was apparent. Along with the standard well-paying job, he had also done well in both the stock market and in real estate. But it wasn't just the money, the opulence, or the wealth that drew Charlotte in; they were kind people. Her mother would be so surprised that a family like this, with "so much," as her mother would put it, was so down to Earth. Her mother believed that money changed people, that they thought too highly of themselves, and that they were unaware of the real world. This family was debunking every comment her mother had made with every minute that went by, and Charlotte couldn't be falling in love any faster.

As she reflected, the thought presented itself. If only she had known that marrying a judge's son who had access to so much would cause her so much grief. Charles had so many unresolved issues that at the time were unbeknownst to her. Had she known what was ahead, she would never have agreed to go to that brunch, to fall in love with his family, and to fall in love with him.

They were engaged quickly and they agreed that she would continue her last few classes, study for the bar, and then join Charles in practicing law. Ultimately, she hoped to join the firm as a partner. It all sounded so perfect.

Increasingly distracted with wedding plans, she wrapped up her internship, got married, and nine months later their first son, Max, was born. Life as she'd planned it, quickly changed.

Being here at the meeting with all of these accomplished people gave her a glimmer of hope that what she had once wanted to do wasn't gone forever. The thought that she could actually practice law seemed to come from nowhere; but everywhere. She hadn't had that thought in over a decade when she and Charles agreed that she wouldn't study to pass the bar after all, but that she would stay home to care for this new but unplanned child whom they both loved so dearly.

At that moment, when she had just been thinking about her law degree and how unexpectedly things had changed, someone entered the powder room and said hello, interrupting her thoughts.

She immediately stood from the couch, and it was like a splash of cold water had hit her face. *How long had I been sitting there?* she wondered. She didn't even remember sitting down. She stood, checked her watch, and then checked her face in the mirror before she exited the powder room. It was time for the next session to begin.

DARBY

Darby wondered what all the fuss was about. The woman with the "B" on her nametag was so fidgety at lunch when they started talking about "higher-ups" being present at these sessions. She knew that something was rumbling. There was more to Charlotte, certainly more to Brandi, and truth be told, more to her. What was it about this event that seemed to be shaking things up? Some people seemed to be a little edgy. Was it nerves or just a result of the unfamiliar territory?

She knew that for herself, seeing all of the beauty and level of detail brought her back to when she was a young girl. When it was time for a wedding, she and her cousins would hide behind the curtains that had been erected to separate the soon-to-be bride from the rest of the family. There were boxes of jewels, colorful saris, and stations for a makeup artist and hairstylist in preparation for the multi-day affair that would include many of the traditional ceremonial events.

Darby and her cousins giggled when the *haldi* ceremony would take place because they enjoyed seeing the soon-to-be bride and groom get the turmeric, oil, and water mixture rubbed on their faces. They anxiously waited for the surprises that came out of the *mehndi* party. This painting of the bride's hands and feet was always so intricate and unique. Sometimes, the initials would be woven somewhere within the painting, and they liked to try to find them while the bride was getting her hair and makeup done.

Like every family, there were some traditions that were modified and others that were untouched and followed to the letter of the law. For Darby's family, her name, for one, was clearly not a traditional Indian name, but her sister's bridal weekend was an example of the expected opulence and grandeur where no expense was spared.

For her sister's *baraat*—a time when the groom makes his way to the bride's family accompanied by his own—both families were beautifully dressed. The dancing, the colors, the music, and the food were all a part of just one of the many special ceremonies and parties that would be held over the next several days. Darby had always loved them all, but seeing the beauty on display at today's event was an instant reminder of the weddings. And *that* was a reminder that she was going to have to have a conversation with her parents about Ashton, her now longtime boyfriend who was studying at Stanford.

All of this was on her mind and she continued to reflect. Their relationship was unconventional at best, and complicated at most. Ashton was soon to be a fourth-generation physician whose parents planned to have him return home and take over the multi-million-dollar plastic surgery practice that had grown to be popular in the Bay Area. People flew in from all over the world to have work done by these gifted and talented hands.

Not unlike her own family, Ashton's parents wanted him to marry sooner rather than later. A respected Chinese woman from a notable family was the expected and anticipated choice, and they already had one in mind for their son. During a recent conversation, his mother said, "Ashton, there is someone we would like you to meet the next time you are home. She is beautiful and her family has ties to the mainland that date back to the Ming Dynasty. She is friends with one of those Netflix reality show stars. You know, like the show *Bling Dynasty*. We don't like the show, but anyway, your father and her father have already met several times. We are planning dinner as couples this week and I am looking forward to meeting her mother. I hear that she has impeccable taste and has raised their daughter with a discerning eye. She and I already have tea at The Four Seasons scheduled next week, and I am planning to invite her to join me at The Peninsula Hotel in Beverly Hills for my charity event."

The way his mother was going on and on, Ashton could hear the excitement in her voice, which was not just about meeting these people. What he detected was what she didn't say. He knew that his parents hoped that the two families would soon be joining to form one of the most influential "partnerships" the Asian community had seen in decades.

The problem was that he was not interested. Not even in the least. He was in love with Darby, and he just didn't know how to tell them. He had often wondered if maybe, just maybe, if he brought a girlfriend home to meet them, they would see that he was capable of finding his own wife. Now that he had met and fallen in love with Darby, there was an actual person to consider. He didn't want them to associate her with the demise of their dream, so he avoided them meeting like the plague. They knew he dated around but firmly believed that these relationships were of no consequence whatsoever. Surely, they thought, that once he graduated and he met a suitable, approved, and predetermined companion, all of it would come to an end.

When Ashton first told Darby about his parents and their plans for him, she couldn't help but laugh. His first response was to take immediate offense. "Are you kidding me? You're laughing? You're seriously laughing right now? What could you possibly find funny about any of this, Darby? Really? This is serious" he said between her few random moments of silence before she would burst into laughter again. As Darby worked to compose herself, her laughter made way for a few tears.

"This is unbelievable. Absolutely unbelievable," she said. "Of all the people, in all of the world, only WE would choose someone whose parents already have someone in mind for them to marry. I mean it's not like this is the twenty-first century or anything, or that we would be capable of finding the love of our life on our own. I mean, you wanted us to BE like Americans and to have every opportunity. You wanted us to pursue higher education and to become people with notable careers, to make the family proud. But there's nothing further from traditional American culture than an arranged marriage!" With her voice escalating with every phrase, she spewed the words out, barely making time to take a breath during her outburst. Watching her riff was like watching Olivia Pope of the television series *Scandal* light into a person with a long oration, her words piercing to the depths of their being.

"Whoa! Whoa! Whoa! What?!" Ashton said with his voice now equally intense. "Are you telling me that YOUR parents have already got you hitched in the back of their minds, too?! That they have plans for you to marry someone that they have chosen?" His face planted into both palms of his hands, elbows on his knees. "Now it's my turn to cry," he said.

Darby was walking back into the next session in a mood that was a bit more serene. Remembering all of this now wasn't exactly the best timing, but being here was a result of her wanting to be accepted into the mentorship program, to climb the proverbial ladder... That was the fastest known track to getting into the inner circle—and getting into the inner circle is how she would fast-track her way to the top. She knew that if she was going to have any hope of winning her parents' approval about her wanting a career as an investment banker, future hedge fund partner, and a relationship with her non-Indian boyfriend, she needed to come to the conversation with the decks stacked in her favor.

Since attending this event was now a requirement of her application to even be considered for the mentorship program, she was determined to make the most of it, and that included finding out who the "B" lady was and why she had been so anxious to break away.

BRANDI

"I'm not so sure that this is such a good idea," Brandi explained as she walked and talked quietly on her phone to Quinn even though she was there at the event and in the building with them. She couldn't risk them being seen talking in person because someone may put the pieces together, so she made the call. "Someone is bound to find out who I am and what my position is in the company. Tell me again WHY it is necessary for ME to attend this series of meetings."

"First, let me ask you this," Quinn responded quietly. "Are you not impressed, in the least? I mean, everything is top-notch, no expense has been spared. The invoice for this whole training is enough to pay for a year of college tuition at an Ivy League school, and from the reviews I read and the first session we have just been through, I'm even more convinced that we're going to see positive results, and it's just day one!"

"I do have to admit that I am impressed, yes. They haven't missed a detail, and I understand that we—well I mean the firm—paid a pretty penny for all of this detail. It's just that having to be here with the other employees is a bit uncomfortable, and this whole 'don't let them know who you are game' that they are playing seems a bit juvenile. I know that as a firm we have to keep a low profile, and this DawnToday group has explained why they are keeping the names and titles in the background instead of the typical 'in your face' approach, but the combination of the two is a bit much!"

"Your position isn't a secret," Quinn said. "In our initial meetings with their team, Dawn explained the rationale. It's part of their process to have titles and positions remain anonymous. I'm sure that it doesn't last all six weeks."

"Well, there is a young woman here whose curiosity rivals that of a dog with a bone. She doesn't want to let up and she already started with an inquisition over lunch," Brandi said with a sharp tone before pushing the red *End* button on her phone, signaling that the conversation was over. Quinn didn't bother to mention that a quick search on Google or LinkedIn would link her to the firm. *Oh well*, she thought, while rolling her eyes.

Brandi placed the phone in the slip pocket of her black Chanel GST and headed toward the powder room. When she saw Darby leaving, she made a quick spin to the right to avoid being seen. Success! She made her way back to the meeting room and found a quiet corner where she again opened her phone if only to appear busy and avoid the possibility of being approached. She kept her head down and didn't make eye contact with anyone. But even though her head was down she could sense the enthusiasm of the people in the room. There were people from the mailroom who had applied for new positions, applicants for administrative, management, and even senior management positions were here too, and she remembered how eager and excited she had been years ago when she was like them; bright-eyed, and full of hope.

Her personality and smile were infectious, and she had always been a hard worker. When she first started out in her career, she was determined to remove every possible obstacle to what she considered to be a success, including her appearance. She couldn't change the color of her beautiful caramel skin, nor did she want to, but the comments and the oversights because of her race along with her appearance at the time were things that she knew that she would have to overcome.

She started by getting Invisalign when she was in grad school. It was her first job with benefits since her other jobs had always been part-time. Her family hadn't had the best insurance growing up, and sometimes they didn't have it at all, which meant that getting braces wasn't part of the conversation, ever.

When she landed her first job after grad school, the benefits were even better so she tackled her weight. She was never labeled obese by her doctor, but being part of a family with a history of diabetes along with being blessed with curves, and a larger frame and bone structure overall, meant that she had to gain control over her yearly weight gain or it would soon control her. She enrolled in every fitness class that she could find and tried aerobics, Pilates, barre and HIIT classes before hiring a personal trainer. She found cycling and running to be her favorites, but she also loved a good yoga class. Now that her life was so full, she had a Peloton and the Mirror by Lululemon in her home gym to save time and to afford her the privacy of working out at home. This arrangement also allowed her to spend more time with her kids while giving her the opportunity to work out before she even left for the office.

She had reached her ideal weight years ago, and it was about this time that she received her first bonus check. While at the mall, she connected with a sales associate at one of the major upscale department stores. The woman brought a few designer pieces into the dressing room. Brandi loved the quality and the feel of the clothes, but even more so, she enjoyed the individualized attention she was getting. She also noticed that other people seemed to be paying attention to what she was trying on. She heard voices outside of the fitting room door making comments like, "Who is trying on the new Gucci cardigan?" or "Is she trying on that new Veronica Beard ensemble?" And just like that, she was "seen" and she felt important.

No stranger to a client who had recently come into money, the sales associate kindly guided this naïve young woman and consulted with her about the latest and greatest. The other customers in the fitting room area looked on, curiously, when they passed by. There were sales associates gathered around Brandi when she left the dressing room to look in the large three-way mirror, and all these reactions were all that Brandi needed to see. She was sold. "I'll take it all!" she said, and things grew from there.

She remembered what it had felt like to be overlooked in her younger years and how she never really knew what the right thing was to wear. Even if she did know, she didn't have the money to do anything about it. So, that very first time with the sales associate was the beginning of the "New Brandi," as she referred to herself. Not having these things had never stopped her from going after what she wanted. In fact, it made her work even harder. But now that she had the wherewithal to buy what she wanted, she was on a mission to show the world what all of her hard work had produced. She was going to *make* them notice her!

Being here at this meeting, seeing and overhearing these people, reminded her that it hadn't always been about trying to climb a ladder or get a seat at the table. At one point, she had just wanted to help people. She wanted to learn the business to help people change their lives and their financial future.

Investment banking and hedge funds were never a part of her family's conversations, and she knew that she wasn't alone in this. There were lots of families unaware of this path to wealth-building. When she learned about it in school, her interest was piqued and she chose to follow this path. Her original intent was to enter this world of high finance to be in a position to improve her own financial situation. The more she learned, the more she wanted to bring this information to communities—specifically women—to give them the tools to be financially independent. She wanted women and families who lacked exposure to learn about this seemingly hidden opportunity. *When had things changed?* she wondered.

For some reason, being here was shining an LED light in some areas and it took her by surprise. In all of her efforts to "make it," she had lost her focus. She became self-centered and started enjoying the looks and the attention. There were perks to having a personal sales associate at so many major department stores across the country. She was privy to limited editions, hard-to-find pieces, and things that were coveted by other fashion-lovers or collectors. Thanks to the travel that she did regularly for her job, she was starting to create a list of associates in other parts of the world too. She could buy all of the designer pieces that she had never been able to buy as a teenager or college student, and she wanted the world to see that Brandi was on the scene.

Everyone stared when she entered a room. She was the "it" girl now and she let everyone know it. She wore designer clothes from head to toe, even on casual days when she accompanied her children to a sporting event or on a family trip. She was always dripping in logos, and she felt great about every single one. She'd moved on from Tiffany & Co to Cartier and had her sights set on Van Cleef & Arpels. The Coach store had been her first stop in college, before moving on to Gucci and then Louis Vuitton, but now Chanel was on regular rotation, and she even attended Fashion Week in Paris with personalized VIP status. Her current list of handbags to acquire included both the coveted Hermes Birkin and Kelly, each with a price tag that started at $20,000 and went up from there. The idea of buying from the pre-loved market wasn't something she would entertain. She wanted the whole experience and that included purchasing in-store. She planned to add them to her collection and had no intention of stopping there. On occasion, she would throw in a piece from Zara or even Amazon, but she wouldn't wear those pieces without an Alexander McQueen piece or something similar to keep that high-end vibe.

Somehow, being here, mingling with the people who were right where she had been—hardworking and on the rise, attending this session—awakened something in her that she hadn't been in touch with in what seemed like forever.

It wasn't bad to focus on herself or to buy what made her happy, but somewhere along the way, she stopped caring about people, and that was a problem.

With an interest that she hadn't anticipated, she was looking forward to the afternoon session. She locked her phone and put it back in her bag before standing up. Adjusting her skirt before taking her first step, she made her way toward the meeting room for the next session.

Afternoon Session

DAWN

"Welcome back! I hope you enjoyed your lunch and had a nice break. I want to be sure we stay on track, so I am going to jump right in and explain our first exercise.

"We are going to learn more about your awareness of the Power of Clothing and Personal Packaging. We will work in small groups and what I am asking you to share is:

- What is your current perception of the Power of Clothing and Personal Packaging?
- When you heard that your company was enrolling you in a personal development program, what was your first reaction?
- Now that you have heard me share why I created DawnToday, what is your first reaction? What do you think we do, or how do you think we go about implementing the principles shared?

"You will find a reminder of the questions on the screens in front of and behind you."

With that, screens lowered from the ceiling and the questions were easily seen from wherever you were seated. With this setup, there was no need to move your chair to the left or right for a better view. Those who were five-foot-two could easily see around the six-foot-two person who would have otherwise blocked their view. Once again, every detail had been carefully considered.

"Now, let's get started!"

Each table completed the exercise, and it was interesting for the participants to hear the answers that were shared. When the time was called, Dawn began speaking again.

"Thank you for completing that first group activity. Oftentimes, people in a session have similar answers, but I'm always excited when I hear something unique and different, and you have provided that for me today. So, thank you for your candor. I appreciate your willingness to share and I look forward to getting started.

"Despite having just heard some of your answers to the questions— and some were amazing, by the way—I'm going to assume that you haven't investigated the topics of the Power of Clothing and Personal Packaging, and so I'll start from the beginning.

"From a dictionary standpoint, we know how the words 'power,' 'clothing,' and 'packaging' are defined, but I want to bring that into the context of what it is my team and I do. To achieve this, I am going to do what you just did. I am going to share a bit more about me and my first two encounters with the Power of Clothing and Personal Packaging. At the time, I did not have a name for it, but after hearing this, I am confident you will have a deeper understanding.

"I attended an all-girls Catholic high school that required us to wear a uniform. This would be the first time since first grade I would not be able to choose what I wanted to wear every day.

"I remember getting ready for the school year. I always went shopping for back-to-school clothes with my mom, but this year we were headed to the uniform store instead of the department store. When we arrived at the small, one-room store, we told the salesperson the name of the school and they directed us as to where to find the assigned uniform and any approved accessories.

"As we walked by the different rounders of hanging items like dresses, jumpers, and skirts, I saw different color combinations and fun socks with logos. There were lots of greens, yellows, and blues in different hues. Then, we got to the section for my school.

"I had visited the school, but for some reason I had forgotten the colors the girls were wearing. Or maybe I just overlooked it. There's a lot to take in as a visitor, but how had I missed what they were wearing?! Of all the colors in the rainbow and beyond, someone chose *this* color combination for girls to wear? It wasn't just ugly, it was ridiculously ugly. No school uniform is haute couture, nor is it intended to be. I get it. The purpose of the uniform is to keep the students focused on education, and to remove any bias, privilege, or other distractions while reducing peer pressure and bullying. This is done by placing students on the same level. Wearing uniforms enhances school pride, unity, and community spirit—or so I heard.

"For some schools, you might get navy blue pants or a skirt, and maybe even shorts with a choice of shirts and sweaters to pair them with. But the school I was headed to had chosen brown! Brown? For teenage girls? Clearly the emphasis was to downplay the importance of fashion! Ugh!

"As a clothes-loving teenage girl in the 80s, brown was not my go-to color of choice for clothing. The trend of wearing neutrals head-to-toe was not what it is today. The monochromatic neutral tones were not 'on trend' then the way they are at the time of this meeting.

"Even if the current trend was at play back then, the skirt was not just brown, it was plaid. The brown was *complemented* by another shade of brown that could be mistaken for grey or some un-named shade. These colors were accented with a few squares of white. Oh, and to add a little pizazz (are you picking up on my sarcasm here?) we had a stripe of yellow as a highlight! Pretty racy for a uniform (more sarcasm on my part, of course)!

"It was awful. I would be attending a new school, which for me wasn't a big deal because we were all starting at a new school as freshmen, and I enjoy meeting new people. But this uniform? This was a problem! I promise you, pride, unity, and school spirit were the furthest things from my mind, so I had to come up with a plan.

"At the end of the first day of school, I took it upon myself to eliminate any possible lifelong scars of being seen outside the walls of this place in this ridiculous outfit. I went to the school office and called my grandmother because my mom was at work. She didn't live far from us, and we were all within ten miles of the school. I asked her, with full sincerity, to meet me one block from school to give me a ride home because I just couldn't be seen walking home or riding the bus in this skirt. What if someone, anyone, saw me?!

"I can only imagine the laughs the adults must have had when they discussed this. In fact, I have since confirmed the details with my mother, who still laughs about it to this day.

"Now remember, this is freshman year of high school that I am talking about which means that I am the wise age of fourteen at the time, and I have devised a plan to hide from *whom*?! Whom was I hiding from? Everyone else my age was in school. My school dismissed thirty minutes before the other schools in the area, which would have been plenty of time to make it home, unseen. However, in my mind this was a necessary, covert operation that needed to be handled with great sensitivity and care, and I needed my grandmother's help to pull this off.

"My plan included her dropping me off at my house—in the back, of course. This meant I would be changed by the time everyone else in the neighborhood got home. Don't laugh too hard! I'm sure that you've got your own teenage-wisdom stories to share!

"I've always been a confident person and I've been interested in clothing as far back as I can remember, but the idea of being seen in this was just more than I had the words to articulate. Are you feeling my pain, yet? I couldn't do it. I just couldn't bear to be seen in the neighborhood in this thing.

"Looking back, no one was looking at or for me. Not only were they not looking, they were at school navigating their own teenage drama and likely too absorbed in what they thought people were thinking about them.

"That's easy to say as an adult, and especially as one who understands the power that clothes yield, but in the mind of a fourteen-year-old who loved clothes and fashion, the entire planet was going to be looking at me in this plaid skirt!

"Thankfully, I worked through my drama and found ways to make the skirt unique by pushing the envelope as far as I could. I found different versions of the tops we were allowed to wear or the shoes or accessories I chose. By the end of the semester, I'd settled into this new situation, and all was right with the world.

"Fast-forward twenty years, and I am one of many facilitators at a large women's group. It wasn't uncommon to have one hundred and fifty to two hundred in attendance. At the end of every quarter, all the leaders would present with their group's participants or with other leaders.

"For the year I am sharing the details about, all of the leaders were placed into small groups of six. Each group drew a piece of paper from a box and each paper had a different word, title, or phrase on it. Our *assignment* was to dress and perform a small skit that represented what was on the paper, and the large group would then have to guess what word we'd chosen. It was a version of charades, and in just a few weeks we would present our skit to the large group of women.

"Our group did not pull the name or title of someone or something amazing and fabulous. Nope. Not this time. What did we draw from the pile? We picked the word 'nerds'!

"So, what do I get to wear? You guessed it! It was back to the plaid skirt for me! I didn't have my school uniform on hand, but I did find one at a local thrift shop. First off, I'm always game for dressing up, but I refused to buy another new brown plaid skirt or to even borrow one from a former classmate. Did I mention that I, and many of my classmates, didn't wear brown for YEARS after high school? Literally. I'm talking decades here. After four years of brown and tan, it's enough to make you run for the brightest thing you can find. So, for this event, I bought a plaid skirt, but this time I got it in red!

"The skirt fell just beneath my knees. It was a traditional, tartan plaid and it wasn't bad. You've likely seen one, whether or not you recognize that description. The pattern is often popular at

Christmastime. I am not against plaid. In fact, J.Crew, The Gap, Eddie Bauer, Talbots, Tommy Hilfiger, and Ralph Lauren have all done a classic plaid that works.

"On the day of the event, I put the skirt on with a white button-front blouse, which I wore buttoned all the way to the top. With my neck asking for mercy because of the tightness of the shirt, I paired it with a black cardigan, which I also wore buttoned. I had on white, knee-high socks and loafers. I styled my hair into two braided ponytails that hung in front of my shoulders and then added a pair of black prescription eyeglasses I still had on hand. To add a finishing touch, I wrapped a piece of masking tape around the bridge of the glasses as if they were broken and needed to be held together. Are you getting the visual here? I've got the whole thing down, right?

"Since no gathering is complete without snacks, there was a sign-up that we operated from on a weekly rotation to remind us who would bring what. For special events, the number of participants increased by at least thirty percent, so for these occasions all the leaders brought something to share to be sure there would be more than enough.

"Like others, I was on rotation twice a month and I usually stopped at the grocery store on the way to the meeting to pick up my snack. I don't recall what I brought that day, but I do remember that I went to the same grocery store I went to every week, and for some reason that day, I felt invisible.

"As is often the case when you go to the same store, you start to see the same faces.

"The staff and I had moved from exchanging pleasantries to exchanging ideas and thoughts about current events. Now we were on to details about our families or our frustrations at work that day. As a mom of four, two of whom were growing boys, I was in the store several times a week. I always made a point to say how much I appreciated them being there. In turn, they would thank me for my kindness to them. I share this to paint a picture of how things were when I visited the store. I wasn't a stranger.

"When the day of the event came and I walked into the store, I didn't realize that I had done such a good job disguising myself. That was not my intent. I was simply dressing for a part in a skit, and even though I was the same person on the inside, evidently, I was not recognizable on the outside.

"I was dressed in a way that was as far from my normal style as the east is from the west. I thought my outfit might strike up a conversation with the folks in the store. *They're going to get a kick out of this*, I thought. But this couldn't have been further from the truth. Not one of them recognized me! Not only did they not recognize me, but they didn't even acknowledge me. I got nothing from them when it came to interaction; not even a hello. In fact, they barely made eye contact with me when *I* said hello. I couldn't believe what was happening. I'm guessing that all of the introverts in the room are wondering, 'Why is it a problem that they didn't talk to you or make eye contact? Sounds like Heaven to me!' But for a person who loves to engage with others and gets pure joy from bringing a smile to someone's day, it didn't feel good at all. I didn't understand it at the time, but I knew that something was going on. Was it me?

"I got back to my car and thought, *what in the world just happened?* I got a glimpse of myself in the rearview mirror as I prepared to back out of my parking spot and startled myself! Then, I looked down at the skirt and realized, 'Oh my gosh, they didn't speak to me because they didn't recognize me?! Not only did they not recognize me, they didn't really *see* me!'

"The person they saw didn't prompt them to engage in conversation. They didn't feel drawn to say hello. I saw them looking at me. I know that they saw the outfit.

"Although I didn't have a title for it at the time, I knew that what I wore and how I carried myself had affected the way others perceived and interacted with me. This was a phenomenon I would later call the Power of Clothing and Personal Packaging.

"But I'm getting a little ahead of myself.

"If you would allow me, I'd like to start at the beginning of my career when I was a personal shopper.

"My first client was a woman who worked for what was then Northwest Airlines. You may know it now as Delta Airlines, which absorbed the company. This client was strikingly beautiful, had a happy marriage, and loved her job. Looking at her, it would be easy to assume that finding things to wear came easily, but she hated to shop. At the time, it was beyond me that anyone could possibly hate shopping, but after spending some time with her I gained an understanding.

"She was very petite and, in her words, 'built like a boy.' Curves weren't abundant, but they were there. Her frustration was that shopping felt like a treasure hunt; it was like looking for a needle in a haystack, she would say. Finding pieces that complemented her slim frame was a challenge, and she would often leave the mall feeling overwhelmed, disappointed, or defeated. Over time, when she started feeling this way, she counteracted this by buying shoes—lots and lots of shoes. She had over 200 pairs! 'They're easy to find, always fit, and I can leave the mall feeling accomplished,' was what she shared with me.

"During one of our conversations, I mentioned that I enjoyed shopping probably as much as she hated it. I had an idea and we decided to give it a whirl. I would shop for her while she was away on her next trip. When I was done, I would leave the items I had chosen for her with the store's staff. I would leave both of our names so when she returned she could go into the store, sort through the things I had selected, and choose what she liked. Essentially, she could pay and be on her way.

"For both of us, this was like gold. I got to be in the mall and choose fabulous, versatile, and practical pieces on someone else's budget. I was thrilled that she loved the pieces and was so happy. Knowing I was instrumental in her finding things that made her feel confident was the highlight.

"She enjoyed the experience and was grateful to put an end to the sense of overwhelm and frustration. No more shuffling through racks upon racks of clothes in hopes of finding pieces that fit her small frame. She no longer had to shop.

"I loved that I got the thrill of shopping and I didn't have to pay for it—but I got paid, instead! We were a perfect match!

"Fast-forward a bit, and I had now learned that there were lots of women who would absolutely love to have this service, and I decided to provide it.

"After decades of helping women, I encountered a new client who shared how thrilled she was to have saved $700 by opening up a credit card when she checked out at one of the stores I had taken her to.

"Keep in mind, that was twenty years ago, and because the value of money doubles every ten years, that $700 savings was actually a $2,800 savings in today's dollars. It would be a $2,800 savings on a $7,000 purchase.

"There are thousands of women who make purchases like this every day. That wasn't what got my attention. What rang true for me was this: there are countless women who would love to have even a fraction of the amount she *saved* to spend on themselves.

"It was at that moment I realized the women who need services like this likely couldn't afford them.

"And I felt compelled to do something about it.

"My first step was to gather information, learn, and make connections. Next, I became a volunteer. I wanted to immerse myself in what was required to provide a service for women, for free, and starting as a volunteer was a good place to start.

"At two of the organizations, my job was to help pick out clothing items for women, many of whom were nervous about their new job, their upcoming interview, the onboarding processes, etcetera. Some were feeling uncomfortable, even ashamed, about the idea of having to pick out and try on clothes that had been donated.

"While we often had to go through several racks of clothing, the space was set up like a boutique, and the clothes were organized by size and color and beautifully displayed. So, the typical 'thrift store fragrance' wasn't looming in the air, and we didn't have to dig through barrels of dirty, dingy clothes.

"However, it was not uncommon to have the women come to me with tears in their eyes and say 'I can't believe that I can't fit in this. I really thought it would fit.'

"The problem? Let me explain.

"The size on the tag showed size ten and this woman is a size eight. Naturally, one would assume that item would be too large.

"But, in this case, and in many others just like them, it didn't fit. It was too small. Sometimes, we would go to a size twelve, and an item still didn't fit. And that could be for several different reasons.

"Perhaps she didn't know her size; maybe these were vintage pieces; perhaps the quality just wasn't there and the piece did not hold up well; the piece could have been damaged; perhaps it had been put in the dryer and it shrunk; or maybe it happened over time.

"As a result of one, or a combination of these factors, the size on the tag didn't match the size of the item.

"And the previous owner likely knew that, which could have been one of the reasons why it was donated in the first place.

"It happens more often than you may realize. A person decides to donate an ill-fitting item not realizing the consternation they may cause for the new owner.

"I touched on this in the morning session as well, but it bears repeating. Have you ever been asked to donate food or clothing? When you are looking for items to donate what do you do? Do you go to the grocery store to buy canned goods? Do you go pick out your favorite things or order something great online? While I am not pointing the finger, I would venture to guess that most of us do not. Most times, we go to our own cabinets or pantry and we find the dented, dusty pinto beans that nobody in the house is going to eat, or a can of something that we bought for a recipe we planned to make but never got around to it. We decide that this unwanted can of whatever, and others like it, is what we will donate.

"Why is it that our first inclination isn't to purchase something new for someone else? Why is it that we think that they want something we don't? There is something to be said for sharing from a position of excess or abundance, but outside of that realm, the average person equates the idea of donations with what they don't want. And that's where we'll end to take a fifteen-minute break: with the dented, dusty can of pinto beans."

The Afternoon Session Continues

"Diving back in, let's start where we left off: talking about the dirty, dusty cans of pinto beans.

"Now, I realize and agree with the statement, 'One woman's trash is another woman's treasure,' or 'one person's discarding is another's discovery,' and yes, old things can be given new life. I'd be the first to tell you that thrifting, consignment shops, flea markets, or antique stores can be fun, economical, and go a long way toward helping to keep things out of landfills.

"But I want to say something, and I want you to hear and understand my heart behind this thought.

"I'm *not* suggesting that we shouldn't be generous, or that we shouldn't get rid of things we don't want or need. What I *am* suggesting is that when we *do* give something to someone else, it should be something of quality, and not our junk.

"If you don't know the difference between the two, simply ask yourself this: 'would I be embarrassed to have it posted somewhere that this was something I donated?'

"Listen, I love a good re-make or upcycle, and I have found some treasures on the curb that would make your head spin. However, when it comes to helping others, I believe that it's critically important that we give in the same way we want to receive.

"The agencies I volunteered with did their best to offer quality pieces, but let's face it, some things slipped through the net. From time to time we would have a volunteer who wasn't quite concerned about what went on the racks. After seeing so many frustrated and disappointed women on the receiving end of a sweater that didn't survive the dryer or a blazer that no longer fit quite right, I was now frustrated, too.

"It was this revelation that motivated me to create a nonprofit that I also call DawnToday!

"This is a division of the company that helps women who are starting or want to advance their career, or who want or need to return to the workforce but don't have the financial capacity to invest in a proper wardrobe. They are likely not eligible for any socio-economic assistance, and consequently fall between the cracks. What that means is that most never qualify to get the help they need, and those who do are subject to the effects of used, donated clothing which we already discussed.

"By the way, when I say 'proper wardrobe,' I'm speaking of the kind of clothing that would communicate the right message to her, and to the people around her. That's what I've termed 'The Power of Clothing and Personal Packaging,' and we'll talk more about that as we go through our sessions.

"Suffice it to say, that after seeing the negative emotional impact of receiving used, donated clothing, and the toll it took on each woman's confidence and self-esteem, I made the critical decision that this organization would only accept donations of brand-new clothing. This is one of the things that makes us unique and differentiates us from most other nonprofits in this arena.

"I say it was a critical decision because it really opened my eyes to the impact of the Power of Clothing and Personal Packaging. I saw with my own eyes what I had read in so many scientific studies over the years. As a result, this became the foundation upon which I built both the for-profit and non-profit sides of the company.

"Now that you've got some background about where my passion comes from and where things started, I want to talk about the science behind the Power of Clothing and Personal Packaging.

"Remember what I shared with you about my experience with the plaid skirts? Well, at that time, I didn't know there was science to back up the way I felt and everything I had experienced. However, while researching to prepare for a number of presentations early in my career, I uncovered it.

"I won't go into all of the science with you right now. I simply want you to be aware that there is science-backed data to support the claim that what you wear really does make a difference. To do that, I will share the findings from just one of the studies I came across.

"As part of a research project, scientists conducted several experiments. It was there that they observed groups of people as they completed a series of tasks. The participants were given different articles of clothing to wear while completing them and then data was collected by the researchers.

"The scientists recorded what the participants were wearing and how it impacted their mood. They tested their blood pressure, their heart rate, their success rates while working, and their interactions with other people. They found that what the participants wore really did make a difference.

"For one of the experiments in the study, scientists asked a group of people to put on a white lab coat while completing various tasks while another group of people kept their regular street clothes on for the experiment.

"The scientists found that those who were in the lab coats said they were able to come up with ideas that they ordinarily wouldn't have thought of; they said they were surprising themselves with the solutions they came up with.

"The participants said they thought of themselves as scientists; as 'answer people,' while those who were in regular street clothes complained about the fact that the experiments were outside of their realm of expertise or that they simply didn't have the tools to be able to solve the problem.

"This further showed the scientists that a simple piece of clothing really did have an impact on their working theory, and that what people wore had a direct impact on the outcome of what they were working on.

"Before we wrap up for the day, I'm going to leave you with something to ponder.

"I don't know how many of you spend time with children. Depending on your age, you may have younger brothers or sisters, nieces and nephews, children, or even grandchildren of your own.

"Whatever the case, I am confident that if you put a young child in a tutu and ballet slippers, it is almost impossible for them to sit still or to walk without twirling, and if they have been exposed to ballet, they may even spin uncontrollably, point their toes, and *become* a ballerina!

"Similarly, if you put a cape on a child, you have an instant super-hero. It isn't uncommon to hear children say things like, 'Don't call me Dylan. I am so-and-so,' taking on the name of whomever this particular superhero or dancer whose costume they are now wearing represents.

"It could be a performer, fireman, judge, or famous chef. When you put a costume on a child, they often embody that person's characteristics.

"My point in sharing the example of children is to show the ease with which children take on the character, and that sometimes as adults, we can overcomplicate things. Being reminded of how easy it is to make a change, to embody the person we really want to be, can start with something as simple as putting on a new costume.

"After thirty years in the fashion industry and personally styling thousands (twenty thousand at the time of this meeting) both in-person and online, I have had the opportunity to work with men and women, teens, and children. However, right now, my primary focus is on women. As a result, I have discovered a number of common mistakes that women make with their clothes every single day.

"This does not mean that men are off the hook, of course. In fact, to all the men in the room, I will let you in on a little secret: what YOU think is attractive and what others find attractive are two different things. You are sending a message with the clothes that you choose, as well. Is it the one you intend to send?

"When we think of body shame and physical insecurities, most people think of women. Yet, a study conducted by Chapman University found that only twenty-eight percent of men are very satisfied with their appearance and weight.

"This dissatisfaction and insecurity lead to them trying to compensate with their clothes and personal packaging, and unknowingly committing many of these same mistakes.

"The critical mistakes I am referring to have an impact on confidence, relationships, and income-earning potential. Some of you may be making them as well.

"It all happens within seven seconds. That's right. It's another scientific fact. In less than ten seconds we make judgments about people, and they make judgments about us, and most of the time we don't even know that it's happening. But for you, that's about to change.

"These critical mistakes can negatively affect both your personal and your professional life. These are seemingly innocent mistakes, and I've seen them cause women (and men) to lose motivation, undermine their self-esteem, negatively affect the experiences that they have in life, and even reduce the quality of their lives in many other ways.

"To keep that from happening to you, I am sharing a short email series with you, and this is how we're going to end our time together today.

"This series is something I share often, and it is typically in the form of a challenge. It has a set of actions to take that accompany these common mistakes. Many have participated and have seen phenomenal results.

"For our purposes, I am only going to send the mistakes for you to read. No challenge, since you are already participating in these meetings with me weekly. By reading them daily, you will come to know the five common clothing mistakes women make that can ruin their lives and their careers and how to avoid them.

"In closing, I want to give you a couple of quick metaphors that will help you to better understand the concepts that I will be sharing in the emails.

"I shared earlier about the ballerina tutu and the superhero cape, but now I want you to think about the practice of a play, a television show, or a movie. It is another way to help you to see just how powerful clothing can be.

"Even in the very early stages of a theatrical production, professional actors come to rehearsal wearing the character's costume because they say it makes them feel more like the character they are playing.

"Perhaps you have listened to an interview with a celebrity who is a television or movie actor. When the interviewer asks how they prepared for the role or how they knew how to walk, talk, or act like the character they were playing, their answers vary.

"Some of them had to lose weight, like Anne Hathaway for her role in *The Devil Wears Prada* or *The Dark Knight Rises* so the clothes fit a certain way. The same is true for Beyoncé, who lost weight for her role in the movie *DreamGirls*. There are others who had to gain weight like Viola Davis for her role in *Ma Rainey's Black Bottom*.

"Some say they didn't just watch other movies about being a police officer, but they wore the uniform and rode in a squad car to really embrace the role.

"Some of you may be too young to remember the show *Mr. Rogers' Neighborhood*. In this made-for-children PBS production, every episode started with the main character, Mr. Rogers, walking into his home, presumably from work. He would close the door behind him and effortlessly remove his blazer, hang it on a nearby wall hook, and replace it with a cardigan. The point of this action was to signify to the viewer that by changing his clothes, he was now changing his role. He was no longer in work mode, but he was now just a neighbor; approachable and ready to talk to you, his neighbor.

"I want you to remember that five-year-old child who put on the superhero costume, was given a sword or a light saber, or put on a pair of shoes like the character. Once this happens, the transformation begins. Can you see it? The same child who was sitting at the kitchen table just moments before now morphs into a brave warrior ready for action. They raise their shoulders and stick out their chest like a peacock, moving around the house with confidence and swagger.

"The same holds true with the clothes we wear in everyday life. Unfortunately, most of us have little or no understanding of this fact or how to benefit from it, and consequently, we continue making a number of mistakes with our clothing.

"You will begin receiving emails every day at 12:01 a.m., so please be sure to check your inbox. If you haven't already, add us to your email's 'safe mail.' Your assignment for the week is to simply read the email and get everything you can from it. Embrace what's inside, and if you are compelled—and I am guessing that you will be—apply what you've read and then keep track of your results.

"I also want you to begin to think about your mindset around clothing. What changes do you see in yourself or others as a result of your new knowledge? Are you seeing things that you didn't see before?

Keep track of these things—the notebook provided is a great place for this.

"It has been my privilege to spend time with you. If you have any questions, you can find our contact information throughout the materials you have been given today. My team members and I are happy to help.

"I look forward to seeing you next week to continue our discussion. Thank you. Have a great weekend."

For some reason, we all started clapping. It wasn't planned, but we all seemed to be excited, energized, and encouraged. When Dawn stopped talking, we collectively felt compelled to show her our thanks and we instinctively did this by applauding loudly. What a day!

Picking Up the Packets

QUINN

As this first session came to a close, we were told we would be receiving a packet of information to bring home.

Usually, when someone says "packet," you think of a manila envelope filled with paperwork to complete. But this was something no one expected. Consistent with everything else we had experienced, this "packet" was actually a package.

The company name was emblazoned across a black and white, lidded box about the size of two shoeboxes in height, width, and depth—likely twenty-four inches all around.

There was no disguising that it was something special, but when Darby, who was headed home via the train, saw it, she mumbled, "Great! How am I going to get this home without making a complete spectacle of myself or inflicting bodily harm to myself or the other passengers?" She let out a loud sigh before deciding to call a car service.

The entire day had been more than anyone expected; almost overwhelming. Despite that, it wasn't something you wouldn't do all over again if given the opportunity. From the information and revelations to the welcoming hospitality, delicious lunch, and generous gifts, Brandi's annoyance over the mandatory attendance was moving further and further into the background.

Her kids were at a Jack and Jill meeting with the nanny, and her husband was working late. It was rare to be home alone, so she chose to use the time to reflect on everything that she had heard and learned while opening the package.

She lifted the lid from the box and found coordinating confetti sprinkled across the top. Phrases like, You Are Special, 7 Seconds, Brighter Future, Change Your Mind, Change Your Clothes, Change Your Life, Power of Clothing, and Personal Packaging were the words she found repeated in this decorative touch.

She smiled and then set the lid down on the floor next to her. Layers of beautifully scented tissue paper were the first thing she noticed. The paper had been sprayed with the popular Jo Malone fragrance, Wood Sage and Sea Salt. It was like opening one of her fragrance purchases from Nordstrom. It was fantastic!

She peeled back the first layer of the custom tissue paper that displayed the DawnToday logo and the phrase, "Your Brighter Future Begins Today." Again, Brandi caught herself smiling at the attention to detail. It reminded her of unpacking a new Chanel bag. She wondered how the other participants, especially the younger woman she had met at lunch, were enjoying this experience. Did other people even notice the thoughtful details?

She would later learn that at this same time, Darby was also digging into her box. She had opened hers with much less precision and care, so she was glad she was sitting on her bed; it's what prevented the candle inside from breaking.

The smell of the candle was amazing, and it instantly reminded Darby of one of her aunt's events. It almost seemed like the paper was scented. It wasn't until she spoke with another participant at the next session that she learned that indeed, it *was* scented. She made note of the fragrance the person shared with her.

Mmm, she thought to herself as she held it closer to her nose and inhaled the lovely scent. She hadn't really cared too much about perfume since high school, and it felt strange that she was paying such close attention to all the details of this box. *Maybe it was all of the grandeur of the day*, she thought. It really did bring back good memories.

After opening this breakable item, she began opening things with a little more care. She was glad to have made that decision because the next item she opened was a mirror. A gold rim framed this 8x10 beauty with the words "YOU are your Brighter Future" at the top and a small DawnToday logo at the bottom right corner.

After putting the kids down to bed, Charlotte was finally able to dig into her package. She was thrilled to find the small box inside that mirrored the larger one. On the top of this lid, there were two capital letter C's, with the words "Confidence Collection" underneath with the DawnToday logo creatively intertwined. She lifted the lid to find a heavily weighted card on the top with the words "Confidence Cards."

The instructions below the card directed them to, "Read this out loud daily to change your thoughts and to remind yourself that your brighter future begins today!"

Once the shrink-wrapped stack of cards was removed from the plastic, she found a coupon for a percentage off the full collection of the cards. Evidently, this was just a small sample.

There were four different patterns to choose from, and after reading more about the purpose of the cards, Charlotte learned that these were perfect for hanging on a mirror or in your closet. They also worked well as gifts, or to place in your calendar, organizer, or on your desk.

In the small jewelry-sized box, Charlotte found a necklace with the DawnToday logo and a small card that said, "Wear this as a daily reminder that your brighter future begins today!" There were a few other things in this Confidence Collection:

- A custom notebook filled with lined pages, some of which had journal prompts
- A beautiful pen
- A custom Oli Clip
- A black and white DawnToday T-shirt. The logo was on the front and the phrase "My Brighter Future Begins Today" was on the back. There was also an accompanying tag to exchange at the DawnToday office if the size wasn't quite right. Participant sizes had been noted on their forms, so this was obviously a precautionary measure
- A 5x7 acrylic clipboard-style frame to hold one of the Confidence Cards
- A copy of the book *The Power of Clothing and Personal Packaging* (with a 20% off discount code for another one of Dawn's books, *Mistakes Women Make When Choosing a Personal Stylist and How to Avoid Them*, or another title of our choosing)
- A host of body care products like Kiehl's Lotion, Brazilian Bum Bum Body Cream, Origins Shower Gel, Laneige Water Sleeping Lip Mask, Moroccan Oil, and Sunday Riley Vitamin C Moisturizer. All the products were contained in a branded and wipeable cosmetics pouch that had likely been donated by a sponsor or business partnership
- A custom measuring tape and card to record measurements

- A coupon card for 20% off the purchase of one item from the DawnToday online boutique
- A coupon card for 20% off the purchase of a one-hour Private Coaching session
- A coupon card for 20% off the purchase of any DawnToday online course

There was no doubt that this was a treat. It was created to make the person feel special and it did not disappoint. But Charlotte was also excited about the 5 Mistakes email series, and she couldn't wait to get the first one, which was scheduled to arrive the following day.

She set her alarm thirty minutes earlier than usual so that she would have time to read it before or after her morning three-and-a-half-mile run.

The Email Series:
Mistake Number One

BRANDI

Relaxing after having said goodnight to her children, Brandi was in the sitting room of her primary suite. She picked up the iPad Pro that she kept by her chair. Its sole purpose was for occasional late-night browsing and shopping.

She was thinking about what she had heard and learned during the meeting today. Initially, she thought that she would just attend one session to appease everyone and then convince them that she was needed in the office as a way of excusing herself from any additional meetings.

But something had started to shift, and she found herself increasingly interested in what was next. It was now just before midnight, and she waited until the clock said 12:01 a.m. so that she could look at the Five Mistakes email series to see what in the world mistake number one could possibly be.

Dawn had really piqued her interest because she was a clothes horse. She had all the "right" clothes, all of the "right" bags, and all the trendy, of-the-moment designer names. She joined the right sororities and had been in all the right social clubs. And now, she had her children participating in similar groups. She wanted them to network with the "right" kids and the "right" families, and get into the best schools, on and on.

Despite her money, possessions, and exposure, she had been intrigued by what Dawn shared in their first session about the messages that clothes send that may be unintentional. So, she opened the email out of curiosity as soon as it came into her inbox.

Mistake #1: Not realizing that your clothing can affect the way you think.

"Did you know that people who dress in formal business clothing can think faster on their feet and have more creative ideas? It's true. And it's backed by science."

Brandi remembered Dawn mentioning that this information was something that had been proven by science as she continued to read.

"Current research concludes that how you dress can change your perception of the objects, people, and even the events around you, stimulating fresh ideas and new points of view. This means that you must be more intentional about what you wear and how you dress. How do you benefit? The research also shows that you will have reinforced problem-solving abilities, enhanced creativity, improved decision-making, and a better capability to understand new things. You will also be less likely to get manipulated by others. How's that for making a real difference? Amazing, right? That's it for today, we'll continue tomorrow. I'll meet you back here. Same place. Same time."

Setting the iPad down on her lap, Brandi whispered, "Wow!" She continued to be taken aback by this whole situation. She was irritated, interested, frustrated, and empowered all at the same time.

To convince herself that she wasn't losing her edge, she said aloud with a little bite in her tone, "I know how to create an intentional outfit all right," before walking over to her closet to begin assembling an outfit for the next day.

She pulled out her Veronica Beard blazer and paired it with her Akris blouse before adding a strand. "Nope, I'll go for two or maybe three…" She picked up three strands of long Chanel necklaces with the signature logo CCs embellished all the way around.

Then she selected a bag from her collection of over thirty designer options. "Now, for the shoes…" She pulled down a pair of Louboutins from her wall of shoes. The signature red bottoms of the patent leather heels matched the red, floral blouse she had chosen.

Cut with a deep V-neckline, the blouse was a bit tight. She had heard that less is more, but to her, more was more! With that in mind, she decided to change things up by adding a purple pencil skirt.

It was an interesting contrast that could have worked with just a little tweaking. Changing an outfit without a purpose and adding something, just for the sake of adding it, was her typical M.O. She had no idea that oftentimes the whole thing was just too much, especially for a conservative office setting. Of course, no one would dare say a word; well, at least to her face.

The Email Series: Mistake Number Two

CHARLOTTE

With her daily run under her belt, she showered and anticipated reading the next day's email. Since setting her alarm thirty minutes earlier had worked for her the day before, she did it again today. This extra time gave her the opportunity to read without interruption since her kids wouldn't be up for at least an hour.

The first meeting at DawnToday had stirred emotions and thoughts that she hadn't expected. She still couldn't believe how she had gotten lost in her thoughts while she was in the powder room before the afternoon session.

Now, she found herself thinking about what she had been wearing recently compared to how she used to dress. Not only that, but she was also thinking about her life before kids; before the end of the marriage—and the beginning of it all; when things changed, for that matter.

At that time, she had been full of hope and anticipation about the future, but somewhere along the way she seemed to have changed without realizing it had happened.

Throughout her life women would mention that they no longer felt like themselves or that they used to be this way or that. How had this happened to *her*? She had always thought she would never be one of *those* women.

She could hardly wait to read the next email because the first one had been so impactful. So, with anticipation and curiosity, she opened her laptop to read about the next mistake.

Mistake #2: Not realizing that what you wear can affect your mood.

The email read, "Quick question. What are you wearing right now?"

Charlotte looked down at her T-shirt and shorts with a frown. "Well, actually, an old, grey college T-shirt and a pair of old running shorts. I just got back from a run and a shower. What do you expect, a prom gown?!" she barked at her laptop. The shirt had permanent stains from when her children were infants, and the shorts were threadbare in spots.

She continued reading. "How does what you are wearing make you feel?"

Charlotte paused to think about her answer and then continued to read the email.

"Here's why I'm asking that question. Research by Dr. Alastair Tombs, Senior Marketing Lecturer at the University of Queensland Business School, backs up the fact that there is a strong link between women's emotions and their clothes. He states, 'By interviewing thirty women, we found that outfit choices are made to match one's mood and as a form of self-expression. But we've also found that clothing is used to control or to mask emotions.'

"Science has also concluded that memories or emotions attached to our clothes can evoke good or bad feelings when we wear them. For instance, if someone is complimented on their clothing, then the good feelings they experience often come back when they look at that article of clothing and they are more inclined to wear it again, subconsciously seeking those same good feelings.

"By the same token, if something negative has happened while wearing a particular outfit, like experiencing a bad breakup or losing a job, many women can't wear that outfit again. Bottom line, you want to create a 'happy wardrobe.' Talk to you tomorrow!"

"Ah! That's it?!" Charlotte couldn't believe how quickly she had been drawn in and how much she didn't want the email to end. She enjoyed learning that there was science behind all of these claims, and she wanted to learn more. She had never considered that her clothes could have such an impact.

Was this an answer to so much of what she was facing in her life right now? The divorce, being a single parent, a new job, and all of the baggage and emotion that she had yet to deal with? She hadn't realized the problems that she still had to face. She had chosen to ignore some of the legalities that were hovering under the surface.

Financially, she and her children continued to be taken care of in the manner they had been during the marriage. However, the thought of the rug ever being pulled out from under her again was incomprehensible, which is why she started looking for a job immediately after the divorce.

At the time she felt powerless—seemingly out of control—because the divorce and all that came with it was such a complete surprise. She was working to regain a sense of self-sufficiency. Being equipped with this new information was giving her the confidence she hadn't realized she was missing. This idea of controlling her emotions was something that she could actually take charge of. She could now see that she was not operating at her fullest potential, and it left her with questions.

When she thought back to how things could have been different, she didn't regret having her children, not even for a moment. She loved them dearly. She wasn't questioning herself because of her husband's actions. No, she knew that he was just a jerk. Period. His decision to cheat (more than once, she had learned) reflected his moral character, state of mind, and lack of resolution about having been abandoned and then adopted. These were his issues, not hers. It didn't make the reality of the situation less painful, and she certainly would not excuse his behavior, but months of counseling and therapy had helped her identify the issues and come to terms with them.

It had been her strong belief that she was made for more, but she had let that go somewhere along the way, and that is what she was grappling with now.

She looked back at her computer screen to re-read the lines of the email that resonated with her. "If someone is complimented on their clothing, then the good feelings they experienced come back. But if something negative happened while wearing a particular outfit, they may not want to wear that outfit again."

She bolted out of bed, jumped over to her closet, and pushed every-thing over to the left. On the far right, she found that navy blue Hugo Boss suit with the beautifully cut, fabulous fabric. It was the only suit like this that she had. She had intended to wear it to one of her inter-views when she started looking for positions right after the divorce, but she made the decision not to because she remembered the comments her mom had made in the past like, "Charlotte, you really don't need to go overboard. It's just a bit much. Don't you think that's a bit ostentatious? It's not the best cut for you. Why do you have to have something so expensive? A respectable woman of your age who's been married and is now a single mother of three young children really needs to dress more appropriately. It's not like they're going to hire you to be an attorney or anything..."

Wow, what a gut-punch. Her mom knew how close she had been to becoming a lawyer, but she was an old-school traditionalist who felt that Charles' career was most important and should take the foreground. She had shared these sentiments with Charlotte while mixing them with joy at the birth of her first grandchild.

She knew her mom loved her and that the comments she had made over the years were not mean-spirited; they were from a place of concern.

Despite that, the words were swimming below the surface, and they would rise when she least expected it. During her first interview at the firm, she was asked if there were any other positions within the company that she thought she may be qualified for. It was as if, somehow, they could see that there was more to her.

She had, in fact, looked at all the positions available before applying, and several caught her attention. She was interested, but for some reason, she couldn't apply.

It had been a gracious opportunity on the part of the interviewer to offer this potential detour and to make more of this interview. They were giving her an occasion to speak up for herself, and her first instinct was to reply with "yes." But as soon as that thought came, it left and was replaced with doubt, so she simply replied, "No. Thank you for asking," and added, "Entry-level is where I should probably be."

Amazing! She actually had a connection to the idea of this clothing-emotion-action thing that she had just read. How had she missed this before? Her mother's comments, her past and present choices about what to wear, her confidence—they had all joined together to form her current opinion of herself.

While this was not the most pleasant of revelations to have, Charlotte was excited to have something to add to the conversation—even the one running in her own mind. She was going to have an example to share at the next meeting that would put emphasis on what they were learning.

It was likely that she wouldn't actually share, but just knowing that she could relate was exciting. It also added to her anticipation for tomorrow's email. She was now even more convinced that there may really be something to this DawnToday, Power of Clothing and Personal Packaging "thing."

The Email Series: Mistake Number Three

CHARLOTTE

Charlotte couldn't believe how intrigued she was by these emails. She fell asleep waiting, but her body clock woke her the next morning and she read the next email in the series.

Mistake #3: Not realizing that clothing affects your confidence!

"Oh. My. Gosh! Are you kidding me?!" she yelled out loud and then quickly covered her mouth to restrain herself from waking her kids. She was treasuring this time to herself before they were up and headed into their day. She was almost sure that at least one of them would have heard that outburst, so with her hands still covering her mouth, she continued to read.

"Hey, friend, in another study, scientists have shown that the way we feel about ourselves is often directly linked to our appearance. Clothing influences behavior and attitude because it carries a symbolic meaning. So, what you wear is subconsciously changing how you act.

"When you wear an outfit that you associate with intelligence and power, you're likely to do better and feel better than when you wear clothing that you associate with sloppiness or low-skilled work. It's like the actor we talked about, putting on a costume to get into character for a performance. By dressing to *be* that character, you expect to have a better performance, making you more mentally prepared for the task.

"You're over halfway through the Five Mistakes, friend, so stay tuned to your inbox and I'll talk to you tomorrow."

Charlotte couldn't believe what she had just read. She read it a second time, a third, and then a fourth. This had to have been the eighth time that she read that line, "clothing influences behavior and attitude because it carries a symbolic meaning."

She looked at her Hugo Boss suit. It had made it from the far back corner to the front of the closet, and now it was hanging outside of the door.

It felt as if the suit was calling her names like "stupid," "deficient," and "unworthy." It called her a chicken for not wearing it, daring her to try it on just to see how she felt in it.

She thought about all the comments her mom had made about it, which, of course, caused her to think about all the thoughts that had come rushing back while she was in the restroom lounge at the offices of DawnToday.

The suit represented who she had planned to be, and now it hung there, daring her to change her life. Was she up for the challenge that it brought; to be who she was meant to be? Would it end up back in the closet, or worse, would she get rid of it altogether and stay in this position that she had never planned to be in forever?

The Email Series:
Mistake Number Four

DARBY

Darby had to admit that she'd grown increasingly interested in this entire subject. Never in a million years would she have believed that clothing was anything more than just something that you had to contend with every single day. Choosing an outfit was drudgery. Not only did it require choosing pieces that coordinated, but they also had to be appropriate, clean, and unwrinkled, and she liked pieces that masked what she wanted to hide because her inherited curves didn't match the highly touted all-American figure.

Once all the choosing was done, you had to launder it—or take it to the dry cleaners, for crying out loud! That was a mistake that she would hope to never make again: purchasing something that you had to continuously pay to take care of.

Despite this, she was increasingly intrigued by her new exposure to the Power of Clothing and Personal Packaging shared at the first meeting and now through the daily emails.

She opened the next one and read,

Mistake #4: Not understanding that your clothing can affect your performance.

"Image scientists call this phenomenon 'Enclothed Cognition.' But here, at DawnToday, we call it the 'Power of Clothing.' In her book

Mind What You Wear, Fashion Psychology Professor Karen Pine states, 'When we put on a piece of clothing, we cannot help but adopt the characteristics associated with it even if we are unaware of it.'

"This is just one of the many reasons I tell my clients how important it is to get up and get dressed. That simple act can help you to feel beautiful, confident, and strong. You have got to change out of those sweats and put on the clothes that wake up your superpowers just like Wonder Woman going from her Diana Prince uniform to her Wonder Woman costume. You need to do the same thing in order to wake up your own superpowers.

"Speaking of superpowers, researchers conducting a study at the University of Hertfordshire asked a group of people to wear a Superman T-shirt and concluded that the participants believed they were stronger when they were dressed like a superhero. This translated into more confidence and the belief that they could achieve more. My point? Not only should you dress for how you want to *feel*, but you also need to dress for how you want to *act*.

"Okay, tomorrow we will cover the last mistake. I hope that you are learning something each day that is provoking you to take action. Talk to you tomorrow!"

Darby was in shock and thought, *Okay, it's backed by science*. She had heard this mentioned at the first session and even read it in the previous day's emails, but the evidence was compounding, and there was no more denying that there was something to this. Somehow, today's email was the push that she needed, and she decided to give this a try by putting it into action.

She was not one to be easily swayed by fashion fads or crowd-pleasing, but when someone could show scientific evidence to support what was being presented, she was willing to listen and learn. She was, in her own words, practical.

She decided that she was going to do something with her long black hair. Its natural wave pattern made it easy enough to style, and she followed its seemingly permanent side part and let the front pieces hang behind her shoulders.

She decided to wear one of the outfits she had gotten when her mom took her shopping after graduation. "Darby, you're going to need some new clothing to have that business look. You really want to make an impact," her mother had said. Turns out she was right.

Reluctantly, Darby had gone shopping with her mom—really just to appease her—and she ended up with bags of clothes. Some of them she had never worn. In fact, the tags were still on most of them.

She wasn't ungrateful for the clothes, but at the time, she was on a mission to reject anything that even resembled a particular "look." She especially avoided anything that seemed to appease her parents' goal: to get her married and into the family of their choosing—by way of an arranged marriage, of course.

She decided that she would break out a few of the pieces since this was backed by science and all. She decided to see if her attitude about work, her coworkers, and life in general would change as a result of changing what she wore.

She was determined to land a spot in the firm's mentorship program, and if changing her clothes was going to help (and based on what she was learning, it would), she was all in.

The Email Series:
Mistake Number Five

All three of the ladies were eager to read the last of the daily emails. Even Brandi, who was averse at the start, was curious. They had been challenged to look at not only what they were wearing, but *why* they were wearing it. With great anticipation they each opened their email boxes to find the last email:

"Hello and welcome back! If you have followed along this week, congratulations on making it all the way through! While some of you may be shocked, concerned, or excited, it is also likely that some of you may have made some changes as a result of what you learned. If not, that's okay. Enjoy this final email.

Mistake #5: Not Understanding That the Clothes You Wear Affect How You Are Perceived by Others!

"Have you ever heard or used these phrases?

- She looks fantastic
- She's so driven
- She's not my type
- She doesn't like to talk to people
- She's not afraid to talk to anyone
- She couldn't hack it
- She looks friendly
- She looks like a hard worker

- She's an extrovert

"Studies show that 80% of communication is non-verbal. That means people will 'SEE' you long before they 'HEAR' what you have to say.

"You don't get a second chance to make a first impression, and people make snap judgments based on what you are wearing. Remember this: you only have seven seconds to make a first impression. This means that the clothes you wear could determine whether others:

- comply with your request(s)
- trust you with information
- purchase your products or services
- pay you a certain salary or fee for contracted services

"It's ALL directly related to your image, your performance, and how you are perceived.

"The question isn't whether or not you care about fashion. The question is, what are you communicating with your choices?

"What's the bottom line? Like it or not, the clothes that you wear can mean the difference between whether you succeed or fail in your career, your relationships, and in your life.

"It's called The Power of Clothing and Personal Packaging. It's time to get that power working *for* you instead of *against* you, don't you agree?

"I hope you have enjoyed our time together throughout this series, and that while learning about these mistakes you have also learned a little more about yourself.

"Your brighter future begins today,

"Dawn"

And with that, the email series came to a close.

The Weeks Continue at DawnToday

QUINN

So, then what happened? Well, with curiosity, anticipation, and excitement, it was time to move on to weeks two through six. The hours that we spent at DawnToday moved quickly, but each week was filled with information that connected with the week before. While every detail won't be shared here, read on to discover some of what we learned.

> Whatever the mind can conceive and believe it can achieve.
>
> —Napoleon Hill

Session Two
Mindset

DAWN

"Welcome back! I am happy to see you all and I enjoyed visiting with some of you before things began today. I am glad to hear that you enjoyed the email series and gained greater insight. Today we are going to start by talking about mindset. Let's get started, shall we?

"Mindset is everything. You have the power to change things, and it all starts with you!

"What do you think about yourself? Who do you say you are? Do you believe that you are worthy of having, doing, and being more?

"If not, it's okay. Most of us have an area or two, or ten, we need to work on. This one is crucial. Do the work to get to a place where you believe in your value. It may not happen overnight, but it's important that you get here. The truth is, YOU MATTER, and the world would not be the same without you. Who you are has the power to make the world a better place. We need you.

"Following are some journaling questions that will help you to move toward a mindset that says, 'I am enough, I am worthy, and what I have to share matters.'"

JOURNALING QUESTIONS

- For what are you grateful?
- Who do you believe you are (powerful, resourceful, intelligent, friendly...)?
- What challenges have you overcome? You survived "THAT?" Wow! You're a star and I hope that you can hear me cheering you on, wildly!
- What makes you strong?
- What makes you unique?
- What helps you believe in yourself?
- Who is the 'real' you?
- What do you feel like when you are being that person (excited, strong, capable)?
- When you are feeling your best and at the top of your game, what do you spend your time thinking about, how are you feeling, what kinds of things are you doing?
- How does your current personal style represent who you are; and, if it does not currently represent who you are, what steps do you need to take to make this a reality?
- What are a few words that describe how you want to be seen or perceived to be (classy, smart, healthy, wise, leader, informed...)?
- What does the confident version of you wear?
- Where does the confident version of you shop?
- If you were to present or introduce yourself in the form of three songs, what would they be?
- What are some of the things that cause you to feel bad or that

drain energy from you?

- What is something that motivates you?
- Who is someone who motivates you?
- Who are three people who currently showcase or exude the confidence you want to grow to?
- Who are three people who currently encapsulate the style that you are after?
- What excites you?
- What are some areas that you are holding back from being the confident or authentic version of yourself?
- What skills would you like to learn to feel more confident in a particular area?
- How would the most confident version of you go about making this a reality?
- How does the most confident version of you want to be addressed? How does that version of you dress?

"You may come up with additional thoughts and questions and you can add them to your notebook.

"As you complete this work don't forget the power of the word 'YET!'

"Always remember to add this to the end of your sentences when something seems discouraging. Here are a few examples:

- I'm not good at this, YET!
- I don't understand how to do this, YET!
- I haven't been promoted, YET!
- I don't have the right clothes, YET!
- I don't have enough money, YET!

"One more thing as we wrap up this session. Always remember that every day you wake up is a new opportunity—it is literally, a new Dawn, Today. Your Brighter Future Begins TODAY!"

...if the packaging of products has an impact on how people regard a particular product, then the packaging of people must have an impact on how others regard those people.

—Dan Kennedy

Session Three
Personal Packaging

DAWN

"Okay! Let's get to it, everyone! Are you ready?" Dawn said as she walked back to the center of the room to address us. We all replied with heads nodding and some giving a loud, "Yes!" to the question, and we dove right in.

"What is your personal package? Do you have a signature look or style? For what are you known?

"I have heard it said repeatedly that what you wear doesn't really matter, and that focusing on the clothing and the outside appearance is superficial, superfluous, and distracts from what really matters; or it's an excuse to compensate for something missing or a reason to spend money.

"These sorts of claims seem to have some weight behind them, and they impact the receiver when they are spoken by a person in authority, someone with a strong opinion, or a big personality. The unfortunate thing about opinions that are not backed by science is that they are often logical fallacies.

"The truth is that there is actual data that supports the contrary. One example is Dan Kennedy. He is a multi-millionaire entrepreneur who is a highly paid and sought-after marketing and business strategist. He has delivered over two thousand compensated presentations, and over the course of his career, his popular books have been favorably recognized by magazines like *Forbes*, *Bloomberg Businessweek*, and *Entrepreneur Magazine*.

"According to his personal bio, he has helped thousands of entrepreneurs build businesses worth millions. He has also worked with former presidents, athletes, and actors. It came as a surprise to me when I read his quote, '...if the packaging of products has an impact on how people regard a particular product, then the packaging of people must have an impact on how others regard those people.'

"The words themselves weren't a surprise, but the person delivering them was.

"I was only slightly familiar with his work and had read a few excerpts of his books. However, I have family members and colleagues who are fans and have followed his work for decades. They have experienced success as a result of applying the principles they learned from him.

"Interestingly, only one of them mentioned a particular chapter in his book that supported my findings of the Power of Clothing and Personal Packaging. It is very possible that because this isn't something other readers were focused on, it didn't really stand out.

"As powerful as his stories and experiences with personal packaging are, others continued to read it without pause. I immediately zeroed in on what he was sharing, and I felt like I knew what he was going to say before finishing a sentence or a paragraph.

"This is because I had been studying and immersing myself in the topic of personal packaging, which has a direct link to the Power of Clothing. It isn't until you see something and become aware of it that it then stands out to you.

"Fascinated by this principle, I wanted to understand more about why this happens. Why did we all read the same book and have different things stand out to us? I have learned that there is generally an answer as to why we do what we do. So, I did some light research and learned that the Baader-Meinhof Phenomenon, also known as the 'Frequency Illusion' or 'Recency Bias,' is the term that psychologists use to describe these situations that we all experience.

"Because our brains are constantly being bombarded with things to look at, it filters things out and focuses on the things that we acknowledge and pay attention to. It's like when you choose to buy or even consider buying a particular kind of car and then you seemingly start to see it everywhere. Frequency illusion is considered a cognitive bias. This explains why, after noticing something for the first time, there is a tendency to notice it more often.

"In one of Dan Kennedy's books, *No B.S. Sales Success In the New Economy*, he shares how he once encountered a private banker who wouldn't give him the time of day.

"He was dressed rather casually, but after giving the banker his business card, the banker questioned him and said that there must be some mistake because his attire said otherwise. In other words, his business card was impressive, but he was not! You can read the chapter, or the book for that matter, to learn the details of what happened. Spoiler alert: Dan made the necessary clothing changes, returned, and got the loan.

"After a few instances like this, Dan quickly learned that 'For every one person who says it, there are somewhere between 10 and 10,000 who think it.' This is a premise that marketing research is based on.

"He knew that if a few people were thinking and saying that his personal package didn't match what was on paper, in the bank, in books, or in presentation content, that there were countless others who felt the same way.

"How would you feel if you went to an appointment with your doctor and instead of showing up in a lab coat, they were dressed up in full makeup like Gene Simmons from the 70s rock band KISS? Or, if you went to dinner and the server brought your food out wearing a dirty mechanics jumpsuit with fresh oil stains and the smells to match?

"Might these situations give you a reason for pause? These are some of the reasons to consider the audience you will be addressing when choosing an outfit.

"You may have encountered a newer dress code at work, as many companies, depending on the industry, have a 'dress for your day' policy.

"The point is to dress for the event.

"You see, you have biases. They may be subconscious but they're there. We all have them.

"By wearing a *costume* to play the role of the part you're performing helps not only you, but the people you will encounter. It's easier to see you as the character when you're dressed for the part.

"It's difficult to get past the idea of a construction worker dressed as a ballerina for a scene in *The Nutcracker* or *Pas de Quatre*, or a bodyboarder dressed in a football uniform while on a surfboard riding a wave in the ocean. It just doesn't work.

"Now, back to Dan. During the course of the 2,000+ talks that Dan has given, he decided to experiment. He concluded that his sales were exponentially higher when he wore a suit and tie compared to when he wore a sports coat and pants. Keep in mind that this book was written in 2010, and while employee dress culture has changed, the principles remain the same.

"In addition to what he wore, Dan also noticed a difference based on geography. He concluded that he would wear different clothing while working and presenting in California than he would when giving a talk to a group in Massachusetts.

"In Dan's book, *No B.S. Sales Success In the New Economy*, he shared, 'There is no doubt in my mind that the clothes and accessories you wear, the briefcase you carry, the pen you write with, and the car you drive all combine to communicate a message to others that can hurt or help you. To deny it, resist it, or to ignore it is self-destructive.'

"That is powerful, and I quote it often because I encounter people who want to debate or try to prove that they are 'different' and that these principles don't apply to them. You may be feeling that way right now.

"The goal is not to convince you or rattle the earth with this information. The goal is to help you stack the odds of success in your favor and to help you to stop missing out on opportunities for more money, more success, better relationships, and reaching your highest potential. The way we'll do that is to create a powerful personal package.

"Dan continued to say, 'Know this, too: people prefer dealing with successful people. I want my insurance agent, my real estate agent, my accountant, my lawyer, my doctor, and my public relations consultant to be doing well. The fact that they are doing well indicates that many others agree with my choice and judgment.'

"Dan also observed over time that he is given more courtesy by people that he interacts with—everyone from store clerks to airline attendants when he dresses professionally versus when he is dressed casually.

"When I read this, it reminded me of the story I shared with you about me dressing up in a red plaid skirt and going to the grocery store. Do you remember that?"

Some nodded, while others answered audibly as Dawn continued.

"Dan created different uniforms for different occasions—just like we teach at DawnToday. Dan had an outfit for new clients, one for speaking, one for selling, and so on.

"As you looked through the questions in the handouts from session two, this is one of the things you were prompted to work through: who and what does the person you see yourself as, or want to become, wear...? This is another reason to work through those questions. It will help you understand which uniform or costume you're going to wear on a given day or for a particular occasion.

"In his final example about this, Dan shared that at one time he had produced an infomercial that was going to be hosted by a well-known actor at the time. As they prepared for the recording, they were discussing the part that the actor would play and what he would wear. Interestingly, the actor said, 'How about I wear my *Basic TV Star Uniform*?' and then explained what it was.

"You see, this is a universal principle that can be applied to so many different lines of work. Would a scaffolder take a new hire seriously if they showed up wearing a tuxedo or a full-length ball gown?

"Let's take another short break. I'll see you back here in ten minutes."

Post-It Note Activity

QUINN

Dawn had shared with me that this was the week that things could get a little dicey, emotional, and certainly transparent. It was the week that things got *real*.

Past participants had shared with their team that they had assumptions about what people thought of them, but actually reading it, hearing it, and taking ownership of it was something different.

When we returned from the break, we noticed the room was a bit different. Whiteboards lined the wall behind where Dawn usually stood, and each person's seat had a small drawstring bag placed on it.

Dawn began by sharing with the group that this would likely be groundbreaking, motivating, and memorable.

"Let's get started. We're going to mix things up a little and move into an activity. Don't worry. It won't be one of those group activities like the ones we all *loved* so much in high school or college, where there was always that one person who never pulled their weight or the one who decided to be the self-appointed leader. You know the one—they would take over and start doling out instructions to the rest of the group as if they were the assistant teacher or professor.

"I hear a few giggles and see your smiles, so I know you understand what I mean.

"Instead of that experience, we're going to spend some time on the messages that we are actually sending with our clothes versus the messages that we think we are sending, and we are going to do this three different ways.

"First, I would like you to find the black Post-It notes in the bag that was placed at your seat. Inside you will also find a gel pen with white ink and a pencil with white lead. Both will write on the black paper with ease.

"I'm going to set a timer and I would like you to list at least five of the messages that you intend to send with the outfits that you wear.

"What message are you looking to convey to others when you walk out of the door? You have had enough exposure to how our clothing can impact others, so write words or statements that would tell someone who can't see you what message your look is sending. Any questions? No? Then, let's begin."

Most wrote feverishly, but some pondered before getting started. Eventually, the tables were covered in black Post-Its!

When Dawn called time, she asked again if anyone had any questions before moving on. The room was silent, and people seemed to be curious about what was next.

"Let's get started with the next portion of the exercises. I would like you to take a white Post-It note and write at least five messages that you think you are *actually* sending with the clothes you wear. For some of you, it may be the same as what you just wrote, and for others this may be completely different.

"For example, you may think that you're sending the message that you are a well-informed researcher or scientist, but you now know that you may be giving off Luke Skywalker or Bart Simpson vibes."

Again, the tables became filled, this time with white Post-It notes with black ink.

"Finally, the third exercise is for you to fill out a pink Post-It note with black ink. You're going to write on separate Post-It notes, and you will complete at least three. For each person at your table, you will write out the messages they are sending with the clothes that they're wearing.

"Be honest but not intentionally hurtful. For instance, you can write 'romantic' or 'boho' instead of 'you look like you are playing the character of a milkmaid in a high school play.'"

Small laughs were heard but concern was evident. Once this was done, Dawn continued with the next set of instructions.

"Great job, everyone. I understand that can be uncomfortable. Now I want you to do that last exercise again, but this time please share what you think the person does for a living—where you think they work, what position you think they hold—based on the messages they are sending with their clothes.

"While this may seem similar, it will look a little like this: I think that Dawn is a teacher and the message her clothes send is that she is a bit quirky—that purple tail she has pinned to her clothes says that she is on her way to be a character at a child's birthday party. Or you can keep it simple and write something like this: character at a child's birthday party for a career—Dawn."

When the time came, participants placed pink Post-It notes that were clearly labeled with another person's name into a basket and the team collected them. At the end of the session, everyone would leave with the Post-It notes others had written about them.

The team did this to be sure that hurtful notes could be filtered out if, for some reason, someone was a little overzealous about sharing their thoughts and didn't do so in a respectful manner.

Dawn had access to a few of the Post-Its and shared that some of the words were: flamboyant, confident, casual, serious, timid, boss, thoughtful, too small, and considerate.

"I'm guessing you may be wondering, 'could that be about me?' It's possible, of course. Keep an open mind. Be aware that even though these may not have been the messages you wanted to send, now you know. To make the necessary changes, be willing to take an honest look at the pieces you've worn to the meetings in the past and what you are wearing today.

"I appreciate your participation in this activity. When you read through the words and phrases your peers have shared, remember how they fit into the whole picture of the Power of Clothing and Personal Packaging.

"Remember the Baader-Meinhof principle, the experiments that Dan did with his audiences, and the scientific data that supports and reinforces the principles we discussed this morning.

"That's it for today. Please be sure to pick up a copy of the questions which are part of your homework for this week. These have also been made available via email.

"Thank you for your time and please let us know what questions you may have. We are here to help."

And with that, another session wrapped up, and it was apparent that it had really gotten people thinking. There were a few who gathered to discuss the day's topics while others seemed to be in deep thought, already pondering the questions on the handout that had been made available. I took a few extras, just in case.

Quinn Shares the Questions with You, the Reader. Enjoy!

I'm guessing you may be curious about the homework so here's a brief glimpse of a few of the questions on the handout:

- How do I feel about the way that I am currently dressing?
- What do my outfits say about me?
- Does what I wear accurately show who I am inside?
- What message do I want to send to the world with the way that I dress every day?
- Do I feel confident in the outfits that I wear?
- Do the clothes that I wear flatter me?
- Do the clothes that I wear align with my current lifestyle?
- What can I wear that supports my confidence?

Session Four
Body Type

"Welcome back! I am glad to see you and I trust that things are going well with your work from the previous sessions.

"Today we are zeroing in on ways to stack the odds in our favor. We are doing this to increase opportunities in our relationships, our work, and our finances and we will start by learning how to:

- Choose pieces that fit us well and support our intent to send certain messages
- Choose pieces that help increase the good feelings and minimize the bad ones
- Optimize our 'seven seconds'—the time it takes for someone to make a judgment call about who we are, what we do, and what we have to offer the world

"As you can see from your agenda, today we will be focusing on BODY TYPE. You will quickly see that there are lots of terms and classifications used. Please remember that we are describing bodies, not personalities. It is very important that you don't get hung up on the names and titles, but that you focus on the concepts.

"Although we have a plethora of words at our disposal, I am highlighting three of the common ways people have combined words to separate, highlight, and identify different body shapes and types.

"In addition to body types and shapes, we can also consider face shape, clothing color analysis, and wardrobe personality.

"All of this can seem a bit overwhelming the first time around, so I am going to start with a general overview of the areas we will touch on, and then I will divide things into categories. From there, we will break some of those concepts into bite-sized pieces.

"This is by far one of the more intense days. You are not expected to retain or even understand everything. For some, this may be your first exposure to the fact that these concepts even exist. That's okay. You can always go over your notes and the information provided.

"We are condensing what is typically a three- or four-session meeting into one day, so we will be driving fast. Buckle your seat belts, and let's get started!

"The first reference of body shapes and sizes we will touch on is from a scientific point of view that refers to the way the body is built.

"If you have ever worked with a personal trainer at a gym or a health club, or maybe through physical therapy, it is likely that she or he will create a plan based on your somatotype. Some of you may remember the term from a high school or college science class.

"The three terms used to classify a body type within the somatotype are Ectomorph, Endomorph, and Mesomorph.

"Next, we move into references that refer to bodies as geometric shapes and pieces of fruit. Classifications among this group are typically apple, hourglass, triangle, inverted triangle, pear, rectangle, oval, and diamond.

"While some of these are interchangeable, I am presenting all of them simply to make you aware. You may also see iterations of these terms like bell, skittle, or spoon depending on what you are reading or with whom you are speaking.

"The third area we will explore is the thought that bodies can be identified based on the lines of the skeleton and facial features. This system, developed by fashion stylist David Kibbe and thoroughly explained in his book *Metamorphosis: A Personal Image and Style Book for Women*, is a far more robust system than the ones above that are based purely on the silhouette.

"He classifies bodies into these five categories, and very simply put, focuses on working with the body that you have. This is done by concentrating on looks that are balanced and based on the natural lines of the body versus trying to create an 'ideal' shape. According to Kibbe, by creating a natural and unique balance with your clothing, you will, in turn, look very natural.

"Now that we have gone over the three different groups, let's go back to the top and learn a little more about each one.

Somatotypes

"Remember that there are three categories here: Mesomorph, Endomorph, and Ectomorph.

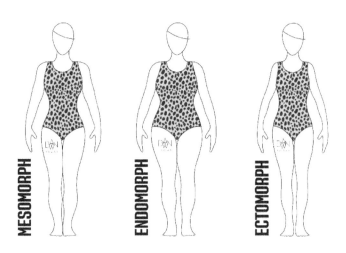

"**Ectomorphs** are generally thin and oftentimes tall. You can expect that they will be pretty slender and narrow with long, lean limbs. Many will have small joints, a thin waist, and some have protruding bones.

"For these folks, it seems they can eat an endless amount of food and never gain a pound. These are the people who must work to gain weight.

"With Google at your fingertips, you can pull up photos of people with these body types. A few celebrities that you may recognize at the time of this session are Taylor Swift and Charlize Theron.

"On the opposite end of the spectrum, we find the **Endomorph**.

Their challenge is typically losing weight based on their soft, round curves. Beyoncé, Salma Hayek, Marilyn Monroe, Sophia Vergara, and Jennifer Lopez come to mind here. They could all be described as curvaceous with small waists. They have medium bone structure and small shoulders.

"**Mesomorphs** fall right in the middle. They don't store as much fat, and they find it equally easy to gain or lose weight. Janet Jackson, Madonna, Angela Bassett, and Tina Turner are celebrities we have seen embrace their beauty at various times in their lives. They have broader shoulders, muscular arms and legs, and typically don't store much body fat.

"Now, let's move on to descriptions that refer to bodies as geometric shapes and pieces of fruit.

Shapes and Fruit

Apple, Pear, Hourglass, Inverted Triangle, Rectangle, and Hourglass.

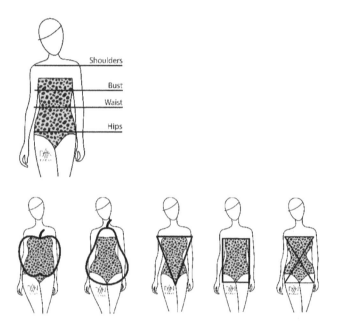

"By looking at the graphic, the shapes are easily identifiable, and many in the fashion industry use these terms to describe different shapes of the women they are working with.

"We will start by discussing those who may fall into the category of a **RECTANGLE**.

"A person with this figure will likely have:

- A straight shoulder line and ribcage
- Hips that are in line with the shoulders
- Bust and hips that are approximately the same width
- A small to an average midriff
- Very little to no waist definition
- Straight hips and bottom
- Lack of curves throughout the body frame
- Weight gains that typically distribute evenly throughout the body
- 'Curvy' is NOT an adjective that you would use to describe this body type

"Some celebrities or well-known names in the media with the rectangle body type are Kate Middleton, Anne Hathaway, and Kate Hudson.

"This rectangle body shape is also known and referred to as a 'ruler' because of the minimal number of curves.

"So, if your hips are in line with your shoulders, and you have a small or average bust, you just may be a rectangle shape.

"There are still other shapes to consider, so don't put your stake in the ground and call this one yours just yet! Let's wait until you have learned about and considered the other ways to define your body shape. An often surprisingly slight change here could mean that you identify more closely with a different shape.

"Those who fall into the category of an **INVERTED TRIANGLE** will likely have:

- Shoulders that are noticeably wider than their hips
- Shoulders that might be straight, squared, and strong looking
- Very little or no waist definition
- A flat bottom and hips that look straight because of their broad shoulders

"You may have a few minor differences from what is found in the descriptions, which might indicate that you are in a different category.

"For instance, even though your shoulders are wider than your hips, your bottom may be the same size as your bust line, which means that you may be an hourglass shape. So, let's continue.

"Those who fall into the category of an **HOURGLASS** will likely have:

- Slightly round shoulders
- Bust and hips that are usually the same width
- A small and defined waist
- A bottom and hips that are rounded
- Fuller thighs
- Features that bring the word 'curvy' to mind

"The hourglass body type is considered the ideal body shape because your proportions are equally balanced. When you gain weight, your curves don't change because the weight is usually distributed evenly all over the body. You also have a well-defined waist that doesn't change when you gain weight.

"As it was with the other body types, the same is true here. There are variations that you want to keep in mind. Remember that even if your bust and bottom are the same sizes, if your shoulders are larger than your hips then you may be an inverted triangle. However, if your shoulders are smaller than your hips, then you may be a pear, which is the next shape we will discuss.

"Those who fall into the category of a **PEAR** will likely have:

- A defined waist that is smaller than the hips
- Hips that are wider than the shoulders
- Hips that are wider than the bust
- Prominent hips that are larger than the shoulders
- Weight that is typically gained in the thighs or bottom

"Once again, remember that every body type has a variation.

"If you have a pear-shaped body, some may refer to it as a triangle since the top part of your body is dramatically smaller than the bottom. To help you visualize, Beyoncé and Jennifer Lopez are two celebrities with this body type.

"Now that we have covered the rectangle, hourglass, and pear shapes, we move on to those whose figure is equated to an apple.

"The **APPLE** shape is also referred to as a 'circle' or 'round' shape. Those who fall into the category of an apple will likely have:

- Shoulders, a bust, and a waistline that are fairly similar. However, sometimes the shoulders and/or the hips may be slightly narrower
- A waistline that is undefined
- A large bust

"Women with this body type tend to appear top heavy since they have little to no waist and fat tends to accumulate in the stomach area.

"Just like the other body types, the apple can also have variations. So, some may have:

- A large ribcage
- Great legs

"Don't forget that these are guidelines and not rules, so if you find that you don't have a full bosom, it does not rule out being an apple shape.

"We have covered the basic shapes and fruits that are commonly used to describe body types. Next, I will address both curvy and petite body types, and how they are commonly classified within these shapes."

Addressing the Confidently Curvy Body Type (AKA Full-Figured)

"Thankfully, times have changed, and many have chosen to embrace the fact that having a fuller figure does not exclude you from fashionable clothing.

"When Ashley Graham, an American supermodel, appeared on the 2016 cover of *Sports Illustrated* magazine, she took the world by storm.

"It was around this time that the industry began referring to full-figured women as 'curvy.' While you may find some stores still call this area of the shop 'plus-size,' at DawnToday we have chosen to adopt the modern term 'curvy' when referring to women with these body types.

"If you have a fuller figure, remember that just like with any other body type, it is important to know your measurements and your body shape.

"Oftentimes the sizing charts for clothes are converted for a fuller figure, so having this information on hand can help to alleviate confusion and frustration.

"How do you know if you fall into the category of curvy or full-figured? Many are often:

- Unable to fit what is considered conventional sizing (0-14)
- More comfortable in clothing found in the "plus size" area of the store because it seems that 'it just fits me better'

"You don't have to be a certain height or weight to be considered curvy or full-figured.

"When choosing your clothes, you want clothes that flatter your figure. So, whether that is something with movement or something fitted, you will be happier with the finished product if you have the proper undergarments, so be sure to start there.

"Did you know that sixty-eight percent of American women wear a size fourteen or above? If this is you, you are not alone. You're in good company!

"One of the reasons that women who fit these clothes have difficulty finding them is because patterns for clothes are typically made in a size two or four. This is more cost-effective for designers who have to create an entire collection for fashion shows.

"Like most things, when you create it to be one size and attempt to change it without modifications, it usually doesn't work.

"Things can get distorted when you don't make tweaks to the original. For instance, when you cook something like oatmeal there is a certain ratio of oats to liquid. If you simply added more liquid to create more oatmeal, you will likely end up with a liquified mess with only remnants of oats to be found.

"It's the same with a pattern. If a pattern is created for a size two and it is simply made larger without accounting for the changes in the body, it doesn't work.

"Patterns are sometimes also made in curvy or plus-size size runs. The challenge is for the people, body shapes, and sizes that fall in between.

"Thankfully, we are seeing changes in the fashion industry to alleviate or eliminate these challenges. Once you know what works for you and your body, you can disregard any meaningless categories such as plus, curvy, or full size and embrace who you are with the tools to shine brightly!

"I strongly recommend looking into Ashely Graham and her story to learn more about how she embraces her curves!"

Powerfully Petite

"How do you know if you fall into the category of petite? Many petite women are often:

- 5'3" or under
- Frustrated when trying on standard sizes because the shoulders and/or pockets are in the wrong place on your body. Sometimes the knees of the pants fall on your shins because they are too long, or the cuff of a jacket falls well beyond the wrist. Skirts and dresses may not fall at a natural point on your body
- Find that cropped bottoms are a better fit

"Not unlike the curvy woman, determining your body shape will also begin with your measurements. Once you've got that down and you determine your body shape, modifications can be made to fit your specific body.

"Petite women come in all different body shapes and sizes, just like curvy women, but your height and your proportions are what classify you as petite.

"Just like other body types, as a petite, you may find exceptions. You may find that you are short but have a long inseam so petite pants don't work, or that you need petite bottoms but standard tops.

"So, remember that the key, for you, is to elongate, and certain styles will help you to do this. You can expect that alterations may be needed, often, so finding a good tailor will make things easier.

"Wearing cropped jackets, three-quarter sleeves, and lighter colors on top are all common recommendations to help accomplish the goal of elongating your figure. However, the most important thing is to know your body type so that you can make an informed decision about what works best for you."

QUINN

After this crash course in body types and the ways to describe them, it was time for a break, and boy, did they need it! Dawn shared that we would reconvene in fifteen minutes.

Who would have known that there was so much to consider when it comes to determining how clothes fit and that it all worked together as a part of the Power of Clothing and Personal Packaging?

We returned from the break ready to dig in and learn more. Dawn started by asking if there were any quick comments or reactions to what was shared before the break, and one participant said, "I honestly thought a white shirt was a white shirt and a pair of black pants was a pair of black pants. I had no idea that one would fit differently based on my body type… I thought that it was just me, picking up the wrong things, but there really is a *best fit* and having these tools is going to make it easier to find them. It's also going to help create a wardrobe that is just for me."

Another participant shared, "It is all new, and it feels like a lot of information, but I am loving every single minute and I am learning a lot! I can hardly wait to get home to review it all! Now I know why half of my clothes don't fit!"

There was lots of head-nodding showing agreement around the room. Then, we got back to work.

The Kibbe Method

DAWN

"Okay, I know that I have just shared quite a bit, but just when you thought there couldn't be more, there is!

"The third category or way of describing body types brings us back to the Kibbe method.

"The theory here is that bodies can be identified based on the lines of the skeleton and facial features. This system, as I previously mentioned, was developed by fashion stylist David Kibbe and thoroughly explained in his book *Metamorphosis*, where he classifies bodies as Dramatic, Natural, Classic, Romantic, and Gamine.

"It is likely that when you pick up a fashion magazine or read a blog, the second category—shapes and fruits, which we discussed before the break—is far more common.

"The categorization of shapes and fruit is also far less complex than that of the Kibbe method, which has several parts to it. I'll do my best to keep this to a minimum as we are working with a condensed version of this training."

Even though she had briefly mentioned that this theory was based on the skeletal system, Dawn continued to explain that Kibbe's theory also considered the balance between yin and yang. Yin represents the feminine energy with soft edges, fitted waists, and curvy lines. While yang was the direct opposite and represented the masculine with sharp edges and strong, crisp lines.

She shared that we could feel free to do our own personal research as to how the yin and yang descriptions come into play within this method and that she would just be going over things with a very broad brush.

And with that, we began a very brief overview of the Kibbe method.

"The Kibbe method is complex, and I will not be going into every detail. I can imagine that based on our English dictionaries and your own personal life experiences, your definition of a Dramatic is: someone who dresses in attention-grabbing outfits or has a dramatic personality. But, in fact, in the Kibbe method these things are completely unrelated.

DRAMATIC

"A Dramatic body type has the following physical characteristics:
Bone Structure:

- They appear very tall, narrow, and elongated
- Their shoulders are narrow with sharp edges
- They have long arms and legs
- Their hands and feet are large and narrow

Body Flesh:

- They have a flat bustline, straight waistline, and straight hips
- The flesh on their bodies is very taut

Facial Features:

- They have prominent, sharp, and angular facial features (nose, cheekbones, jawline)
- They have small, close-spaced eyes, straight, thin lips, and taut cheek flesh

"Are you seeing a parallel to any shapes we discussed earlier?

Moving on, our next stop will be the category of the Natural.

NATURAL

"Those who fall into this category are still angular, however, their edges aren't as sharp. A Natural body type has the following physical characteristics:

Bone Structure:

- They appear tall and broad
- Their shoulders are wide with sharp or blunt edges
- They have long arms and legs
- Their hands and feet are large and wide

Body Flesh:

- They have a wide bustline that leans toward the flat side, a straight and wide waistline, and straight hips
- The flesh on their bodies is taut but muscular

Facial Features:

- They have wide, angular facial features (nose, cheekbones, jawline) with blunt edges
- They have wide-spaced eyes, straight, broad lips, and muscular cheek flesh

"Next, we will move on to learn more about the Classic body type.

CLASSIC

"The Classic body type will appear very symmetrical with moderate features. A Classic body type has the following physical characteristics:

Bone Structure:

- Their shoulders are not fully straight or sloped
- They have moderate arms and legs
- Their hands and feet are proportioned
- Their height is easily guessed

Body Flesh:

- They have an evenly proportioned bustline, waistline, and hips with a slightly smaller waist
- The flesh on their bodies is neither very taut, nor very curvy, but evenly proportioned

Facial Features:

- They have very symmetrical and proportionate facial features (nose, cheekbones, jawline)
- They have moderate eyes, lips, and cheek flesh

"And finally, we come to the Gamine!

GAMINE

"The Gamine is a combination of a few different features and has these characteristics:

Bone Structure:

- They look petite, but their bones are angular and straight
- Their shoulders are sloped and tapered
- They have long arms and legs
- Their hands and feet are small and delicate

Body Flesh:

- They have a straight bust line, waistline, and hips
- The flesh on their bodies is quite lean

Facial Features:

- They have angular facial features (nose, cheekbones, jawline)
- They have large eyes, moderate to thin lips, and taut cheek flesh

"Let's move on to learn a little about the Romantic.

ROMANTIC

"The Romantic will appear very soft with round edges. A Romantic body type has the following physical characteristics:

Bone Structure:

- They appear delicate and shorter than they are
- Their shoulders are sloped with round edges
- They have short arms and legs
- Their hands and feet are small

Body Flesh:

- They have a full bustline, a full hourglass figure, and curvy, rounded hips
- The flesh on their bodies is very soft, voluptuous, and fleshy (even when at ideal weight)

Facial Features:

- They have small, delicate facial features (nose, cheekbones, jawline) with round edges

- They have large, rounded eyes, full lips, and round cheekbones

"We have covered the basic categories of the Kibbe method but there are several components within each that give even more detail. As I mentioned, we won't dig deep here. I am sharing an overview so that you are familiar with the fact that there are several ways to describe the body as you learn about best fits, etcetera.

"Before wrapping up, let's touch on one last piece of the Kibbe method.

YIN/YANG

"It's likely that you have heard the words "yin" and "yang." Maybe you've seen the black-and-white symbol, or seen the words used when describing interior decorating.

"In the Kibbe method, it's about the direct contrast that runs throughout. Think, if you will, of the actress Keira Knightly. If you are not familiar with who she is, take a moment to look her up online. You will see that her features are very sharp. She would be placed on one end of a horizontal line. In direct contrast, Beyoncé with her soft features would be placed at the opposite end of the line.

"Using Kibbe's terms, Kierra Knightly would be described as yang while Beyoncé would be considered yin. We can then place others on this imaginary line based on their degrees of yin and yang. The Classic sits right in the middle with the yin (soft and curvy) being the Romantic on one end and yang being the Dramatic on the other end.

"The Kibbe method looks at the differences in bone structure, body flesh, and facial features—like the amount of flesh on the face—to mark the differences in body types.

"All three of these areas can have a different yin (straight and narrow, not too much flesh) and yang (soft and curvy). These variations are what make up the different body types. If a person has all three of these areas with the same balance, they are considered to be the purest form of that description, e.g. Classic, Dramatic, etcetera.

"You will find examples of each of these body types on the screens and in your handouts. These concepts may take a while to sink in, so reviewing them along with the visuals may be helpful.

"I know this has been a long day with lots of information, but it is an important piece of the puzzle we are putting together. Thank you for your time and attention. We'll put things into action in the next session. I look forward to seeing you there."

QUINN

Admittedly, this session was one of the most in-depth introductions any of us had had about dressing our bodies. By the end of this week's session, everyone seemed to be exhausted because it can take energy to learn something new. As the time concluded, Dawn explained a few details about how to determine which of these classifications best described our body type and reminded us that we would receive a printed version of what she had just shared.

It was no surprise that all the handouts continued to fit into the disc-bound-style notebooks that we were given on the first day. By this time in the program, we had gotten into a routine of receiving our handouts and placing them into the notebook. During the break, as we picked up our handouts, the conversation veered to this disc-bound notebook style.

While this style of a notebook was new to some of us, Brandi was, of course, familiar with it. One of the most recent owners of the company that owned the patent for this style of a paper-binding system had been a client at one of her previous companies.

As it turned out, this way of binding papers wasn't so new after all. The first patent was filed and sold in 1948. Through a series of business transactions, patent purchases, transfers, and eventually a lawsuit, the disc-bound system was now a widespread tool that could be purchased at local office supply chains, which is where Charlotte had picked up a version of the system without knowing that there was much history to the concept.

There were a few conversations during breaks about the differences between the binding system and the three-ring binder system, which is where both Brandi and Charlotte chimed in. They had found the sleek, yet easy to maneuver inserts to be a far cry from their own days of using the three-ring binder system when they were in school.

Another participant added, "Back then, the loud sound of prying open a three-ring binder could be disruptive and it didn't come without its own set of challenges. After accomplishing the feat of getting this contraption open, it was a known fact that you had to close it with preciseness and perfect timing to avoid getting your fingers pinched in the rings that you had worked so hard to open. I mean, did anyone ever use those tabs at the top and bottom of the three rings?!"

Another person added, "There was always a student who had to take a trip to the school nurse for a Band-Aid because of a finger that got caught in the 'trap' of this required school supply. I may or may not have been one of those students."

The small group shared a quick laugh with empathy, knowing all too well the details being shared.

Someone else chimed in, "Yes! I can relate! Trying to close a three-ring binder without getting your finger caught would, at best, lead to a blister and at worst, cause your finger to bleed. Unfortunately, it was usually on the sheet of paper you had worked so hard to add to the binder in the first place! It was awful!" More head nods of agreement, smiles, and laughter continued within the small group. It was nice to see folks connecting as I stood close by.

Charlotte shared that she had recently enrolled in a subscription service with a company by the name of Cloth & Paper. It was a female-founded, minority-owned brand that sent some of the chicest, clean-lined organizational tools that she had seen in a long time. This company offered a similar style of binders and inserts to this disc-bound system, and she was really enjoying their products. A few people took out their phones or jotted down the name in their notebook.

As we looked through the handouts that followed this information-packed session about body types, we found the instructions on how to classify which fruit and/or geometric shape we identified with, as well as the terms introduced about the Kibbe method and how to determine which one best represented our own bodies.

The handouts also covered things like which tools we may want to use to measure ourselves, how to measure our bodies, and a worksheet to record our findings for both methods, along with a few drawings of body types, and photos of current and former celebrities who showcase the essence of each of the categories. There were also resources listed as to how to purchase a copy of *The Biggest Mistakes*

Women Make When Choosing A Stylist: How Many Are You Making?—a book Dawn wrote for her clients and the general consumer to give an understanding of how to choose someone to work with who could help us reach our goals. There was also a link to a coaching question-naire about style, a discount code for the mini-course about conduct-ing a closet audit, and a few other helpful links.

We were being armed with the tools to make an informed decision as to whether we wanted to brave this new terrain on our own or with the help of a trained professional.

We spent some time working individually on questions that Dawn provided her clients, such as:

- When I get dressed and interact with other people, how do I want to feel?
- Does my clothing accurately showcase who I want to become?
- Who do I want people to perceive me to be?
- Am I dressed like that person?
- Who do others think I am?
- What do they think I do for a living?
- Is this the look I was going for; the message I want to send?
- Most importantly, who am I, what do I bring to the world, and what can I wear today that lets that shine through?

Dawn highlighted a few of the chapters of the book and then told us that during our last hour we would have time for Q and A.

We wrapped up our session and went our separate ways with plenty to work on and lots to consider. It seemed that with every week we were together, we learned more about ourselves, each other, and the Power of Clothing and Personal Packaging.

Once we had wrapped up the questions, our time came to an end. It was amazing to see how quickly the weeks passed and how much we were able to accomplish during our time together. While it may have been hard to believe at the start that we would be feeling this way, it was going to be difficult to see all of this come to an end.

Session Five
The Big Reveal

QUINN

In this session, Dawn shared the importance of pressing pause to assess what is currently in our closet.

For some of us, that meant that we had a lot of work ahead simply because we owned a lot of clothes. For others, this would be a task that we could complete with ease because we didn't have much to sort through. We were also taught about the importance of a regular closet audit and how to complete one on our own.

We had grown accustomed to receiving handouts and materials, so it was no surprise at this point that we were given supplemental information. Any handouts we were given were added to our binders from the first day, which were now full of useful tools, tips, and tricks.

After completing this exercise, we moved into the topic of what to buy, and from there we talked about getting help while doing so.

As it turns out, not all sales associates and store stylists deliver service equally. We learned about the different types of stylists available—most of us didn't even have a clue that there was more than one type. Well, of course, Brandi knew.

As it turns out, some sales associates or stylists will sell you things that you DON'T look good in. It was disheartening to hear, but we were grateful for the information.

In addition to learning about the different types of stylists, we were given a few bullet points on how to choose the right one for us if we decided that we wanted to go that route.

It was a pleasant reminder that among the many things we received on day one, there was a card with a discount code for the book *The Biggest Mistakes Women Make When Choosing a Stylist—How Many Are You Making?* if we wanted to learn more.

I saw people making notes to themselves when this was mentioned—inferring several people were interested.

Before closing out the session, we were also reminded that to get the maximum benefit of Power of Clothing and Personal Packaging, it was best to use all of the information from the sessions as a package.

Dawn concluded this portion by sharing that if or until we decided to work with a stylist, we should always bear in mind that we should buy the best quality our budget would allow. There was no need to overspend or to add anxious pressure to buy things that we could not afford. Again, this embraced the idea of this whole package. "Buying something expensive doesn't make it right. There are pieces to this puzzle, and like most things, you want to make the best choices with the money you have."

We were surprised that this session was so short by comparison to the others. We learned that there was a reason for this when Dawn surprised those in the room with an announcement. She shared that she would be hosting the next portion of this session at an off-site location that evening at a restaurant in town called Bellemore.

This was not on the agenda because it was completely voluntary as to whether we would attend. The invitation was presented as a continuation of the topic of a closet audit with a few very important surprises.

We were told this had been part of the plan all along and that she had already informed our employers about this event at the time of contracting with them. They, too, knew that this would be a voluntary session and that our attendance would not have any bearing on the successful completion of our time at DawnToday. She did not, however, tell them *when* this would be taking place, so the timing was a surprise to everyone, even me.

With some private schedule juggling, all the ladies from the firm— Brandi, Charlotte, and Darby—were able to attend.

Charlotte's mom was already planning to go through the after-school routine with the kids and even prep for dinner. After Charlotte's call, she agreed to stay a bit longer, take the next step, and make sure that the kids were all fed and in bed on time.

Brandi checked her family's online calendar to see if her husband had plans to be out. This would tell her if she would be contacting him or their nanny about her change of plans. As it turned out her husband was home for the night, so she called him. He was supportive but surprised about her choice to attend, especially since she had been so adamantly against her mandatory attendance in the first place. He had to admit, he had noticed changes over the last few weeks, and he didn't hide the fact that Brandi was more like her 'old self'—she had a new level of energy, purpose, and drive. She had never stopped being friendly or welcoming, but it was nice to see her a bit more light-hearted and down to earth these days. He was glad to hear that she was going to this event. He could hear the excitement in her voice when he told her again about the positive changes he was seeing, and her enthusiasm increased when she mentioned something about a big reveal that would happen that night. He let her know that he was happy for her. She smiled and agreed that she was seeing the changes, too, then she disconnected the call.

As a young, single woman who was not going to pass up an opportunity to prove her commitment and hopefully impress her bosses at the firm, Darby made the instant decision to join in on what sounded like an interesting way to spend an evening.

As the coordinator and originator of this connection of employees to DawnToday, I wasn't going to miss a minute. When we contracted with Dawn and her team, I knew that tonight was going to be an interesting one. Dawn had shared that it was one of her favorite portions of the series. I was one of the first to arrive at Bellemore.

After exchanging pleasantries with many of the attendees, I joined the table with Brandi, Charlotte, Darby, and a few others. Dawn shared again that this was not something that the firm would be counting as attendance and that it was merely a time for them to get to know each other a little better. The "big reveal," as she referred to it, would also happen tonight and her address to us began like this:

"For many of you, as we get closer to the end of our time together, things may have started to change. As you have embraced the principles you have learned over the last several weeks and put some into action, things can really start to shift. It isn't uncommon for people to start going through what they own to see what they can change about an outfit, or to purge their old belongings altogether. They are enjoying how they feel after making even small changes, and they want more. This domino effect spreads to other areas, and before you know it, things are really looking up; you're having brighter days, and these are just a glimpse of your future!

"Sometimes, it can be challenging to explain how you are feeling—both inside and out—and the details of what you are experiencing to someone who hasn't taken part in all of our meetings. So, this more laid-back approach to a session is also a time to check in with your peers and get to know them. You can ask what changes they have noticed, personally, and ask how they are feeling about those changes. This is also the time for the 'big reveal,'" she said with a subtle laugh, using her pointer and middle fingers to create air quotes.

"When we first started our time together, I mentioned that there was a reason for the secrecy, and that there was a specific time you would be given the 'okay' to share the details of who you are.

"You are a smart and bright group, so many of you may have already put the pieces together. But tonight it becomes official, and you will reveal your real names (beyond an initial). You will also share a few other details that you will learn about as the evening progresses. I am excited for you!" Dawn said as she smiled.

"You are seated where you are seated for a reason. Any empty place settings near you have the information about those who chose not to or were unable to attend on the underside of the place setting. Your table coordinator will reveal them when the time comes."

The participants couldn't believe it. They had become so accustomed to using these "pretend names" and seeing just a person's initials on their name badge that they had almost forgotten about any "reveal" that may or may not happen. Well, except for Darby, who if you remember was eager to undermine the entire plan at lunch the first day.

"You may be surprised about what you have in common!" Dawn said with raised eyebrows. This was likely because she had seen that Brandi, Charlotte, and Darby had become chatty with one another over the recent weeks.

Then Dawn shifted back into the session and started with the next topic on the agenda: how to effectively conduct a closet audit. We took notes between bites of our appetizers and sips of drinks. Her approach seemed to be less formal but certainly not less impactful. This was likely a strategic move on the part of the DawnToday team. Everything we had encountered to this point was strategic—with purpose and intention to guide us toward a certain outcome.

A short and informal Q and A period followed the presentation, and true to form, there was a reminder that there was a coupon code in the original packets from the first day. The coupon was for a workbook titled *The Wrong Way and the Right Way to Audit Your Closet.* We were told it would reinforce what we had just learned.

Dawn shared that she was aware people were likely a little preoccupied and most interested in what would be revealed about the other participants. This is one of the reasons she and her team were offering a discount on this valuable tool. Again, nothing was done without purpose and intention to steer us in the right direction.

Table by table, and then one person at a time, participants stood to share their real name, where they worked, how long they had been at the company they worked for, and the position they had applied for that caused them to be a candidate to attend the sessions at

DawnToday. This led everyone to believe each company had this personal development requirement for applicants.

When the time came for Brandi to stand and share, Charlotte immediately flashed back to having seen her in the parking garage on her first day. "It was *her*!" she said audibly but quietly, and she glanced over at Darby who gave her that knowing look of *I told you!* as she reflected on Brandi's interaction with them at lunch the first day.

Charlotte followed after the next two participants and shared her first name followed by an explanation.

"My name is Charlotte Whitlock, but most of my close friends call me Charlie. I am new to the firm. When I originally applied and received the entry-level position, I had a lot going on in my personal life. Once I started working, I realized that I had undervalued myself by applying for the job, although I couldn't articulate these feelings at that time. I'm not quite sure what prompted me to apply for a transfer to a more challenging position."

There were a few perplexed looks as she spoke because it was obvious there was more to the story. Brandi and Darby were both shocked that Charlotte worked at the same company as Brandi, but Darby was the most taken aback because only she knew about the information bomb she was about to drop.

When she stood and told the group what her name was, she added that she had recently graduated and passed the MCAT. This was news to everyone, including Quinn, and any other People and Culture/Human Resources employees. She had intentionally omitted this from her resume and didn't mention it in any of her interviews.

There were immediate looks of confusion and raised eyebrows as she continued to share. They learned that this potentially future physician had rejected several offers from top-tier medical schools. It was clear to everyone that Darby had clearly been misjudged and that this was a living example of the Power of Clothing and Personal Packaging in action.

There was nothing about her appearance or conversation that fit the stereotypical ideas of what a medical student might say, do, or be in terms of personal packaging. In her attempt to hide this from everyone, she had created a new message that she presented to the world, and it was working—even though she'd done it subconsciously.

She knew they were likely wondering, "Was it some sort of pre-requisite, or had she taken a gap-year...?" The questions reeling through their minds were written all over their faces. She answered their looks of confusion about why a medical student would be at these meetings.

Darby's passion to succeed in unchartered waters, to take on a new career path that didn't have her family's footprint all over it, and to pursue her strong desire for independence were only a few of the reasons she shared.

She explained that she felt the pull to something other than medicine while she was at school. For most medical students, forty-nine percent major in biology, while only seven percent major in other intense areas like engineering, which is what she had done. To keep her options wide, she also took on a minor in finance.

Her explanation eased their furrowed brows as she continued. She shared that she was determined to gain independence in more than one area of her life, and that pursuing a career in a different field was one way that she saw best suited her plans.

The looks of surprise on people's faces didn't outshine the looks of shock and awe on Brandi and Charlotte's faces as Darby revealed that she, too, was an employee at the firm! How could they have missed seeing each other? How did they not know this was the case? It was all so wild! Talk about an incredible night of "reveals!"

Darby explained that a move to the finance industry was where she saw an opportunity to jump-start the changes she wanted to make. Even though these changes weren't all financially driven but equally personal, too, brought a bit of understanding to everyone listening.

Darby had shared more personal information than the others, and it was clear, there was more to her story, too. She was younger than Brandi and Charlotte, but they saw in her a similar drive and passion. There was an unspoken depth to her, and it was being masked by her personal package.

This observation and Darby's obvious determination didn't go unnoticed, and the fact she was also employed at this top-ranked firm was what prompted Charlotte to slip a note to both Darby and Brandi. She requested they exchange contact information at the end of the meeting.

The looks on Brandi and Charlotte's faces brought a glimmer to Dawn's eye as she watched their reactions.

Dawn had conveyed at the time of the contract signing with the firm that this was one of her favorite events in the series. These moments were topped only by the transformation stories that would be shared at the last meeting.

Before wrapping up for the night, Dawn shared a bit more and reminded us that the closet audit process would look very different for each of us, and that there were a variety of budgets represented in the room and at the meetings as a whole.

"For some of you, you may need an hour to complete this while others may need a few days or even a week to complete this process," she said. "Don't be too hard on yourselves, and remember that you now have the real names of your peers. Some of you may want to trade contact information."

Brandi, Charlotte, and Darby exchanged a quick look at one another.

"Use the tools we have provided," Dawn continued, "and utilize your peers as a sounding board if you find yourself getting stuck on whether to keep an item. They may not be stylists, but they will likely be able to empathize on the mindset piece as you have all had your own personal transformations happening."

To say that the evening was a surprise is an understatement. Everyone left the meeting in a state of bewilderment and joy; confusion and confirmation. If there remained even the smallest sliver of doubt about the Power of Clothing and Personal Packaging, it had been erased and eradicated by the end of the big reveal!

Brandi's Closet Audit Leads to Brunch

BRANDI

Walking into a quiet house after a night full of surprises wasn't ideal. Even after the drive home, Brandi was still excited and full of energy.

She was looking forward to sharing the details with her husband in person, so she sent a text before leaving the restaurant's parking lot to let him know she was on her way and to ask if he was still awake. When he replied with a thumbs-up emoji, it didn't really answer her question. An emoji could mean he heard the notification and replied quickly, or he could be in the middle of a show or the replay of a game. He could have been answering quickly so he wouldn't miss anything, but either way, she hoped he would be awake and ready to listen when she walked in.

To her surprise, the phone system in the car alerted her—she had a call coming in, and it was from her husband.

Her voice must have been in a high register because when she answered the call, he said, "Wow! You sound excited! How'd it go? Can you talk?"

That was all the invitation she needed, and she jumped right in. "You're *never* going to believe what happened tonight!" She talked for almost the entire forty-minute drive home before they ended the call.

When she approached their neighborhood, and then finally the driveway, she pressed the button overhead to open the garage door. Gathering all her things from the car, she walked in.

She made her way to the staircase separating the two sides of the house. When she reached the top of the stairs, she set her things down on the long, narrow table that lined the wall. Glancing above, she saw the framed oil painting of their family and she smiled. It had been a gift, and she couldn't have loved it more. It was one of those things you see so often it can almost seem invisible, but when it does catch your attention, it makes you stop and take it all in.

This was one of her favorite family photos, and an artist from Lisbon, whose card they had gotten on their ten-year anniversary trip, was the artist. Her attention to detail was second to none, and unlike so many oil paintings that can go bad, this one depicted the heart of each person. The gold display light above the painting shone down and highlighted their bright smiles and the sparkle in each of their eyes.

Brandi made a stop to check in on the kids. She pivoted right and walked down the hall to peek into their rooms. They were both sound asleep, so she decided not to go in. She remembered her last attempt to navigate their rooms in the dark. The Lego Friends piece that lodged its way into her foot couldn't hold a candle to the dismembered keyboard parts that were splayed across the floor and attempted to make a permanent home in her toes. As a part of a science project, the sharp pieces had been left out for the next day's work. The memory alone of her screaming in pain and waking the entire household was reminder enough that entering either of these kids' rooms without the flashlight from her phone could end badly. So, she closed each door quietly while bidding them a whispered goodnight.

Making her way back down the hall, she grabbed her things from the table as she headed toward their primary suite. She saw a light on in the sitting area of the suite, which meant her husband might still be awake.

Turning the brass knob on one of the double doors, she entered and found the lamp by the loveseat on, but there was no one sitting there. Clearly, her husband had left the light on for her.

As she reached down to turn the lamp off, she noticed the light from the sleeping area illuminating the floor beneath the next set of double doors.

She guessed she would find him here—iPad in hand—and she was right. Adrenaline still pumping from the big reveal, it was hard to think of sleep, so she was glad to see he was awake; even though they had talked almost the entire drive home.

After greeting each other she asked, "Can you believe it? Isn't it a wild twist in all of this? I mean two of the women working at the firm, right there under my nose this entire time?! I *told* Quinn that this could happen. But you know what? It doesn't even bother me anymore. Hearing everyone share even a small piece of their experience with the Power of Clothing and Personal Packaging and how it has impacted them was incredible! It has made all the difference!"

"Wow, you are actually using the phrase 'Power of Clothing and Personal Packaging' in a positive light? Talk about a transformation. Phew! That's great, Brandi. This *reveal* sounds like it made a big impact!" She could tell he was sincere, but she didn't think he really *got* it.

"I know you're excited," he continued, "but I've got an early meeting tomorrow and then I am flying out for an overnight trip, so I've got to get some sleep. I wanted to see you and to say congratulations on this event tonight and all the growth you've experienced over the last several weeks. We can talk about it more tomorrow on my way to the airport if you want to. Just let me know what time works for you."

Even after sharing, in great detail, what she learned about the people in attendance, specifically Charlotte and Darby, she was still pretty tightly wound, and sleep was the furthest thing from her mind. Her husband may have been ready for bed, but she still found it difficult to wind down.

She tried reading and found herself reviewing the materials from all the sessions, especially tonight's meeting about the closet audit.

She had been slowly removing pieces from her closet over the last several weeks of meetings. There were lots of pieces she felt were no longer quite right. After tonight's meeting, the supplemental handouts, and this amazing reveal, her head was still spinning.

She looked over and saw that her husband was almost asleep. Touching his shoulder to say a few words, she hadn't expected the monologue that followed, "My mind is still reeling from it all; not just tonight's events, but everything. It's all starting to add up and it's hard to imagine it coming to a close. I'm not sure if I am more excited about the ladies I exchanged information with—you know, the ones I mentioned to you. I still can't believe we have been working under the same roof! Did I mention that Darby was accepted into more than one top-ranked medical school and she turned them all down?! Can you believe it?!"

Her husband was listening as intently as he could. Even though he knew the question was rhetorical, he answered with a quick, "Yes, you *have* mentioned it. In fact, I think this may be the third time, or wait, maybe it was the fifth time you've mentioned it. It's hard to keep track. I mean it's all so incredibly unbelievable!" He ended with a wink, a smirk, and a lot of sarcasm. "I mean, how can we keep it all straight?" he continued, trying to keep a straight face as he teased. "With all the secrecy and mystery, it's like living in the middle of a Steven King novel. I just can't believe this power of clothing!" He raised his eyebrows and opened his eyes widely for emphasis as he said the last sentence. He could not hold back the laughter any longer and he doubled over as it fell out of his mouth.

She knew there was no harm in his teasing. Sarcasm was just one of the things they had in common. She got the joke and had to smirk and laugh a little herself. Hearing him mock her about this made the whole thing sound funny.

Checking her reaction—to be sure she knew he was kidding—and confirming she was not offended, he put the finishing touch on this little performance by saying, "You told me about it while you were in the car, you mentioned it when you walked in, you told me again just now, and I'm *pretty* sure, if I wait long enough, you will tell me again. Wow, Brandi, this has really made an impact on you."

She playfully hit him with a pillow as he continued to laugh. "All jokes aside, Brandi, this has been one of the most transformative things that has happened to and for you. I mean next to marrying me, of course," he said, winking again.

They both laughed, and Brandi added, "The birth of our kids, sir! I'd say that was pretty transformative, too!" And they both smiled.

As she finished that last sentence, Brandi swung her long legs over the side of the bed and her feet touched the floor. She told her husband she was going to spend some time in her closet, putting some of this new knowledge about a closet audit to work. "Go ahead and go to sleep. Thanks for staying up with me, and for listening, like you always do. I appreciate it. I'll see you in the morning," she said, looking back one last time with a smile.

It wasn't long after entering the closet that she saw the pile of clothes on the floor. She had started adding pieces that no longer fit her based on what she had been learning.

Seeing the pile grow, she got frustrated and emotional thinking about the sales associates she had worked with over the years and how they had guided (or misguided), supported, and even sometimes encouraged her to make these purchases. Some of the associates she had really come to like, and she wondered what would have to happen for them to learn about the principles she now knew.

She wanted them to do well and she started to brainstorm ideas about how to connect them with DawnToday. As her thoughts continued, so did the mound of clothes she was creating.

She finished all the hanging items and was ready to move on to the folded pieces. These were kept in the wire baskets she had ordered and installed when she first moved in. It was one of the only modifications she had to make to this almost-perfect built-in closet system.

At first, she only eliminated a few things from her regular rotation. As the weeks went on, she shifted and started choosing what to wear based on the messages she wanted to send, her body type, how she wanted to feel, and the role she wanted to play that day.

Now, the piles on the floor resembled sand dunes, and as she looked back at what remained in the drawers and on the racks, she saw more wall space and wire shelving than she had seen since moving in.

The room was easily the size of a small bedroom or nursery, and she sat in the middle on the tufted bench. She looked at the spoils of the purchases she had made over the years, and it felt like that woman—the one who had done all of the buying—was different than the woman who sat here now.

She vacillated about what to do with everything that sat on the floor. She didn't dare calculate the value; it would have made her sick to her stomach. She remembered some of the words from the meetings, how what she had may be exactly what someone else needed or wanted. And *this* wasn't junk! So many of these things still had the tags on them. And for most of the shoes and accessories, the original packaging was still in her possession.

She liked the feel of having her own boutique in her closet. She also knew the value of the re-sale market and that pieces in their original packaging had a higher perceived value and commanded a higher price. So she usually hung on to them.

Instead of wallowing and being frustrated, she used this as ammunition to continue working on herself—she was "changing her mind, her clothes, and her life..."

"I'm pretty sure Dawn didn't mean we were supposed to empty our closets in one night. Nothing in the closet audit said anything about coming up empty, but none of this works!" Brandi said to herself.

She quietly walked over to grab her iPad from her nightstand and then went back to her spot in the closet with the hopes of not waking her husband. She typed in the words "storage bins" in the search bar. After viewing a few popular sites, she ended with orders from the Container Store website.

Labels and a label maker were added to the cart, but she quickly removed them after remembering their nanny had purchased a replacement model for the house. Brandi was insistent on organization, and they used one often to help organize some of the kids' things.

After clicking "Add to Cart" and completing the order, she felt a sense of overwhelm had lifted.

She wanted to talk about all the changes and transformations—both big and small—and she knew her husband would gladly listen and support her. But she wanted to talk to someone who had been there; someone who could validate or understand what she was experiencing right now.

She had intentionally not synced her iPad with her phone—in another attempt at work-life balance—so she walked back to the digital charging station in her closet. She had been trying to do a better job of not keeping it on her nightstand when she went to bed after learning it can interrupt sleep cycles. She removed the phone from the docking station.

Knowing their phone numbers were added to her phone tonight, she started a group text with Charlotte and Darby, surprising herself at how excited she was about it. "Anyone else having trouble winding down after tonight's meeting?" she typed before pressing send.

Surprised at how quickly they both responded, she smiled when she heard the beeping and saw her phone light up as they replied almost simultaneously. She hurried to turn her ringer and alerts off before reading them. She had forgotten to do it when she placed it on the charger. Tonight had been a full one, and clearly the noises the phone might make wasn't what was on her radar!

Reading their replies, both women chimed in with unanimous agreement. Charlotte said, "I am, for sure!!!" Darby sent an emoji with the raised hand. While Brandi was smiling and thinking about if or what she wanted to say next, Darby sent a GIF with a person lying in bed, kicking in frustration at not being able to sleep. Brandi laughed out loud and thought, *I really like this girl!* Then she told them about her restlessness, the piles on the floor of her closet, and then explained what she was doing.

Charlotte said she had lost count as to how many hours she spent reviewing her materials. She said she was still in shock about the fact that they all worked at the same place. She was a bit sheepish after learning about Brandi's title and position but continued to interact in the conversation. Brandi's present-time text messages didn't match her title and previous demeanor, and this put Charlotte at ease.

Darby shared that she had just been debriefing with her boyfriend via Facetime. After several messages back and forth between the three of them, it was hard to believe that almost forty-five minutes had gone by. Brandi admitted to having a full day ahead and her need to at least *try* to get some sleep.

She let them know how much she had appreciated the conversation; having someone to talk to who had been through the last several weeks and tonight's events had been great. They said goodbye and each of them headed to bed with a smile, equally as happy about the conversation.

The next morning, Brandi walked into her closet and saw the piles and they reminded her of the jokes she had exchanged with Charlotte and Darby during last night's conversation.

She picked up her phone to revisit the conversation, and after re-reading the thread, she made the impulsive decision to invite them both to her home for Sunday brunch that weekend. She sent a text right away, and before leaving for the office her phone was illumi-nated with updated messages. Both of them had replied with an em-phatic yes to her invitation.

They both asked what she would like them to bring. Knowing an or-der would be placed for prepared foods, Brandi didn't need them to bring anything. She also knew that oftentimes people don't like to ar-rive empty-handed when they visit someone's home, so she asked both of them to bring their favorite juice. It was something easy for most, and her usual response when people asked.

Brunch at the St. James Home

Sunday morning came and Darby headed out in a car driven by a Lyft driver. There were no bus routes in the area she was going, and the train (or "L") only operated Monday through Friday in that area. Even if it did run on the weekends, it would only get her to the commuter station where people parked their cars before getting on and off the train. So, after a bit of researching, she decided to reserve a car the night before.

As the car approached the brick exterior of the home, she looked out of the window and smiled. *It looks just like her*, she thought.

Before she could ring the bell, the family dog came dutifully running and barking toward the wrought iron screen that framed the large double-door entry.

Darby heard Brandi call out to what must have been one of her kids, telling them to get the short-haired—but furry and well-groomed—family member. Tail wagging, the dog stopped barking when he was joined by his young male friend. *Well trained. Impressive*, Darby thought as she watched Brandi approach just seconds later. Darby was quickly introduced to Brandi's son, Landon. She wasn't surprised that the young man looked her directly in the eyes while giving her a firm handshake. Darby moved the bag and the flowers she was carrying to her left arm so she could take his hand with her right.

"What kind of dog do you have there?" she asked.

"He's an Airedale Terrier. It's nice to meet you, Ms. Darby. I'm going to get him out of the way now. Have fun, Mom!" he said as he turned and ran down the hall with his four-legged companion by his side.

Darby didn't know if she was more shocked by this obedient dog, who looked a little like the family butler, or the son's manners. She quickly remembered where she was and whose house she was visiting, and it all made sense.

Before they turned to walk away from the entry, they noticed a van pull up in the driveway. Assuming it to be Charlotte, they stood and watched.

After exiting the driver's side, she walked around the back of the van to the passenger door. She opened it and loaded her arms with a gift bag and what looked like a bouquet of flowers. As she walked towards the door, she slowed her pace to take note of the precisely trimmed hedges, the varieties of mature Hosta that lined the front of the house, and the overall landscaping. Watching Charlotte through the large screen, Darby realized she had overlooked this from the backseat of the car she was riding in. The front lawn was, indeed, a showstopper.

Charlotte was so busy admiring the beauty and taking it all in that she didn't see the two of them in the doorway, watching her. She approached ready to look for the doorbell when one side of the screen opened.

Startled, she smiled, said hello, and made her way inside. Handing the bouquet of flowers to Brandi, she turned to see Darby standing there. "Oh, wow! I didn't realize that you were already here. Hi!" she offered with a smile equally as wide as the one she had shared with Brandi.

"I usually like to take the train, but the one from the city that comes out here is a commuter route. It only operates during the week, so I decided to call a Lyft. That's why you didn't see a car in the driveway."

"Well, I'm glad you're both here," Brandi said as she motioned them to follow her.

She slowly led the way down the long hall. The pace allowed time for a small peek into some of the rooms along the way. On the right, a large, sun-filled room with a fireplace and book-lined walls had a window facing the front yard. As they passed a room on the left, a shiny black baby grand piano sat across from a guitar stand with multiple guitars. A violin sat atop its case, and a music stand filled with books stood nearby.

Reaching the end of the hall was like approaching a T in the road. The space was large and open; clearly a family gathering spot. The kitchen was on the left, complete with a double island—one with a built-in cooler down the center, the other with a prep sink and large eat-in space surrounded by leather stools. The high-end appliances were eye-catching, and everything displayed was like viewing a well-curated work of art.

What separated the kitchen from the great room directly across from it was the expansive space with wide-plank hardwood floors where they now stood.

A large cloud sofa looked inviting, and despite its massive footprint in the room, this well-appointed gathering area could have been on the cover of *Architectural Digest* magazine.

The sofa seemed to be big enough for a team of large football or basketball players. It was huge! As Charlotte and Darby were taking it all in, they saw a framed family photo that covered a third of one wall; this explained the size of the sofa.

Brandi was tall, but her husband was even taller. He must have been at least six-foot-five, if a person had to guess. In the photo, the family stood barefoot in the sand in front of the ocean, her husband's height hovering over Brandi. "What a beautiful family," Darby said at the same time Charlotte was complimenting her on her home and how beautiful it was.

If anyone else had said these words that followed thank you, it may have seemed pretentious. But in her Gucci slides and casual attire, Brandi's comments seemed natural and sincere. After saying thank you to both of them, she continued, "I thought we'd eat out on the terrace; it overlooks the garden."

Charlotte and Darby looked at each other and smiled.

"Oh! Would you like us to bring the juice out there or leave it here on the island?" Darby asked after seeing the beverages standing in the ice-filled cooler that ran down the center of the island. Brandi had forgotten that she had mentioned them bringing anything but quickly replied, "Sure! Let's bring them out with us."

Entering the terrace, their eyes went as wide as saucers. The colorful array of charcuterie boards, bowls of fresh fruit, and small chafing dishes to keep the hot food was more than either of them expected. The food was displayed on a beautiful sideboard and a credenza held the beverages—which included coffee, tea, and carafes of lemon- and mint-infused water, another with orange slices, and another with cucumbers, along with a few choices for sparkling water.

Upbeat jazz music filled the space, and it was a perfect way to set the mood for the day. Brandi took the juices from their hands, thanked them both for the lovely flowers they brought, and told them to get started with the food while she put the flowers in water.

Being the gracious host she was, she returned with the store-bought flowers beautifully displayed in a Baccarat crystal vase that instantly elevated them and made them look even more beautiful. "They'll be right at home out here!" Brandi said with a smile when she returned.

She motioned the two women to follow her with their plates in hand. They rounded the corner to find a small and intimate French-inspired table. The table was in a three-season porch adjacent to the terrace, and the view surrounding it was breathtaking. It was clear that either someone in Brandi's family had majored in horticulture, had an amazing green thumb, or they had the best gardener in town.

All the grass on the property rivaled that of a championship golf course, and the flowers were stunning. How they managed to pull this off in the Midwest was beyond these guests. Charlotte had often had similar thoughts about her former in-laws' property, but whenever she mentioned it to any of the family members, the topic seemed to land on uninterested ears.

The way Brandi seamlessly incorporated their floral contribution into the space let them know she had been in this position many times before. She was no stranger to the scenario of incorporating store-bought flowers into this beautifully landscaped space abundant in flowers of its own. The ones they brought were arranged and placed as if they had been freshly cut from this gardener's dream.

After placing the flowers just so, Brandi prepared a plate of food for herself and then joined them at the table. Conversation erupted after

Brandi broke the ice. Even in this beautiful and well-appointed space, she had the ability to make it feel warm and inviting. The three talked non-stop, and no one could believe hours had passed when someone entered the space, bursting them out of their conversation bubble.

A young girl bounced in with sparkling eyes. It was Brandi's daughter, who had just returned from a birthday party. Following close behind was the tall man from the photo. Both had come in to say hello and meet Brandi's guests. When they saw her husband bend into what seemed almost like a bridge to reach down to kiss Brandi on the cheek, any questions about his height, especially based on the family photo they saw on the wall of the family room, were immediately put to rest.

"Nice arrangement." His deep voice surprised them. He smiled and pointed to the vase with the flowers from Charlotte and Darby.

Wow, this guy knew how to read a room. Both Darby and Charlotte knew they shared the sentiment, catching each other's eye. With all the flowers around them, he saw the ones they brought? Surely this couple had to have had similar situations in the past and discussed this before.

Introductions and pleasantries exchanged, Brandi was thrilled he would now have faces to put to the names she had been talking about since the big reveal.

The break in their conversation prompted visits to the restroom, refreshing their beverages, and some checked their phones. When they settled back into their seats, a new topic arose; they started a discussion about how things had changed for them as a result of the sessions at DawnToday. They talked about how they had each landed at the firm, and nothing was held back. Well, Brandi did have some legal and positional obligations that kept her from being completely transparent, but she was able to navigate it in a way that didn't feel awkward and kept her included in the conversation.

She told them she had transferred from another state and how much she had been looking forward to working there. Then, she jumped into her feelings and how she had no idea about the messages she was sending with her clothes and personal package.

A tear streamed down her cheek as she began to quote one of the lines that had resonated with her the most. "It was something like, 'I can communicate my goals with my outfits,' or something like that." She couldn't remember the words exactly, so she said, "I'll be right back. I'm going to grab my cards."

The rustling of Brandi's feet in the house must have queued her husband and kids. They entered the room and asked if the ladies would mind if they interrupted and grabbed a bite to eat.

There was enough for a party of eight, and the three women had spent more time talking than eating, so as Brandi came walking back into the room behind them, she said, "Of course! Help yourselves," to the hungry trio and they dove into the food.

The ladies heard the kids' excitement when they saw the juice Charlotte and Brandi had brought. The enthusiasm made it obvious that these brands weren't common at this house. The smiles made the ladies feel even more comfortable here.

Charlotte and Darby smiled when they saw Brandi return with the stack of cards. They recognized them as part of the Confidence Collection Card sample pack they had all received in their packets weeks before.

"Okay, now, let me show you which ones meant the most to me from this pack," Brandi said as her crew was finishing up. "Did you two look at your cards? Do you have favorites?"

"Absolutely!" Charlotte said. "I've actually got my favorites in my planner." Then she stood and walked over to the small table where she had placed her bag.

When she returned, Darby was scrolling through her phone. "I'll pull mine up. I ended up purchasing the entire online pack," she said, and they all smiled.

Brandi started talking and said, "Okay, I was trying to remember one, in particular, but I'll just read a few of the ones I look at most."

- "Do we not express ourselves through the clothes we wear as much as what we say and do?" —Mary Brooks Picken
- "Fashion is a way of communicating ideas, values, and aspirations through clothes." —Richard Thompson Ford
- "Through our attire, we announce who we are, what we care about, and where we belong—or aspire to belong—in society." —Richard Thompson Ford

Then, Darby shared hers:

- "Your daily outfits determine how seriously you take yourself."
- "Getting dressed allows me the ability to show up for who I want to be or what I want to accomplish that day."
- "Clothing manages your mood, and helps you feel better about yourself."
- "Style matters because your outfits determine how you carry yourself every day."

- "Think of the person you need to be in any particular situation. Then dress, groom, and accessorize in a way that helps you mentally step into that personality." —Molly St. Louis
- "Style matters because your daily outfits determine how you envision your future."

"Did you guys know about any of the authors quoted on these cards or the scientific study about Enclothed Cognition?" Charlotte asked, chiming in.

"I feel like I've been living under a rock, and someone has come to rescue me," Darby added.

"I had no idea my ego had gotten so big. I am a people person, and I had no intention of coming across the way I was. My insecurities obviously joined my wallet and partnered to create a new version of me I didn't even realize existed!" Brandi said.

Charlotte laughed and shared that she felt similarly except that it was in reverse. "I had so many negative thoughts about abundance and openly showing it that even though I have seen and experienced so much, this bothered me. Marrying Charles meant entering a whole new world. I didn't grow up affluent; not by any stretch of the imagination. I can definitely relate to becoming someone else without even knowing that it's happening."

Darby shared that for her it was more about what she wanted to avoid. She shared the backstory of her parents' intended arranged marriage and her plans to get around it.

She also talked about what her childhood had been like, what the clothes represented to her, and how even at a young age, she had devised a plan to oppose it all. Unfortunately, she was unaware that her idea was actually working *against* her, and it certainly wouldn't have helped in her pursuit of the internship.

They sat, looking at each other, processing. How nice, they had agreed at some point in the afternoon, that their personalities gelled and not one of them felt the need to fill every quiet moment with words or idle chatter.

After a few moments, the conversation turned to what they hoped to accomplish by taking the next step at the firm.

Of course, Brandi was unable to share details, but at the end of this topic of conversation, they all had a greater understanding of each other's story. Aware of her position at the firm, they accomplished this without crossing any lines or creating any conflicts of interest on Brandi's part.

The piece of personal information Brandi *did* share was that her focus right now was to be a partner at the firm. It had been a career goal for over a decade. She hoped that at the end of this series of meetings at DawnToday, the timing for it to finally happen would be just right.

What she didn't share was that she knew conversations were already taking place between the current partners, but she couldn't divulge these confidential details.

Shocking both Charlotte and Darby, Brandi talked about why and how she had originally gotten into the field. There were some very interesting reasons, and it did cause them to look at her in a different light.

She said she hadn't been able to pinpoint when all the clothes and accessories started going to her head. In fact, she didn't even know they had, until now. The fact that this was even a point of discussion was a revelation for her. Her other eye-opener was the way she was perceived when she was wearing the clothes she had assumed were giving her an edge.

At this point she hadn't determined if she was more upset about the messages she learned she was sending or the fact she didn't know. She had always attributed the looks and the rumblings behind her back to admiration or just jealousy.

The Post-It note exercise was the point at which she first learned what people thought about her—not as a person, but about what she was wearing—and how she was being perceived.

"Do you remember how the team at DawnToday sorted through all the notes before giving us access to them?" she asked. Watching Charlotte and Darby nod, she continued. "The night I read the notes, I was shocked. I had absolutely no idea I was coming across that way or sending any messages at all, let alone what was written on these little slips of paper I was reading!"

She told them how she had home the night of the Post-It note activity and she was moved to add up everything she had learned so far, from the one-week email series, the live sessions, and the Post-It note activity, and she used the journal that had been provided to process it all.

It was like a glass of cold water had been thrown in her face, and she could see how much she had changed. She decided to put some of what she was learning into action. The positive reactions to the changes she made were motivating. The way she felt about herself was even more encouraging. Both led her to make more changes, and those changes spurred on more. Little by little she could see the positive momentum building.

"At this point," she said, "I have cleared out more of my clothes and accessories than I care to admit but..." She paused before continuing. "Let me show you something." She stood and gestured for the ladies to follow her.

Secretly excited to see more of this gorgeous home, they both followed, leaving their cloth napkins in their chairs as they walked away. They passed by the rest of the family, who was watching TV on the comfy, oversized sofa they had seen earlier.

Getting a second glance at the piece, Charlotte thought the sofa looked like one she had seen during one of her late-night YouTube binges. *I knew that piece looked familiar,* she thought.

She wasn't really into YouTube, or television, but in the time period between the break-up and the divorce, she often found herself attached to a screen as a way of escape after putting the kids to bed.

Obviously, this episode had made an impression because she still remembered this sofa over a year later. It was featured during the tour of a home that belonged to Heather Dubrow. Heather is one of the stars of the show *The Real Housewives of Orange County*, which Charlotte learned after Googling to see who this woman was.

In the video, Heather and her husband, Dr. Terry Dubrow, a plastic and reconstructive surgeon, shared their 22,000-square-foot home. They made quite a big deal about the decision-making process they went through to find a piece large enough for the enormous family room. Not long after seeing the episode, Charlotte's neighbor Alex invited her to come and see their newly remodeled family room.

When she visited her neighbor, Charlotte recognized the sofa immediately and mentioned where she had seen it. Alex laughed, telling her that Heather's home had been the inspiration behind her selections, and that everything was from Restoration Hardware. Charlotte was used to this kind of conversation—where women would slip small details in to seemingly impress people or to stroke their own ego.

Here at Brandi's, it was different. No less impressive, in fact, this home rivaled—and in some areas surpassed—some she had seen while married to Charles. It made sense that this couch was here. They were a tall family. They had the square footage, and Brandi's taste in decorating seemed to be similar to Heather's in many ways. Charlotte wondered if Brandi was a fan of this television series. If she was, it would explain a lot.

Charlotte had been trying to put her finger on a way to describe Brandi to her mom, and quite frankly to herself. If Brandi was a fan of the Housewives franchise, so many of her questions about her would all start to make sense. Her choice of clothes, the opulence, and how she presented herself when they first met could have easily been influenced by the women she saw on the show. She inwardly agreed with Brandi; the changes she saw her making now were obvious. She saw a difference not just in her clothes, but in the way she was carrying herself.

They entered a room at the back of the house, and what they saw when Brandi opened the door was anything but common. Most homes have a place in a garage, a shed, or a small storage space under the stairs to store unused items. But in the St. James home, this multipurpose room was different. It served as a place for out-of-season equipment in sizes for every member of the family, and apparently, some for guests, too. Cross-country and downhill skis, snowboards and snowshoes, helmets, cleats, elbow and knee pads, tennis rackets, and fishing poles filled one side of the room. The organization and display made it look as if you were in a boutique-style sporting goods store, and seeing the room as a whole, it all made sense.

The space was shared with a large gift-wrapping and counter-height craft station. Stools with leather seats were tightly tucked beneath it. Not too far from the hot glue guns, scissors, and ribbons sat a row of clear containers. This made it easy to see the designer boxes and shopping bags with logos from departments stores and multiple fashion houses. Next to the shelf were two rolls of double-sided, industrial-sized rolls of wrapping paper to accommodate almost any occasion. The tag from JAM Paper & Envelope company hung on the wall-mounted paper dispenser roll.

Apart from the flowers in the yard, this was the most colorful room in the house—everything else they'd seen was on a neutral palette. Charlotte was always amazed at people who dared to have this much beige, white, and cream in a house with kids and a dog!

One of the walls of the room had been outfitted with industrial wire shelving, and one-third of the shelves was filled with clearly marked and precisely stacked clear storage bins.

"Here, just look. This is what happens when your shopping habits take on a life of their own," Brandi said, pointing to the bins as the trio made their way into the room.

Quizzical looks on their faces, they looked back and forth between the wall and Brandi. The space was so precisely curated it looked like yet another photo in a magazine; this time one of the home organizing options often at the grocery store checkout. *Is there no end to this perfection?* It was a rhetorical question Darby mulled over in her mind while taking it all in.

Brandi continued, "I shopped and shopped and now I can see that subconsciously, I was trying to fill a hole. Funny thing is, I didn't even realize it was there. It's like the clothes filled a void and somewhere along the way, things got tangled into a web I am still working to unwind. There's so much more to this than clothes.

"Sadly, so many of these pieces were 'highly suggested' or recommended for me at the store. It's like a gut punch knowing I have been sending messages without even knowing it. The kicker is, the messages didn't even represent who I am or who I thought I had to be in my role. I was sending a message that was the complete opposite of who I *really* am. How did things get so twisted?"

Concerned, Charlotte spoke, interrupting Brandi's soliloquy. "I hope you remember, this is new for all of us. Dawn mentioned it was likely we may be impacted, and each of us in different ways. For some it would happen right away, for some over time, and still some who may not even realize the impact until months after the meetings. She said things may come in waves as welcomed epiphanies or like a mixed bag all at once. However they come, our job is to use the tools we've been given to process them and make the changes at our own pace. Don't be too hard on yourself, Brandi. I hope you're able to see the good that comes from all of this.

"So, what's the deal with these pieces?" Darby asked in her matter-of-fact tone. "You said you pulled them from your closet and put them here. By the way, the section of the wall here," she said, pointing to the rows of bins, "is bigger than all the closet spaces *combined* in my condo." She said this with a laugh, bringing a breath of fresh air to the suddenly serious moment. "Are these pieces you have to go through again because you know they were sending the wrong message, or what's the plan?"

"No," Brandi quickly answered, clearly a little lighter after this brief interaction with them. "These are pieces from my closet that I bought after being told by one sales associate or another that they were perfect for me and that I looked great in them!

"Clothes that I was snickered at when I wore them. These are pieces I bought thinking they were what was getting me promotions and helping me with all the deals I was closing. Now I know the deals were closing *despite* these pieces.

"I didn't realize it, but I became one of those people who wanted to impress everyone with a designer name, logo, or something that let people know I had spent a lot of money on a piece, and that's just not who I am."

She continued to explain how things had evolved from her humble beginnings to earning more money than she had imagined and somehow changing who she was along the way. At her core, she was a kind and intelligent person with a big heart who wanted everyone to win.

"So, these are pieces that I am getting rid of." She could see the looks of shock and awe on their faces—and understandably so. There were at least twenty large bins carefully labeled by season, color, and type, and each was filled to the brim. They saw shoeboxes, sequins, patterned pieces with wild prints, and solids. It really was a sight to see. This was not the contents of her closet; this was just what she was getting rid of!

"Do you two have any interest in any of this?" she said while moving her open palm from left to right as if she were a salesperson pointing out a display or a television game show host speaking to a contestant.

"We all know the three of us have different body types and obvious height differences, but we have learned about modifying things to fit our shape and there are lots of accessories here," she said, pointing to the bins again. "And jewelry almost always fits! You may be able to work with some of this stuff. There's absolutely nothing wrong with it and some of it still has the tags attached. I've never worn it.

"While I was sorting, I got into a mood and honestly didn't want anything to do with some of this because I remember how I was feeling when I bought them or the circumstances under which I was strongly encouraged to buy them. They are beautiful pieces, they're just not for me.

"As I contemplated what to do with everything, I distinctly remembered Dawn talking about not giving away junk. Ladies, this is probably as far as a person can get from junk." Realizing that may have come across as a bit pretentious, she added, "I mean, I just want you to know there's nothing functionally wrong with these things."

Looking a little embarrassed, she continued, "I am an hourglass shape and obviously pretty tall, so the length of most of the pants may not work but you are welcome to go through everything and find some things that you want to try.

"Go ahead and take them. If they don't work, just pass them on to someone you know or donate them. I made sure they wouldn't be examples of Dawn's dirty can of pinto beans example." They all smiled.

It felt so good to have these ladies around who really *got it*! She didn't feel judged; she knew they understood. Things had felt a little awkward for a brief moment, but she quickly realized it had been in her mind because of what happened next.

Charlotte was first to walk over and give Brandi a hug. "This is a huge revelation, Brandi, and it's also a lot of bins! I am so sorry. These pieces probably meant a lot to you at one time. You spent a lot of money and invested your time and trust in people you thought were helping you. At the same time, I am so happy for you to have learned these life-changing concepts that have put you on a path back to who you really are and who you want to be known for. We get it." She looked over at Darby, who was smiling and now creating a group hug.

Brandi insisted that they go through the bins and find some things that made them feel special and represented the messages they wanted to send. They gave each other feedback on each piece that was chosen. Brandi even reclaimed a few pieces after the ladies gave her feedback as to how she could pull it off with this new outlook on life and business.

The gift-wrapping station was within eyesight, and along with the expected tissue paper, bows, and tape there were several large bins that held some of the designer and department store bags and packaging Brandi had saved.

When she made a designer purchase, she knew there was almost always the option to re-sell it. The pre-loved luxury market had taken off in recent years and she had experienced first-hand how easy it was to recoup a large portion of her investment. For this reason, she often saved the tissue paper, ribbons, and boxes they were originally packaged in.

Once her new friends had selected an item from a bin that worked for them, Brandi found the corresponding packaging (or something similar when the original wasn't available). After wrapping the piece in tissue paper, she placed it in a handled bag as if they were visiting a private boutique. Brandi was beaming.

She cheerfully insisted they all continue until every item, in every bin, was touched. Her enthusiasm grew once she saw her new friends were finding things that worked for them—even if some of them did need a few alterations.

While they were sorting through the items in the bins, they came across smaller bags with everything from Fendi headbands to Gucci scarves to Prada sunglasses. A Jacquemus bag, Balenciaga sneakers, and a Louis Vuitton hair clip were bundled together and labeled "accessories."

With a new understanding that one small bag may have several pieces inside, they knew there was no shortage of show-stopping loot to keep them entertained for hours.

While going through the bins, Charlotte shared more about herself. She told them she was just one class away from being able to sit for the bar exam. She explained what she had accomplished before meeting Charles, and how so much had changed as a result of her joining his family. "Do you guys know the Whitlocks?" she asked them.

Darby didn't recognize the last name, so she pulled it up online. As soon as she saw the photo, she blurted out, "This is your family?!" after recognizing the very public figure. She didn't expect a response to the question she already had an answer to. There was a picture of the judge—her former father-in-law—one of him and his wife, and a few pictures at their estate that included the entire family, which at the time included Charlotte.

"Well, I guess you found the pictures," Charlotte said, laughing.

Brandi knew the family name because they had been clients and patrons for years at another top firm. However, she couldn't divulge the details of how their current firm was on a constant quest to lure them away to join their firm, so Brandi smiled and nodded. "Yes, I know the name." She hadn't even thought there may be a connection. Charlotte just didn't *look* like that line of Whitlocks. There wasn't any concern of conniving now that Charlotte was no longer related to them. If she was, her working at the firm could have presented a problem. *Phew! That was a close one*, Brandi thought.

Seeing her expression and hearing Brandi's response was all Charlotte needed to know that there was more to the story. She guessed they were likely past or present clients, and she also knew from her time working at the firm and her own law studies that Brandi was morally and ethically on the up-an-up, reacting the way she did. This was just one more reason she could add to her growing proverbial list—she was really coming to like and respect Brandi.

Knowing the family she was a part of was heavily involved in the legal system and now learning how close she was to her law degree, it didn't add up that she was in the position she was in at the firm. *This* was a question that Brandi *could* ask, and she did.

Charlotte explained that after the birth of their children, she and Charles agreed that she wouldn't go back to school or pursue a career until the kids were a bit older. Then, the agreement shifted to when the kids finished elementary school, then junior, and high school—the deadline kept getting pushed back. Even though her children hadn't reached high school, it was fast approaching for her oldest. The topic had moved from a conversation to more of an expectation and she found herself accepting it, year after year.

She was oblivious as to how this was impacting her confidence. Both her mom and her husband had plenty to say about what the *right* way was to build a strong family. She believed her husband's words—that there would always be a place for her in the family business—and she didn't want to rock the boat, especially knowing his family was so affluent and influential. They were seemingly strong, cohesive; almost story-like.

Her mother's opinion was never a secret, and her words continued to ring in her ear. "You've made it, Charlie." *When did my own mother start referring to me this way?* she would often think.

She remembered thinking, *if this is "making it," then something must be wrong with me!* Clearly, she didn't share the same point of view. Her mom would say that this family—meaning Charles'—was the epitome of the American dream, and so she (Charlotte) should comply, get along, and play the part, despite what Charles was or wasn't doing.

Her mom often suggested she wear the *right* mom clothes—*whatever that was*, Charlotte thought. She should drive the *right* 'mom car,' etcetera. Her mom also told her that pursuing her past life or ambitions would be selfish, and since she didn't need the money it really was unnecessary.

Looking back at her words now, Charlotte had to laugh when telling Brandi and Darby about this because without knowing it, what her mom was doing was encouraging her to utilize the power of clothing and personal packaging. They all laughed a little until Charlotte jumped back to say a little more.

"Gosh, as funny as that is, it's unfortunate that my mom was basically telling me that I didn't matter now that I had kids. Or was it because she felt I had landed a 'golden ticket' by marrying into this family? I know there was no ill intent on her part. She was happy to see that I was going to live well beyond a financially stable lifestyle, and this was something she had never had. Even though we didn't struggle while I was growing up, it's pretty clear the Whitlocks live in a different world."

Continuing on, Charlotte told Brandi and Darby that after a decade of these kinds of messages, she was convinced that any thought she had that conflicted with putting her family, husband, and kids first was selfish, so she worked to bury it immediately.

She told them she needed an outlet. She took up running for some alone time and to clear her head—for a while, at least. Her body type, she now knew, was a classic ruler or rectangle shape, so finding pieces in these bins that worked for her was a bit challenging because of Brandi's tall, hourglass figure. Obviously, the pieces had been purchased to fit her body.

Finding a match among the clothes took some work, without a doubt, but because many of Brandi's pieces were just too tight, they managed to find some tops that would work with minimal alterations, along with a few sweaters that were perfect for an oversized look. There were plenty of accessories to pair with the pieces she was finding. All she would have to do is add her own jeans, pants, or skirt for a complete outfit.

"So, Charlotte, why *are* you in the position you are in at the firm?"

Darby asked, bringing them back to the original question Brandi had asked. They all laughed, realizing they had gone down a rabbit trail. Charlotte explained that she didn't even remember who she had been until attending the trainings at DawnToday.

It was a big step to apply in the first place, but after getting back into the corporate scene she decided she would try for the mentorship program. She was taking baby steps. She explained that she recognized how her mom's comments had played such a big role in her lack of confidence, even though her mom didn't know she was doing it. She had just always been so money-conscious and had a ton of limiting thoughts around money. No doubt this was from her own upbringing.

"When I met Charles, it was like she just wanted to make sure I would fit in and stay in his 'world' of money affluence, etcetera—forever.

"Charles was sincerely concerned about the kids—he wanted things to be the same for his children as they had been in his adoptive family. Everything was pretty traditional in the sense that his dad worked, and his mom was very involved in all the charities. She didn't have a paying job outside of their home. I don't think that was the biggest problem, though.

"He had his own set of issues. Over time, his jealousy about my having accomplished so much at an early age seemed to become a problem. At first, he was impressed. I am almost sure it started to bother him once other people found out that I had accomplished it all without being in a family with similar connections and influence as his. It was like a little jab at him and his own accomplishments in the field.

"People in his circles would say, 'Wow, you have done so much in such a short period of time? That's pretty impressive...and you did this all on your own? Knowing that no one had put in a good word or pushed your applications to the top of a pile—that is even more impressive, Charlie.'

"I believe this kind of thing started the ball rolling. Looking back, I really think he was concerned about me returning to school, getting my law degree, and working outside the home because he guessed I may be convinced or reminded that I was playing small and that I had a bright future, even *with* my kids.

"I'm not making excuses for him. I just see, now, that we weren't a good match from the beginning. I tried not to consider divorce, and clearly, he thought he'd handle it a different way—well several different ways and with several different people," she said, rolling her eyes in a way that implied, there's obviously more to the story.

"When the thought of leaving or going back to school crossed my mind, I would immediately think, 'What would my family, especially my mom, do? What about the kids, how would they fare? How would a divorce affect them?'

"Thinking about all this made it tough to change, so I didn't, and unfortunately, I was the collateral damage. My confidence was shot. I kept telling myself that if a company knew I had gotten so close to a law degree and didn't finish, they wouldn't want me around; they would see me as a quitter.

"This is the lie I told myself over and over. I just didn't have it in me, at the time, to go for a position any higher than I did. So, here I am, starting all over. My mom is beside herself, but surprisingly after I started working, she's gotten better." Another knowing smile was shared between them, and the room was silent.

Darby broke the silence and said, "Well if it makes you feel any better, my mom—well, my parents—have a wedding planned for me. Oh, and I have to mention that it's to someone I don't even have a relationship with!

"I am not the type to say, 'Yeah, but my problem is bigger than yours...That's not what I'm doing by saying this to you. It's just that we're doing all this teenage-girl-slumber-party-bonfire-type-sharing so I thought I'd throw my story in the fire, too!" They laughed, and instantly the mood lightened.

Darby asked Brandi, "Do you mind if I grab something to drink before I share my plight?" She smirked and stood up from the bin she was sitting on.

They had gone through the bins, tried things on, and made their choices. At this point, all their new acquisitions were wrapped as if they were leaving a department store and sitting by the door, and each of the women had found a spot to land.

Brandi had been leaning against the wall where some of the bins had been and Charlotte was sitting on the second step of the small step stool that had been hanging on the side of the built-ins in this room.

They collectively put the bins back onto the shelves lining the wall. After climbing up the step stool to replace a bin, Charlotte imagined Brandi's husband being able to reach the top shelves with ease. *This would make a great hiding spot for gifts*, she thought.

Packages in hand, they walked back into where the brunch food had been earlier that day. Everything had been cleared and the room was spotless. Brandi's family had put everything into the kitchen, placing the things that needed to be refrigerated into the fridge. She found a note on the kitchen counter that said, "Didn't want to interrupt. Took the kids for a bike ride. They seem nice. Have fun!"

Brandi read the note for a second time but this time out loud, and they all smiled at her husband's comment. Looking at the oversized clock that hung on the wall, they were stunned at how much time had passed while they were going through the bins and talking.

Getting lost in conversation seemed to be a recurring theme for them. "Oh wow! I can't believe we have monopolized your whole Sunday, Brandi," Charlotte said.

Darby added, "Yeah, Brandi. I don't want to impose."

"Are you kidding me? This is the best version of therapy I have had in a long time. My therapist should be jealous!" And she smiled, widely.

"It's no imposition, and Darby, we have to hear about what you were going to say. Let's grab a drink and head outside to enjoy the sunshine."

She walked past the kids' drinks that now filled the cooler in the island built-in and went over to the apartment-size beverage refrigerator that had clear glass doors. Filled with such an array of bottled and canned drinks, it resembled a Whole Foods grocery store beverage cooler.

Brandi told them they were no longer guests and to help themselves to whatever they'd like. In hindsight, both Charlotte and Darby could see that Brandi had been the ultimate host by asking them to bring juice. Clearly, she didn't need them to bring anything. She had the meal catered, but she obviously wanted to give them a way to feel like they were contributing. The refrigerator was filled with bottled juices, and it appeared they only drank organic. No wonder her kids were so excited about the popular sugary brand of juice they had both brought.

Bottled water, fresh-squeezed juice, and lemonade in hand, they walked out to the backyard. *Was there no end to the breathtaking views at this house*, they wondered. They sat in furniture that Charlotte recognized from Pottery Barn, Restoration Hardware, and Frontgate. She had been part of more than one of her former mother-in-law's renovations and recognized the brands.

Darby started sharing her story and told them how she had secretly made the decision to pull the plug on her medical career. She explained that both of her parents were successful doctors in their own rights and how they had all talked for years about Darby doing the same.

She explained the accepted expectation of an arranged marriage, and how even as a child she had aspired to be among the limited number of women who were slowly emerging and loosening some of the ties to the older traditions.

She mentioned that while she was in high school and college, she followed Priyanka Chopra's career. While Priyanka was predominantly in the entertainment industry, Darby had admired her for breaking barriers and being an example of a high-achieving woman, and Darby saw how this seemed to give Priyanka options.

Darby also followed the career of Indra Nooyi. This intelligent and highly educated woman became the fourth CEO of Pepsi Co in 2006 and led the company for twelve years. Nooyi worked at Pepsi for twenty-four years in total. What Darby loved about Indra as she read more about her was that she didn't start out as a conformist wanting to cross every 't' and dot every 'i.' By her own admission, Indra shared that she was a rebellious teen who was in a rock band.

That was *all* that Darby needed to know. She had been baited and hooked and couldn't get enough of Indra's story. How had she managed to balance tradition and opportunity? To break free from what could have held her back while still maintaining the respect of her family and her culture? Even though Darby didn't have the right words to ask these questions, or the answers, she kept photos of Priyanka and Indra on her vision board as inspiration. They were the perfect role models, inspiration, and reminders that there was a way to do this; to avoid being part of an arranged marriage.

Then Darby shared with Brandi and Charlotte about her relationship with Ashton, and as she did, both Brandi and Charlotte commented on how she lit up when she talked about him.

Smiling at their comments, she was feeling encouraged and went on. "So, here's the challenge," and she gave a brief but effective and impactful explanation of the history of her culture and expectations. She told them about the looming arranged marriage that hung over her head like a constant cumulus cloud that left her wondering when the rain would start to fall.

To help them get an even better grasp of the idea, she went into detail about what things were like for women in her culture. She pulled up an article that she had saved on her phone and read a quote, "Centuries ago it (arranged marriage) was a way for upper-caste families to maintain their status and consolidate assets. Many times, the arrangement puts the woman in a situation where once she is married, she will either stay home or join the family business."

One woman in the article shared that she took advantage of the opportunity to get an advanced degree. "When my father saw that I was successful," the woman went on to be quoted, "this helped to convince him that there was no need for me to rush into marriage."

"Despite this," Darby said, "by the age of twenty-eight, if a woman isn't married, folks begin to get concerned because if they reach the age of thirty, unmarried, they assume that their chances of getting married are nil, at best.

"For Indra Nooyi, her mother almost forbade her to leave home to attend Yale in the United States because she was not married.

"It was unheard of in 1989 for a good, conservative, south Indian woman to do something like this." Indra had shared this on multiple occasions.

Darby was still talking and she shared a CNN interview quote that she also had saved. "It says here that in the past thirty years, things have changed. According to the articles I've read, the average age for an Indian woman to marry has gone from nineteen in 1990 to twenty-two in 2018. Are you kidding me?!" Darby blurted with her arms and hands joining for emphasis to express her frustration.

Brandi and Charlotte looked on sympathetically and with increased curiosity as they were exposed to this huge and intimate look into Darby's life. They asked if she had spoken with her parents, and if they knew about Ashton.

"...I mean, he sounds like he comes from a successful family," Charlotte said.

Darby laughed and agreed. "Yes! Ashton's family is VERY successful.

They own one of the most popular cosmetic surgery office chains in California, and Ashton is being groomed to take it over. But our story gets crazier. Funny thing is, Ash's family and culture have their own version of an unspoken and arranged marriage—they already know who they want him to marry. Oh, and did I mention that he is of Asian descent? Not Indian, but Chinese???"

She started laughing at the absurdity and unlikeliness of the situation. The other two looked on smiling and bewildered because Darby was laughing. They quickly took on a more somber posture when they saw that this was merely a coping mechanism. A tear rolled down Darby's cheek.

"You see, I just have to get accepted into the mentorship program so I can advance my financial status as soon as possible. I *have* to be financially independent so I can even start a conversation with my parents about not getting married. Well, I mean to someone other than whomever they've chosen for me."

"You're smart, so why is it you decided not to pursue medicine?" Charlotte asked. "It's not like the salary is bad. You would have financial security and you mentioned the other night you were accepted into some high-ranking schools. Why did you decide not to go?" she said, clearly comfortable enough in the conversation to be so straightforward.

"Because it isn't something that I am passionate about. I want to pursue something that will allow me to help other women gain financial independence as well. I can teach this to other women once I understand it and have my footing in this career.

"I know my parents want the best for me and there isn't anything they wouldn't do for me or my siblings. My mom would have a cow if she knew about what was taught at DawnToday and that I had been attending the meetings. She has been trying to get me to change my clothes since high school graduation.

"Actually, we have always been expected to look and dress a certain way. She knew that it was important, but I don't think she understood the why, the how, the power, or the science behind it.

"That's actually what drew me in at DawnToday: the science. I had a wall up when I initially heard about the meetings. I thought the whole thing was going to be about handbags and shoes; designer versus big-box store brands, etcetera. It was really helpful to know there was a reason why clothes were so important because I was like Indra Nooyi in her rebellious stage. By Nooyi's own admission, she was and still is a bit of a rebel—wanting to change things; to shake them up… and I felt just like her. I was unwilling to conform.

"Even as a teen, I wanted no part of this arranged marriage scenario. I took out my aggression and put my stake on the ground by refusing to dress in a way that said yes to *this* way of life. Anything that was remotely similar to the opulence displayed at the ceremonious week-long celebrations was off-limits.

"To me, dressing *well* meant conforming, so there was nothing I was willing to wear that even remotely fit the mold. Absolutely nothing. I wasn't willing to give an inch.

"As a teenager, I wanted to wear what the other girls my age did, but my petite frame made it tough to find clothes and it sucked the joy out of shopping for clothes. I enjoyed hanging out with my friends at the mall, but finding clothes was a pain I didn't want.

"It can be tough to shop. Well, it was until I understood what 'petite' meant in terms of clothes, and how to dress my body type. I am forever grateful to understand how to easily find clothes that fit me well, and that send the right message.

"I didn't realize how much trying to hide behind the clothes to mask my frustration was hurting me and was consequently sending the wrong message. I had a similar experience to you, Brandi, with regard to that Post-It note activity.

"I know that's a very long-winded answer to your question about speaking with my parents. But now I have the courage to talk to them. Between the confidence I gained from the meetings, going through the challenge, and hopefully landing a spot in the mentorship program, I'm feeling pretty good about a conversation with them.

"All these things will help me make the changes I want to make. I have always been a confident person in most areas of my life. My cousins have always looked at me with a side-eye like, 'that's just Darby.' I was always one to rock the boat. When we were kids, I was always the one daring to sneak into areas of a ceremony where I shouldn't have been or to ask 'why' something had to be done a certain way.

"I was asking the questions that generations of women in the room all wanted to know but didn't dare ask out loud. I remember my grandmother saying I would likely be causing trouble for my mother in the future. 'You better get a hold of that one,' she would say in her native language while pointing at me. She knew I wasn't a conformist! Sometimes, I think she forgot I could understand what she was saying. That was probably because my English was so clear; no lingering Indian accent. As a second-generation Indian girl, I spoke English fluently, but my parents made sure Hindi was still a large part of our vernacular.

"As an adult who has worked through a lot of this, I understand that it's okay to question things and challenge traditions. Pushing for more and being willing to make changes for the good of others who will come after me is something I now embrace. I am actually proud of it.

"After working through so many of the journaling prompts, reviewing the lessons, and consuming everything we've learned at the meetings, I feel so much more confident. I leave the house determined to send a message that says I mean business, and this momentum is spilling over into other areas of my life.

"I am ready to have these conversations with my parents and Ashton's parents. Well, as soon as I get into this mentorship program." She winked and they laughed.

Charlotte said, "You're going to be all right, Darby, whether or not you get into the mentorship program. Your determination and drive are sure to get you where you want to go. You've got a prized weapon, the power of clothing and personal packaging, and it sounds like you're doing the mindset work necessary to put it into action. You are transforming into a character—like one of the examples Dawn shared. Remember when she talked about how easily kids take on the persona of the person who wears a particular costume? You are going to embody the person who has these conversations, who makes changes, and you are going to make waves, just like your idol, Ineera. Was that her name?"

"No, it's Indra. Indra Nooyi," Brandi said and smiled.

"Yes, Indra and Priyanka. You're going to make waves that cause a ripple and that has lasting effects," Charlotte said.

Brandi didn't miss a word, but she knew she couldn't comment on Darby's application, the likelihood of her getting the position, or anything about the topic. They understood her position and she let them know she would support them, but it couldn't involve anything about hiring, scaling, or the company in particular. Brandi was all too aware of the scrutiny the firm was under, and she didn't want to say or do anything that would compromise her or her new friends.

After Darby wrapped up her end of the conversation, the afternoon quickly moved toward its end. They all agreed it had been one of the most meaningful experiences each of them had had in a long time.

It was now almost four o'clock, and as they looked at the bags they were leaving with, thanks to Brandi's generosity, Darby pulled out her phone to reserve a Lyft. Charlotte offered to bring her home and Darby accepted. By 4:30, the ladies were on their way. Before leaving Brandi's, they agreed to touch base in a few weeks when the announcements for Charlotte and Darby would be sent out. Brandi did say that she was also awaiting some news and that she would be getting an answer at the same time.

They decided it was best not to get together at the office. This way, they could avoid insinuations of favoritism that would be alluded to because of Brandi's position.

Even though she had nothing to do with the decision-making process, they knew people would create their own stories which could surely lead to problems; problems that could be avoided by keeping things about their friendship quiet until after the sessions at DawnToday were over and the announcements at the firm were made.

They did exchange a few text messages to say hello or to share a photo of an outfit that incorporated a piece that Brandi had given them. But that was the extent of the conversation. There were no lunchtime meet-ups or breakroom chatter.

They each worked on a different floor of the high-rise building, and until recently, they didn't even know they were in the same company, let alone the same building, so it was unlikely they would run into one another. They all had their own busy lives to go back to, but any thought or memory of that Sunday brunch brought a smile to their faces.

There was an obvious difference in the way each of them showed up at the office these days. There was a new sense of confidence and boldness about who they were, what their purpose was, what they could accomplish, and there were no lines drawn as to what was affected. It touched their personal and work lives, and others started to notice it. The combination of their new friendship coupled with the impact of the DawnToday sessions was life-changing!

Change VS Transformation

DARBY

New information at the personal development meetings for work was pushing her to dig deep, and she found herself revisiting the 'why' for doing some of the things she did.

She had made two new friends who were interesting in their own right. Making friends this quickly wasn't a regular occurrence, and even referring to them as such felt a little strange.

The internship opportunity she had applied for came with its own set of expectations. In addition to the mandatory weekly meetings at DawnToday and the assignments that came with that, an upcoming presentation and interview were both components of the process.

She was learning so much from her research, and every week came with its own insights to process, both personally and professionally.

For some people, lots of change all at once can be fun and exhilarating. For others, compounded change can be overwhelming. Darby found herself somewhere between the two.

There was so much to learn at the weekly personal development meetings, and they usually left her doing just that—developing, personally.

Even though what she was finding through her research about the firm was often jaw-dropping, it was the personal development piece that was the biggest weight right now.

Feeling a bit overwhelmed, she brought the subject up during her weekly FaceTime call with Ashton. Last week's call had been shorter than usual so there was even more to catch up on this week.

Naturally she had already texted him about the big reveal that happened and her brunch at Brandi's, but they hadn't had an opportunity to talk via FaceTime so that they could see each other.

She told him how much she had been learning at the weekly meetings, how some things were easier to grasp than others, and how some of the information challenged her.

She talked in greater detail about the big reveal, the brunch at Brandi's, and the notes she had taken about professional stylists. She didn't personally use one, but she was intrigued.

She told him that all these things had conjured up thoughts and memories about her younger years—when she and her cousins would talk about what life would be like as adults. She explicitly remembered saying she would never let anyone else define who she was or what she could, or would, accomplish.

Telling Ashton about the faces her cousins would make after hearing her bold statements made him laugh. "Sometimes they would just sit and stare at me like I had really lost it, and other times they would interrupt me mid-sentence, jumping in to finish my statement along with me. Their mocking tone made it clear that to them, it wasn't possible."

She never let it get to her. Their comments were like kindling, lighting a fire under her.

Most of them couldn't imagine a life like the one she described. Every comment they made in opposition or mockery fanned the flames. Nevertheless, she was determined to challenge the status quo.

Being shown that each day was an opportunity to send an intentional message to the world and all the talk about change and transformation brought up lots of emotion.

She reminded Ashton that initially she didn't see much value in simply changing a shirt—or anything that had to do with her wardrobe at all, for that matter.

"Do you remember how I was going on and on about this when the meetings first started?" she asked him and paused.

A quick "mm hmm" was all Ashton had needed to add for her to continue, and she did.

She told him she could feel herself changing as she implemented the ideas and concepts.

"Things are really starting to pile up, Ash. After the big reveal, meeting up with Brandi and Charlotte, and getting closer and closer to the date the results will be shared, there's just been a lot. It's like trying to drink water from a small fire hose. I feel like I might be losing my edge, or my footing, altogether. I'm just feeling a little out of sorts. Now I feel like I'm rambling!" she said, placing a palm to her forehead, lowering it, and then raising both arms, palms facing upward. "Is any of this making sense?" she asked. Ready for him to respond, she sat silently, watching him. Waiting.

He wasn't one to jump right in with a response. He wanted time to process. She watched him sit in his desk chair, thinking. He replied much faster than usual and what he said surprised her.

"Do you remember when we first met? We were both in a level three psychology class." Darby nodded and he continued.

"Dr. Fenmore gave a lecture on the difference between change and transformation. I think this is what is happening to you right now, Darby.

At the time, the idea was new to all of us, and we took notes, feverishly. During the next class, he read names from a list and told us that our next assignment was a group project."

"Which is how we met," Darby added calmly.

"Exactly," he said with a smile and tone that matched her cadence perfectly.

"The project helped us learn more about the differences between change and transformation. You're not having a problem with transformation, you're simply feeling the impact of the changes required to experience it.

"When we received the project instructions in class that day, we were told to select a business that had undergone a change or transformation that was noticeable to the general public. Our group chose the retail chain Panera Bread. We studied what it looked like when the business opened in 1987, and what it looked like present day.

"In the beginning, most customers saw it as a large, eat-in bakery of sorts, but as it evolved and grew, the menu expanded. As it did, the company wanted us to think of them as a healthy alternative, so they really pushed that angle; but what we learned was that the colors of the plates, the fabric on the seat cushions, and the style of the menu board were all 'changes' that supported the transformation from bakery to restaurant, and then to a healthy food choice for dining in. They were changing as a part of their overall transformation.

"Another group in our class chose the automotive industry. Remember that?" he asked without pausing for an answer. She nodded her head yes, and he knew she was tracking him. "Their project goal was to share how the van transformed from being used exclusively to haul cargo to a multi-purpose option that could move people just as easily as it could move products.

"They shared how it evolved into a family-friendly vehicle in the end, and then grew in popularity when the garage-friendly options were introduced.

"People loved the idea of this extra space and convenience. The Dodge Caravan was part of an entirely new concept that involved both change and transformation.

"Another brand that was part of the change was Volkswagen. I remember how we all found the nickname for the van to be pretty comical. Their research found that if people wanted to transport large groups of people to festivals or protests in the sixties, this was the way to do it. The peace symbols affixed to the outside were just one of the ways it earned the title, 'Hippie Bus!'

"Looking at the progression over the years, the first change was to add seats to the previously large but empty vehicles, making them similar to the concept of a small bus. The target market was the family who typically used a station wagon to accommodate their large group and often had large quantities to move from one place to another.

"While people were excited about the extra space a van provided, there was still the matter of having to park it someplace. It was too big for the typical home's garage, so a carport would have to be added.

"Overcoming that obstacle meant shifting the focus of the family van to the idea of a garage-friendly model.

"When all was said and done, the go-to option for more seating and cargo space had shifted from a station wagon to a minivan with all its bells and whistles. Today's versions allow families to load up children and groceries without even touching the door to get in or out. A click of a button on the key fob makes it all possible. Cupholders, swivel seats, and safety measures make this one of America's favorite options for families. Transformation has taken place.

"Are you tracking with me, Darby? You see where I'm going with all of this. Right?" Darby nodded and he continued.

"You were passionate about the differences between change and transformation, Darby, and you were the one who represented our group when it was time to deliver the presentation.

"You stated it best when you said, 'Change is something you do, and transformation is what other people see as a result of the change.'

"You got a wild round of applause from our peers, and Dr. Fenmore emailed you a separate invitation to join the debate team he facilitated on campus. You really took that project to heart!

"Darby, because of the way you stood your ground to argue the case for transformation over change, it is almost unbelievable to me that this didn't come to mind. You were so confident and convincing. I remember thinking, THAT is the kind of woman I want to marry someday. You had a point and you weren't afraid to voice it. In fact, that first debate is what caused our first non-literal sparring match! I've never asked, have you always been a professional debater?"

"Very funny," she replied and then continued, "You're right, I *had* forgotten about the fact that we studied that in undergrad. Gosh, that seems like such a long time ago. It all makes perfect sense when you hold it under that light. But this transformation feels different. It feels personal."

"Of course it does," he said. "Because this time it is about you! It *is* personal. You've got some thoughts and feelings you have been avoiding for quite a while. The exercises at DawnToday are bringing some of your buried thoughts and feelings to the surface. You are going to have to choose if you just want to make a few changes, or if you want an actual transformation. Isn't that what you said that you learned that first day of the sessions?"

He continued, "We are going to have to address the situation of our relationship with both sets of parents. If we want things to go as smoothly as possible, we will need the courage to talk with them, and we're going to have to determine if we want to change or if we want a transformation. Just think of what this will mean for both of our families, our extended families, our children's children, and our communities.

"This is not just about us anymore, Darby. We are really on to something here. Having the skillset to navigate change *and* transformation is proving its weight in gold for us right now. It's helping you, which consequently means me as well. We are becoming different people. I am actually very grateful the opportunity has been presented to us. It didn't come the way we expected it, but it's valuable, nonetheless."

The conversation continued, and when they got off the phone, Darby started to journal about all of the ways that putting in the work would really make a difference.

Being reminded that the small changes she could choose to make could lead to lasting transformations gave her a huge *why* for what she was doing, and she was on board one hundred percent.

She was already excited about what her acceptance into the mentorship program could mean, but after her conversation with Ashton, she had a renewed sense of confidence. Conquering these obstacles would change the trajectory of both of their lives. She was ready for the transformation. The great thing was that it was already happening; she just hadn't realized it!

Session Six
The Wrong way and the Right Way to Choose a Stylist

QUINN

As our sessions with DawnToday were quickly coming to a close, there were a few key takeaways left to share so we could begin, or continue, to take action.

After learning so much about the Power of Clothing and Personal Packaging, including mindset, body type, closet audits, the message(s) we want to send with our clothes, and the options of curating a look on our own or with the help of a stylist, we spent a little more time learning about the field of wardrobe stylists and the different types. As it turns out, they are not all the same.

All three of the ladies were reminded in their own way about all the bins of clothing that Brandi had removed from her closet and the tens of thousands of dollars that were now unusable. Well, for Brandi.

Thankfully, she had already begun recouping some of this money. She consigned some pieces and had her house manager upload pictures of many of them onto some of the online resale market sites. All of this was, of course, after she had been so generous with her two new friends.

We had touched on the subject of hiring a stylist in a previous session, but apparently this was something Dawn and the team really wanted to drive home.

Brandi was familiar with the concept of having this kind of help and had utilized stylists for years. She was now armed with so much new information she had already started to assess the pros and cons of the people she had worked with over the years.

With an understanding that a lot of her clothing did not fit her body type, to add insult to injury, the pieces did not send the message that she wanted to send. In fact, they were doing the opposite. She was disappointed.

Charlotte had always offered a polite, "Thanks, but no thanks," to these kinds of services when she was in a store. When a sales associate mentioned the service or a friend at one of her kids' functions mentioned who they were using, she politely but consistently declined.

She knew she could navigate the store on her own or just order something online. She saw no value in having a stylist involved. It didn't help that her mother had so much to say about her choice of clothes. The idea of yet another opinion about what she *should* be wearing was enough of a deterrent of its own, but now she had a new perspective and had found herself doing a 180 on the subject.

Similarly, Darby had always been adamant about not having another person in her life to tell her all the things that she *should* be doing or buying, so she avoided her mother's recommendations to work with a stylist like a plague.

Because of what she had learned about stylists, along with the science-backed information about the POC and PP, she was convinced that what she wore really did make a difference. She was sure her own confidence levels were increasing with every meeting, and she wanted to keep the upward momentum flowing.

When she got back to her apartment, she pulled out her stack of incentives and coupons from the huge box she had received the first day. She rifled through the papers and cards until she found the one with the discount code she was looking for. She used it to place an online order for the book *Mistakes Women Make When Choosing a Stylist*, which had been mentioned during the meetings.

She was learning so much and she wanted more. Her life had profoundly changed over the course of the last several weeks, and she was determined to stay on this path of self-improvement. She hoped for the best about her application and she planned to take advantage of every opportunity to increase her knowledge, confidence, and potential while she waited.

The Results Are In!

QUINN

Before sharing what happened with the firm, I'll make a quick stop to share a bit about where things were with the ladies.

As the weeks continued, all three had been implementing changes, both inside and out, and they could each attest to their own personal increases in confidence.

The clothes they wore now sent positive messages not only to themselves but to the people they interacted with as well. Things had started changing for the better.

One example of this was a long-overdue conversation that took place between Charlotte and her mother, Marjorie.

For as long as Charlotte could remember, her mother had always had an opinion about what she chose to wear. However, her mother's commentary really seemed to kick into high gear when she introduced her parents to her former husband, Charles.

Marjorie never held her tongue, and consequently, her thoughts about how Charlotte dressed and carried herself were never a secret. Charlotte had learned to keep the conversation to a minimum when the subject arose by offering short answers or changing the subject altogether, leaving her mother's comments dangling in the air.

While this seemed to be an effective method of defense and keeping these kinds of conversations at bay, Charlotte hadn't realized how many of those dangling words had actually landed, taken root, and unfortunately subconsciously settled in her mind, her thoughts, and ultimately her confidence.

Recently, Marjorie noticed changes in Charlotte but had remained uncharacteristically quiet while she observed. Not only had Charlotte's outfits changed, but she seemed to be different overall.

Marjorie loved her time with her grandchildren and had been with them the day Charlotte went to Brandi's for brunch. While she didn't see the haul she returned with, she did see Charlotte on random days she stopped by to pick up the kids, or when she attended one of their sporting events, recitals, or school programs. All the while, she was watching Charlotte and was now keenly aware of the changes she saw in her.

Putting an end to this atypically silent behavior, Marjorie commented on Charlotte's new bag and the outfit she was wearing.

There was no underlying meaning with what Marjorie said, but because Charlotte had become so accustomed to her negativity, she snapped back with a sharp response.

Marjorie was surprised by her daughter's reply. Like Charlotte, she too had grown accustomed to her avoiding the subject.

Marjorie knew that she had been seeing changes in her daughter, and Charlotte responding at all, when she would have otherwise disengaged, was all she needed to confirm her suspicions. Charlotte was no longer changing—she had transformed.

Uncharacteristically, Marjorie calmly responded to Charlotte's comment and said, "I understand why you are defensive, Charlotte. My comments over the years have likely aggravated you. I never meant any harm with the things I said. I have only wanted the best for you and your children. I admit, I was concerned about you—and them—after the divorce, but there is something different about you. You have changed and all my initial concerns have been assuaged. Would you hear me out for a few minutes? There is something I would like to share with you."

Interested, but unsure where this conversation was going, Charlotte agreed, and Marjorie began by reflecting back several years.

"Charlotte, I encouraged your marriage to Charles. I thought it was the 'golden ticket' to a life of abundance and happiness; that his family was the *right* kind of family to be in connection with. When you told me about the divorce, I was concerned about the security of both you and the children."

Charlotte was unsure of where all of this was coming from or where it would lead, but with her new sense of confidence, she let her mother continue uninterrupted.

Marjorie brought up the meetings that Charlotte had been going to every week. She said that she could tell something was happening.

"I can see it. You have changed. It's like a new and adult version of the Charlotte I used to know—the one who announced that she had passed the GMAT with flying colors years ago. That rendition of you re-emerged, but with even more determination. You seem to have gotten back to who you were before marriage—passionate, driven, and confident.

"I realize now that I didn't always support that part of you. I was more concerned about you securing a position both financially and so-cially, and for me, that meant marrying 'right.'

"I grew up in an era where a married woman's expected choices were motherhood or elementary school teacher. Your announcement that you wanted to attend law school just didn't seem to fit the picture in my mind or the messages that had been ingrained in me.

"So, when you married Charles, I assumed you were financially secure and needed to look the part of a respectable suburban wife and mother. At the time, I believed it was best to forget about law school, working, or any other endeavors that would make it appear you didn't need Charles, his money, his family, or their influence in society. I ignored the fact that this came at a cost: your own happiness.

"Charlotte, the way you entered a room back then was like a wilted flower; a gerbera daisy or tulip blocked from the sun.

"When you went back to work, I saw the way you dressed and carried yourself. I thought you were doing the right thing by being demure, dressing conservatively, and not making too much of a fuss about who you were back then. Essentially, I was encouraging you to dim your light. Watching you change over the last several weeks, it has become evident that something is different. It's like you have transformed."

Her mother also shared that she was convinced Charlotte would succeed at whatever she set her mind to. She apologized for her contribution in Charlotte's unhappy times—and here was the real kicker: Marjorie asked, "Would you mind sharing what you learned at those meetings? Is it something you think might work for me?" Eyes filled with tears, Marjorie stopped talking and looked up at Charlotte, surprised by her reaction.

With tears streaming down her face, Charlotte stood in shock and hugged her mom. She was ready to shout it from the rooftops or to do a commercial. She wanted everyone to know there is a life-changing impact in the Power of Clothing and Personal Packaging! It hadn't just changed and transformed her, it had changed her mother's discerning perception of her, and in a way that was so powerful, her mother wanted to change now, too!

Brandi and Darby experienced their own stories of personal change and transformation. But these weren't the only changes that were taking place.

Almost four weeks had passed since the great reveal and the brunch that followed that weekend at Brandi's house.

It was at brunch that the ladies had learned more about each other, their shared experiences and commonalities, and it was there they had cemented their friendship.

Now, it was time for the results from the SEC and the board, which would answer three questions.

First, the firm and the board would learn about the fate of the company. Would they pass all the requirements that had been laid before them just two months before? Would they be allowed to remain in business, or would this be the end of the firm?

Next, the people who had submitted applications within the company and consequently attended the sessions at DawnToday would have an answer. Would they be making a move to a new position, internship, or mentorship, or would they receive a letter of rejection?

And the answer to the final question: after years of training, commitment, and sacrifice, would Brandi St. James receive her long-awaited and highly anticipated offer to join the firm as a partner?

Before announcing the results, the board informed the executive team they had created two plans: Plan A, and Plan B. Selection and implementation of either of these would be based on the results of the SEC report and announcement to the board and partners at the firm.

To that end, letters had been drafted for both scenarios and approved by the legal team, and I held them, ready to be released after our meeting. Once the 'send' button was clicked, predetermined key members of the management team would receive a broad-brush letter highlighting the outcomes and specifics about how to proceed with their applicants.

As the director of People and Culture (Human Resources), I was in the room when the SEC investigators arrived and met with the board of directors and partners to hear the results.

We sat around the custom-designed U-shaped table that sat twenty-four comfortably. Additional chairs regularly lined the walls for executive assistants and key personnel, but since this meeting was so highly confidential, very few were occupied today.

After a two-hour meeting in the largest boardroom in the building, we concluded, and the investigators were escorted to the private executive suite elevators. As they left the room and walked down the hall to the elevators, things seemed to be moving in slow motion when, in fact, they were moving at a normal pace.

It felt as if a collective breath was being held all around the room. We stood and watched them leave through the glass doors—briefcases in hand—until the doors of the elevator slowly met in the middle and closed to begin the descent to the ground floor.

I had stopped by the guard's desk that morning to ask him to call my cell phone once the group left the building. When the call came in, I was standing at the window, with my back to my colleagues. They stood where they had been when the investigators left the room like statues, each in their own spot around the table.

The soles of their feet were seemingly glued to the highly glossed wood floors, and the hyperbolic phrase, "you could hear a pin drop," couldn't have been truer as everyone stood in silence.

I heard the words the guard spoke, but I wanted to see it with my own eyes, so I was focused on the view below. I saw what looked like ants entering a black, chauffeur-driven SUV and I counted as each one got in.

When the last investigator climbed in the truck and the driver closed the door behind her, I turned to face the group. With an audible exhale, a smile, and an excited tone I calmly announced, "Ladies and gentlemen, the SEC team has left the building!"

Applause erupted, corks popped, and some fell into their chairs with a sigh of relief. Many who sat did so with their elbows on the table and their face buried in the palms of their hands while others shared hugs, a high five, or a fist bump with those around them. The cheers were so loud they reverberated down the hall. The firm had passed and would be fully restored to a booming business.

There were a few terms and conditions that would have to be permanent, and some of the old practices would be eradicated, but everyone was thrilled that the requirements to remain in business had all been met. The task of demystifying, simplifying, and disseminating the details would be left to my team and me.

Having been a regular attendee at the weekly DawnToday meetings meant that I had a courtside seat and saw first-hand the changes that were taking place. I got updates from participants along with the ones shared with the team at DawnToday. There was no doubt in my mind this company had been the right choice to take the firm to the finish line.

During our time with the team of investigators on announcement day, they highlighted key areas on a number of different charts. More than one report attributed the high numbers we saw to the outside company we had contracted to fulfill the personal development component.

The path-breaking results and transformations we submitted in our reports were chart-topping. Of course, the investigators cross-referenced and confirmed this information with DawnToday before filing their own results and reporting them as groundbreaking.

This was one of the points that they drove home. In fact, one of the investigators had written in her report that she would highly recommend the services of DawnToday to other high-profile companies in the future. I was excited to share this with Dawn.

A "cheers to Quinn!" was raised in the room. I smiled and accepted the acknowledgment of the integral part I had played with gratitude. Before leaving the boardroom, I went back to my seat at the table, opened my laptop, and released the correct letters to the management team.

On the floors beneath us, the managers shared the good news with their teams, and even though staff members didn't have all the details, they understood that this was good news for everyone. As it is with any gossip, rumors had started to run wild during this time.

Every floor of the building was celebrating in its own way—cake in the breakrooms, congratulations banners arrived across computer screens, and an extra thirty-minute break was given to the call center employees.

Later, as people returned to their respective posts throughout the building, a few bolted from chairs with excitement after opening an email of congratulations about their application to various positions.

Darby was among them, and she surprised herself as she squealed and raised both of her arms over her head, fingers pointing to the sky.

She couldn't contain her excitement! She had been accepted into the mentorship program. The letter stated that the management team had seen an almost unbelievable transformation in her, and they attributed it to her participation in the required personal development program.

They shared that this position had been highly competitive and that they were happy to welcome her into the program.

With enthusiasm and curiosity, Darby walked over to her manager, who she could see ending a conversation down the hall. She wanted to share her excitement and express her gratitude. Unexpectedly, her manager nodded toward an empty office near them, and she and Darby walked in.

Closing the door behind them, her manager shared, in confidence, that the decision-making team had been both surprised and confused as they reviewed her application.

The accolades and accomplishments listed in great detail on her application didn't seem to match the personality or performance of the person they saw day-to-day.

As a result of her time at DawnToday, Darby knew that what her manager couldn't quite articulate was that her personal package and the messages she was sending didn't seem to match the person depicted in the application.

Fortunately for Darby, they were able to verify her claims by confirming with the credible references she had supplied. But even more importantly, they had seen a dramatic transformation because of her time at DawnToday and they were thrilled to see it. They couldn't wait to have her join the team.

Riding the crest of a wave of happiness, Darby almost skipped out of the office. She walked back to her cubicle where the top two-thirds was constructed of clear plexiglass and she sat down. She rolled the office chair toward her desk using the balls of her feet. Reaching the desk's edge, she realized she was just too excited to work.

She picked up her phone to text Brandi and Charlotte the good news. When she unlocked her phone screen with her Face ID, she saw that she had a message in their group chat and the subject line said, 'Great news!!!'

Smiling ear-to-ear, she opened the message and saw that Charlotte had beaten her to it. She shared that she had gotten the promotion! Darby replied with a congratulatory GIF and then stood to make her way to the elevator. With her head down while walking, she texted Charlotte separately to see if they could meet in the break room on the eighth floor.

Brandi hadn't replied to the first message exchange yet. It was likely that she was still busy with the execs upstairs, which was how she rationalized texting Charlotte separately.

Darby had already been on the move when Charlotte began typing her reply, so by the time Charlotte made it to the eighth floor and exited the elevator, Darby was right there. They almost bumped into each other since Darby was still on her phone with her head down.

"Oh, excuse me!" Darby said, still staring at her phone.

"Darby?!" Charlotte said, which caused Darby to finally look up.

"Hi, Charlotte! Congratulations! I am so happy for you! I was just texting Ashton to tell him my good news!" Darby said as she reached out to hug Charlotte. "He's in class right now, but I just couldn't wait! As you know, this news is a huge step in my, well our, future!"

"I am thrilled for you, Darby!"

"I am really excited for you, too!"

As they walked toward the breakroom, Charlotte asked, "Have you heard from Brandi yet? I was going to send a message in the group text to see if the two of you want to join me for happy hour appetizers to celebrate at Bellemore after work. It doesn't seem like much else will be happening at the office today since everyone is in celebration mode. Well, at least it seems that way in my department. How about you? What's it like in your area?"

"Oh, it's definitely high-energy, and I agree that it's unlikely there will be much actual work happening," Darby said.

"It's already two thirty, so how about it? Are you able to leave at three thirty or so?" Charlotte asked. "Actually, now that I say that," she continued, "I realize we have been doing such a good job keeping our professional distances here at the office that I don't even know what time you typically leave. Does that time work for you?"

"Sure! Leaving early works for me and spending some time at Bellemore sounds like a great way to celebrate!" Darby replied. "I would sure love it if Brandi could join us, but I don't dare go up to the executive floor to see if she has checked her phone, especially today."

"I agree. I don't want to make any waves," Charlotte said. "Let's meet at the guard's desk at the main floor lobby. If we haven't heard anything from her when we meet three thirty, we can try reaching her again."

Later, when they met at the guard's desk, they confirmed that neither of them had heard from Brandi.

Charlotte had called her mom to share the good news and ask if she would be willing to pick up the younger two from the carpool line at school. It was their weekend to spend with their father so Charles would be picking them up soon after they got home. Her oldest son, Connor, had already planned to go to a friend's house after baseball practice, and Charles would swing by to pick him up from there. Thankfully, her mom agreed.

"Do you want to ride with me?" Charlotte asked Darby.

"Sure! We can call Brandi from the car," Darby added.

As they made their way to the parking garage, they agreed that the likelihood of Brandi joining them right away wasn't very high. They speculated that she had a far more intricate part to play in today's announcements and may be busy for quite some time.

Charlotte reached into the new OnTheGo Louis Vuitton tote she had been gifted at Brandi's.

Fumbling around for her keys, she said, "I still can't believe that she gave this to me. I know how much these bags cost. I was surrounded by them at functions with Charles' family and lots of the working moms at the kids' schools have started using them instead of the Louis Vuitton Neverfull. As beautiful and as functional as they are, I just never bought one.

"Do you remember what I shared with you and Brandi at brunch about my mom and her consistent comments about my wardrobe choices?" Charlotte asked but didn't wait for an answer before adding, "I'm sure that had something to do with my resistance. Remind me to share an update about that when we get to the restaurant. It will blow you away." Charlotte was alluding to her heart-warming conversation with her mom.

Sensing Charlotte may be feeling a little embarrassed about accepting and using the bag she had been gifted, Darby chimed in.

"It seems almost serendipitous that the bag that was too small for her was perfect for your frame. It happened almost seamlessly. When Brandi was talking about the bag at her house that day, she made it pretty clear that the reason she even had it was because of one of those FOMO (fear of missing out) moments brought on by one of the many sales associates she had. Do you remember that?" Darby asked.

"It wasn't a loss for her, Charlotte," Darby said. "She said it felt great to get rid of the things that didn't represent her well or send the right message. It was a win-win situation."

"You are *so* right about that!" Charlotte replied with a smile while giving the outside of the bag a little pat.

While Charlotte pulled out her keys, Darby reached into her own tote and pulled out a pair of black, Gucci Princetown loafers that coordinated with her outfit.

After their time at DawnToday, Darby understood how having even a slight heel on her shoes changed her posture and worked as part of her new personal package. Despite that, she was glad to have something equally as stylish to change into that provided a bit more comfort.

This was another one of the tips and tricks she now had in her arsenal. It ensured she was presenting herself in a way that accurately told others (and reminded herself) who she was and what she endeavored to accomplish.

The new and unworn pair of shoes Brandi had gifted her came complete with the box and the receipt. They had been a recent purchase, so a call to one of Brandi's S.A.'s at the department store made it easy for Darby to go to the store and exchange them for a different size.

Keys and comfy shoes at the ready, they started towards Charlotte's van. As they were walking, Charlotte saw what looked like Brandi sitting in a car.

"Is that Brandi?" she said and gestured toward a vehicle. They walked towards the car, and as they got closer, they saw it was definitely her and excitedly picked up their pace.

Finding Brandi

QUINN

Charlotte and Darby were elated to share their news with Brandi and to hear hers. Neither of them had any doubt that she had been made partner.

She looked like she was talking to someone on the phone, likely to her husband, Jared. When they met him at the St. James' home, it was evident that he was a huge cheerleader of Brandi's.

With the level of noise, excitement, and high energy inside, coupled with the all-glass offices on the executive floor, it would be no surprise if she wanted to share the news with him in private; hence, her sitting in the car to talk.

To avoid startling her, they called her name as they got closer and then knocked on the back window when they reached the car. She didn't look up.

From farther away, it looked as though she was on the phone because her mouth appeared to be moving. Her hands gestured as if she was in conversation, but now that they had reached the car, there weren't any sounds from another voice. *Maybe she is wearing earbuds*, Darby thought.

Standing side-by-side, Charlotte and Darby knocked on the driver's side window. She looked up, and they saw that her eyes were red and filled with tears. A long stream of eyeliner stained her cheeks. Droplets of the black liner also spotted her white silk blouse.

Unlike her typically well-coiffed hair, Brandi was a bit disheveled and she looked surprised when she saw them. With a puzzled look across her bedraggled face, she pressed the remote start button to start the car so she could roll down the driver's side window.

"Fancy meeting you two here," Brandi said, full of sarcasm.

In complete shock at Brandi's current state and appearance, Charlotte blurted out, "What in the world?!"

Which was followed by Darby's, "Do you need help?" on the heels of her comment.

"I..." Brandi paused and then said, 'They..." And she paused again, clearly trying to compose herself to speak. She started again, "I..." and then the tears took over. She leaned her head into the steering wheel, giving up on trying to pull it together.

"Oh, my goodness!" Charlotte said. "Brandi. *Brandi*. Brandi!" she said, increasing the intensity with which she spoke. Seeing Darby's eyes widen, she lowered her voice and said, "Brandi, unlock the doors. Please, let us in," with a calm, maternal voice.

Hearing other voices and laughter while they stood outside of the car reminded them that they weren't alone in the parking garage. Charlotte and Darby had seen people walking when they stopped for Charlotte to find her keys. It had been just moments before that they had the quick exchange about the bag and the shoes, but this unexpected turn made them quickly forget where they were—until they heard the echo of voices.

Overtaken by tears, Brandi did not respond. So, Darby reached inside the open window and unlocked the doors. Charlotte walked around to the other side of the car and quickly got in on the passenger side. Darby climbed in the back on the driver's side.

Unfamiliar with the car, Charlotte fiddled with the buttons on the console until she figured out how to get the air conditioner going. Simultaneously, she rolled up the windows saying, "Oh my goodness, Brandi! What is going on?"

"What happened?" Darby said as she slid to the middle of the back seat.

A few moments passed. Brandi dabbed her eyes and cleared her throat. She composed herself and shared that she had been overlooked for the position as partner; the position had been given to a man, and to one who was less qualified, at that!

"After all the late nights I've spent here over the years; all of the time that I have put into this firm; the family events I have missed out on… there was absolutely no doubt in my mind that it was going to happen today. I was just so sure that agreeing to attend the personal development meetings at DawnToday had sealed the deal. I was showing my dedicated, selfless commitment to the success of the firm. As a result of my attendance, I was feeling so much more like myself. Initially, I hadn't even wanted to participate, but I changed over the course of those weeks; so much changed. I was so sure!"

Then, Brandi began to rant, saying things that were likely a result of nothing more than human emotion. You know those times that you are upset and you give an audible voice to the ridiculous stories your mind creates when you let it? No filter, just lots of words. Strings of sentences that lead from one thought to the next. It's like once you get going, the tumbleweed starts to outrun you.

Yeah, that's what was going on here, and it was a shock to the ladies when Brandi said, "I should never have changed my outfits. They took me seriously before. They would never have pulled a stunt like this if they still thought that I was a force to be reckoned with. All of this DawnToday, Power of Clothing and Personal Packaging, dress like the message you want to send, personal development rigmarole has gotten me overlooked for a position that was already mine!"

The women sat quietly for a minute. They wanted to give her time to let all of this raw emotion out. After a few moments passed, Darby asked Brandi if she was in the headspace to hear a different perspective.

Reluctantly, Brandi said, "Sure. Why not? There's nothing you could possibly say that is worse than the conversation I just had. Bring it on. I am going to need all of the help I can get to go back in there and face them. To continue working with them, knowing that they have been stringing me along for all of this time, and even while all of this SEC business was going on. I moved my family here!" she blurted to emphasize her frustration.

She took a deep breath and continued. "It's just a lot and I am not sure that I want to. I know I was just bashing the DawnToday stuff, but if I am honest, there were signs all along that they had no intention of giving me that seat.

"Quite frankly, I like that I have gotten back to the real me, and if they don't like it well, they're just going to have to get over it. I'm not going back to the way that I was before the personal development training, and I am not going to accommodate them! They are going to accommodate *me* for a change!" Brandi said emphatically.

Darby realized she no longer needed to say what she had planned—

Brandi had reached the realization herself. So she asked, "What if they don't?"

Frowning, Brandi looked at Darby in the rearview mirror and Charlotte turned to face her with a parental scowl on her face as if to say, "Not now, Darby."

"Hear me out," Darby said. "I mean, what if they *don't* change or accommodate the new, or original-but-improved version of you? You are who you are, Brandi. You're brilliant.

"To prepare for the panel discussion portion of my interview for the mentorship program, I had to study the C-level execs, the partners, and the history of the firm. I know what you bring to the table. I know that it is because of you that this firm has closed some of the most delicate, uncommon, and renowned contracts. You are brilliant at what you do. So, what if you don't *have* to get over it or even work with them at all?"

"Okay, Darby, the timing here is a *bit* insensitive," Charlotte said, no longer choosing to hold her tongue. "Let's give her some time to think about what she wants to do. This is all very new. She may not be interested in moving to another firm right now. We don't know if she will decide that she's going to look for another job right now. She needs time to process."

"That's not what I mean," Darby said.

"Well, what *do* you mean?" Brandi said, jumping into the conversation with a little bite in her tone. "Let's hear it. What's *your* grand plan?" she asked, clearly bothered by the comments.

Without hesitation, Darby jumped back in and said, "Start your own! Start your own wealth management firm."

This time, they *both* snapped their heads around to face Darby.

"What?! Start my own?! What are you talking about? Are you kidding me? You must not know what goes into starting a business; and to compete with such a well-renowned brand, at that! You have no idea what you're talking about!" Brandi was spouting the comments fast and furious.

"Actually, with all due respect, Brandi, I do," Darby quipped. "Please, just hear me out. You bring in over forty percent of new business and you manage almost fifty-two percent of the overall business at the firm. Your clients love you and the in-house annual report addendum showed that you have a ninety-two percent approval rating—the highest in the company. You know this business inside and out, and without you, well, who knows what would happen? You have the talent, the knowledge, and the following to open a firm and be successful. I'm just going to say, I think you would actually blow them out of the water. I suspect that they didn't want you in the position of partner because, quite frankly, you'd be putting a few of them out of a job with that kind of power! You know the good ol' boys have to stick together, to protect each other's secrets. It's been going on for decades, Brandi, you know this. Come on, I know you know this."

Silence filled the car after this monologue that quickly turned into what felt like a presentation. Darby had landed it like Olympic gold medalist Simone Biles, sticking a gymnastic floor routine to the mat for a perfect ten!

Brandi was in a state of shock. Hearing someone else recite her accolades and accomplishments with such confidence was like a splash of cold water hitting her face.

It was encouraging and spun her around like a merry-go-round, landing her right back where she was before this afternoon's news.

Now, she was angry AND encouraged. Darby had just put words to what Brandi knew deep down but had never taken the time to actualize.

"Wow, you really *did* do your homework! I'm guessing that's one of the reasons you got into the program," Brandi said with a slight grin, clearly showing something had shifted.

"When the reports were released and distributed in the meeting, I saw both of your names on the portion that showed which applicants would be making an internal, vertical move. Congratulations to both of you." She smiled as she reached out to grab their hands to give them a quick squeeze.

Now it was Charlotte's turn to speak. "I hope you are able to see things in a different light, soon. Your comment about our time at DawnToday concerns me a little. I mean, I would hate for you to have any ill will about the meetings. After all, if we hadn't all been a part of those sessions, we may not have met."

"That was just raw emotion and frustration talking, Charlotte. You know how that goes, but I appreciate you wanting to clarify, instead of assuming. Thanks for that. To be clear, I am grateful for our time at the meetings, being introduced to the two of you, and to DawnToday overall. I attribute it to re-kindling my confidence in some areas and igniting it in others. If it wasn't for everything I learned during those meetings, I may not have had the courage to do what I am about to do," Brandi said.

With shock-filled faces, Charlotte and Darby replied, almost in unison, "And what's that? What are you about to do?"

"Well," Brandi started, "I want to hear about this idea of yours, Darby. It sounds too well thought out for this to have been a whim or a quick response to this terrible news." She rolled her eyes and shook her head in disbelief that this was actually happening.

"You're right. I have been thinking about this, and quite a bit, actually. When I researched and read about you, your accomplishments, and your contributions to the firm while preparing for the panel to interview me, I was reminded of Indra Nooyi. She's the former Pepsi Co CEO I mentioned when we were at your house. Like her, you have been involved in some groundbreaking, history-making moves that resulted in generating some incredible revenue.

"While I continued to study and gather research about you, thoughts would come to mind. I kept wondering what it would mean for you to be the first woman to run a brokerage of this size. Then, after learning more about what you brought to the table, I couldn't help but see the possibilities and I wondered if you had ever given the idea any thought.

"As I put the pieces together in my mind, I kept thinking, *this woman could run circles around this firm.* The ripple effect that we learned about at our sessions at DawnToday would be life-long, impacting generations, Brandi.

"When you shared a little about why you first got started in this industry, it all made sense to me. I didn't think that it was appropriate or my place to add commentary at the time, so I listened quietly. I haven't stopped wondering if you know it.

"I started to play with the concept, the numbers, and the idea as a whole, and I have to admit, it's pretty amazing," she said with passion.

As Darby was completing her sentence, she heard voices and noticed that more and more people were entering the parking lot.

Darby looked at the clock on the digital display and said, "Ladies, it's quitting time upstairs. May I suggest that we move this little rendezvous to another location? I mean this car is pretty recognizable and likely to draw attention sitting here with the engine running and the three of us in it. It may even look like an invitation to join the crowd!"

"Darby and I were headed to Bellemore for happy hour bites to celebrate," Charlotte said before realizing the word "celebrate" had slipped out. Squirming in her seat, she said, "I'm sorry, Brandi. I just meant, if you want to join us there, it might be a good way to talk through some of what you're feeling and to hear more about what Darby is saying. If we get there early enough, we can request a private room. Do you have all of your things here in the car with you? Do you have a jacket that you can, um..." she said as she gestured towards the stains on Brandi's blouse.

"Sounds perfect. Let's do it! And about this," Brandi said as she looked down, "I keep an extra outfit in my trunk, and I have a gym bag back there too. I put a fresh one in there at the beginning of every week just in case I have to go straight from the office to one of my kid's events.

"I've got everything I need to freshen up, but I'm not going back inside to do it. I can call upstairs and have my assistant gather my things. I'll ask her to have one of the interns bring them down to the guard's desk that's at the private entrance. Then, I'll let the guard know that a colleague will come in to retrieve them. These few extra steps will keep the gossipers at bay. I'll tell you what, how about you drive, Darby? I'll get cleaned up on the way."

Brandi was no stranger to navigating high-profile, time-sensitive, and private situations. She jumped into action without missing a beat. She used the voice-command service in her car to dial her assistant and put the plan in motion. From the deer-in-headlights looks on their faces, it was obvious that Charlotte and Darby were unaware of not only the private entrance, but also what their friend was like when she was in work-mode.

In a matter of minutes, Brandi had put this plan in motion as if it were a regular, everyday occurrence. Given their new friendship and how relaxed Brandi was around them, it was a jolting reminder; she was a force. This quick, bird's eye view of her in action was a reminder of *who* Brandi was and her influence and status at the firm.

"Okay, great. Charlotte, we'll drop you off at your car and meet you there," Brandi said, and the three of them shifted positions in the car. Darby jumped into the driver's seat while Brandi moved to the back, and as they drove off, Charlotte guided them to where her van was parked. Thankfully, they were already on the move as the next elevator full of people descended into the parking garage. The trio remained undetected and unseen.

Brandi and Darby drove in silence. With the exception of the woman with an accent who gave turn-by-turn directions through the car's navigation system, not a word was spoken. Darby tried to decipher whether it was a British or French accent that was so prominent. Hearing the voice for the first time, Darby glanced at the digital display on the dashboard as if the person speaking was there. Smiling at the screen, she gave a quiet chuckle at this oh-so-Brandi touch.

At one point, Brandi told the car's remote system to call her husband. She got his voicemail and quickly left a message. "Hey, babe. Updates to share. Headed out for a bite with the ladies from work. I won't be out late. I'll call you when I get home."

He was out of town, and she knew he would sense that something was going on by the tone in her voice—Jared was good at that. He knew what was happening at her office today and would of course be waiting to hear whatever updates Brandi would share.

What he didn't know was what had just transpired in the office, the car, and what the evening might bring. Even *she* hadn't known the turn the day would take. They would talk later.

Thankfully, for her, the nanny was on duty to handle pick-up, sports practice, and music lessons, so she was able to make this impromptu get-together work. It would give her time to regroup, etcetera.

When she had planned her schedule and availability for the month, she had blocked out today and tonight on the family calendar. Knowing the day would be full of surprises, she wanted to have complete control of her schedule.

Some sort of life change—good or bad—was inevitable today, and she needed the flexibility to be present for whichever way the pendulum would swing. She had played so many scenarios out in her mind about the outcome, but boy, oh boy, she couldn't have dreamt this up.

The happy-hour crowd was just starting to roll in at Bellemore and their early arrival helped them secure one of the popular spaces before it was snapped up. Once they were seated in the private room, the conversation resumed almost immediately.

"So," Brandi started, "I was thinking about Darby's comments while I was driving—well *riding*." She smiled. "Anyway, I have a lot on my mind, obviously, but I just can't seem to shake the idea, and that's saying a lot given what just happened.

"To make this work, I would obviously need a legal team. I know lots of attorneys, but I want someone I can trust; someone with a similar value system, and someone who clearly understands the power of transformation, and there is one person who immediately came to mind. Charlotte, how about you?" Brandi said, looking right at her with a serious face.

Darby smiled. She had placed Charlotte in this role in her mind as she mulled over the details. She had envisioned how this scenario might play out—long before sharing it with either of them.

"Wow, okay. I didn't know that this was what we were doing right now. Did you two drum this up in the car on the way here? I'm going to need to get caught up. What are you talking about, Brandi?" Charlotte immediately responded. She quickly added, "And by the way, you *do* know that I still have one more class to complete, right? Once I finished the class I would have to study for, and then actually *pass* the bar."

Darby immediately jumped into the conversation. She told Charlotte the ride to the restaurant had been a quiet one.

"...Well, other than the fact that our friend, the boss-lady over here, has some kind of French or British assistant who travels with her." She leaned toward the table, nodding her head left as if to point to Brandi. Then she raised an eyebrow and smiled as she took a sip of the complimentary custom mocktail that had just been placed in front of her.

A member of the waitstaff had entered the room carrying a tray with three delectable mood-boosters. The tall, double-walled glasses were clear and slender, offering a perfect view of this Pinterest-worthy beverage. The drink stirrers were filled with fresh blackberries and a large wedge of lime sat on the sugar-rimmed glass.

"A beverage, on the house, in thanks for your continued patronage," he'd said while placing a drink in front of each of them.

"I'm not sure what you mean about a French assistant. Maybe you two can fill me in on that morsel a little later, but right now, what I want to know is, Brandi, where is this talk about my involvement coming from? I have just been given a promotion at the firm, and like I just said, I am NOT licensed. I don't have my degree," Charlotte said as the server left the room, closing the large wooden doors that ran on an overhead track. She reached for her beverage without taking her eyes off Brandi, but hearing Darby's voice chime in, her eyes darted her way.

"Well, after seeing how they have treated our golden girl here," Darby jumped in, "can you trust those jerks to do the right thing by you? I mean, let's not mince words. They are in it for themselves. All of them. They are going to do what's best for them, at any cost. Excuse my frankness, Brandi. I just don't want you to be their patsy, and Charlotte, you've got way too much to offer. They don't deserve you; either of you.

"I know you're excited about your promotion, and congratulations, again. But Charlie, come on, you were made for more. Look at all that you have been through, and now you're killing it, just like you did when you aced the GMAT."

"How did you know that?!" Charlie asked, shaking her head with a grimace.

"Like I said, I've been doing a little extracurricular homework!" Darby said with a mischievous smile. Savoring the flavors of this gratis drink, Darby went on. "Ladies, here's what I'm thinking: we should start our own firm!"

Silence. Again.

Shocked, but caught up in the moment, Charlotte leaned in and planted her elbows on the table. Rotating her wrists simultaneously and opening her palms with a pause at each statement, she replied emphatically, "But I would have to take a class, *remember*? Then, I would have to pass the bar, *remember*?! I have three kids, and a job, *remember*?"

Quiet and seemingly disengaged from the conversation at hand, Brandi's friends would soon learn that this was her posture while pondering and contemplating her insightful and typically poignant replies.

Brandi entered the conversation calmly, adding, "And you've got two new friends who believe in you, *remember*?" And she smiled.

Actually, she didn't remember. In fact, this was news to her. They hadn't discussed it, but she would take it. She knew how much she had enjoyed their time together at brunch, but no one had discussed that the feeling was mutual.

She hadn't felt this empowered since her life before Charles. Today's events happening on the heels of the recent conversation with her mother felt like a dream. Some of the course material encouraged a form of journaling, so she spent time daydreaming and writing. She envisioned a brighter future—a new life altogether—while working through the material, but this—all of this—was more than she had imagined.

She flashed back to her excitement that first day of the meetings; getting lost in her thoughts while she was in the powder room. Never in a million years would Charlotte have imagined she would be having *this* conversation with *these* women, and now they were referring to her as their friend. Wow.

How did they know she had always dreamt of being part of something big?! That this kind of daring and courageous thinking had been part of her drive early on? These thoughts and feelings were part of what made the meetings at DawnToday resonate—because it was tapping into and reminding her of who she really was.

As Darby continued to tell them all the things she had been ruminating over the last several weeks, she closed her thoughts by telling Charlotte that she would gladly help her out with her kids so she could get the school piece done.

Looking directly at her, Darby said, "I have no doubt you're going to ace this, Charlotte. I mean, why else would Charles want to keep you so far away from this line of work? Just like Brandi's situation with the guys at the firm, you are a powerhouse; smart and driven. You would have knocked Charles out of his position at the law firm in no time, and he was probably nervous about it."

Charlotte sat in shock. What Darby said was true and she knew it. Even with all the journaling, growth, and progress she had made, she never allowed herself to stay here—on this exact thought—for long. The idea wasn't new. Something very similar crossed her mind while she was married but she would always shut it down immediately. She felt guilty for even having the thought in the first place. She would hear her mom and her husband in her subconscious saying she was being selfish or that she wasn't thinking about her family...

The timing couldn't have been better. Remembering her mother's words about being wrong... Charlotte couldn't help but think her mom had been wrong about so much when it came to Charles. Thankfully, even in this short time, she had grown to a place where she believed in herself. And not that she needed it, but Darby just validated her and it felt great!

Just when she thought things couldn't get any better, Brandi joined the conversation again.

"You know, Charlotte, I was just thinking about something. There are so many schools that offer credit for the experience these days. I believe some call it credit by exam. Essentially, you test out of the class by proving your mastery of the subject. I've also heard of others receiving credit for experience in the field of study. I'll bet you can apply the hours you have worked at your current job, the position you just got, and any other internship work you did in the past toward that end. Surely you have enough to bypass this last class.

"Additionally, I'm guessing a letter from the firm, on your behalf, would be rather convincing. The letter would be about your own merit—no fluff. It just may do the trick. What do you think?"

"Well," Charlotte said, "when you mentioned a letter from the firm just now, I thought, no. I can't ask you to do that—I would be just like Charles using his dad's name and influence to get ahead. But, I understand that because I am a current employee at the firm, having the letter as confirmation and/or verification would prove to be helpful. I really like this idea! I am going to look into it right away! I also think I am in a state of complete shock." She smiled widely, tears welling up in her eyes.

She thanked them both, and while dabbing her eyes with her napkin, she asked with a little chuckle, "Darby, how do *you* come into play here? There seems to be so much focus on Brandi, and now me. You have a rap sheet on the two of us." She wagged her index finger back and forth from Brandi to herself. "What do you have cooked up for yourself?" she ended without the slightest bit of sarcasm.

"Oh, I am happy to come along for the ride and do PR, or research, or something," Darby stated.

"Not so fast," Brandi said. "You're not the only one who has been researching. I can openly share at this point that I saw the results of your test. You passed with a ninety-eight, Darby. That's impressive! Very, very impressive, in fact. The team responsible for placement is looking to put you on the fast track. Sorry for the spoiler if you didn't already know."

"I did," she said, nodding with a polite and almost bashful grin, remembering the conversation earlier that day with her boss.

"This is something to be proud of, Darby. Not many people are given this opportunity, and not many women, for sure! I remember my group was very small. There were maybe five of us." She paused, looking up as if the answer to her question would be found on this colossal ceiling.

"Wait! *You* were on this track, Brandi? Wow!" she said, slumping back into her seat again. She was overtaken by the news that this enviable and often mimicked powerhouse had once been in the same program. This made the news of her own invitation to the program even sweeter and that much more meaningful.

"You will likely be a junior broker before the others even finish training. Once you've completed your training, you could be an understudy with some of the top brokers on the floor. You are a smart woman who brings a lot to the table, Darby. I wouldn't want you to be our competition! I want you on our team, so let's do this together!

"Just think of what something like this will mean when it comes time to share your progress with your parents. They will see what you've got going and what you've managed to accomplish in such a short period of time. You can almost project what things will look like in a few years."

Darby was touched and got a bit emotional as she realized Brandi and Charlotte had been actively listening when she opened up about the situation with her parents. Telling them about the impending arranged marriage wasn't something she had planned to share, but then again nothing about that day or the past several months had been planned. Everyone was consistently and equally surprised. All the time.

Not only had Brandi been listening to her the day she shared her most pressing challenge, but now she was offering a way to help her overcome it.

A viable and reliable source of self-sufficiency was the most crucial factor involved. Without it, her parents wouldn't even entertain a conversation about changing the plan they had set in motion.

Any hint at backing out of this arranged marriage would have to be heavily weighted, and *this* would be!

Her parent's perspective was that if she repudiated this offer, she may end up alone indefinitely, so she would need to be able to support herself financially for the foreseeable future. Not to mention, whatever took her away from their plan needed to supersede what this potential family had to offer.

It was an old way of thinking, and pride, of course, had something to do with it. But she found it important and respectful to knock this out of the park—her parents had sacrificed so much for her to even have these options.

As much as she wanted to buck the system, she did want them to be proud. Being part owner of a multi-billion-dollar firm would certainly do the trick. She hoped.

After she got the idea for this new company, she started working on a pitch deck. Initially thinking this could be used for her application project at the firm, she put in a lot of work and it was well-researched.

She knew the most important elements to include and zeroed in on the competitive landscape, the team, and projections components of the deck.

The funding portion of the pitch deck was important, of course, but as she worked through how to map things out during a potential presentation, *this* is where she could shave off some time.

Brandi spent lots of time in rooms alongside venture capitalists with deep pockets. Her name carried weight in the industry, and raising capital wouldn't be an issue for a person with her reputation, expertise, and influence.

After bringing her project close to completion, the night of the big reveal happened at Bellemore. Even though she was previously convinced as to who Brandi was, having it confirmed meant she would not use this project as part of her application at the firm. Thankfully, she had a backup plan that was equally as compelling, which she used for her presentation.

Darby had every intention of showing Brandi what her initial project idea had been when the time was right, but sharing her well-laid plans in the backseat of a car wasn't exactly what she had in mind.

She had revised her pitch deck and planned to present it after the results at the firm were in. Knowing it had to be concise yet detailed to make an impact on one of the country's most successful and sought-after wealth managers was imperative, and this made it easy for Brandi to look it over when Darby pulled out her iPad mini. A screen that was just a few inches larger than her cell phone wasn't how she envisioned this first look at her plan, but the momentum was flowing, and surprisingly this *was* the *best time*!

Darby had penciled Charlotte in as head of legal and herself as a highly paid consultant with a recurring contract. Being part owner wasn't on the list.

Seeing the diagrams, Charlotte and Brandi stared at the screen, stunned. Sitting in amazement, Charlotte simply said, "Wow."

Brandi said, "This is exactly what I meant when I said you are one to watch! My next comment is that I want you to replace your title on this organizational chart!"

Despite all her powerhouse moves and enviable successes, Brandi was on board. Ready to move full steam ahead, Charlotte and Darby were now integral parts of the plan. Being a partner in this billion-dollar enterprise was going to be a game changer for all of them!

Darby closed her iPad, and the discussion took a turn.

Charlotte said, "I can hardly believe I am in this conversation. It wasn't that long ago that I was a completely different person." They found themselves discussing how they had each grown, personally, and agreed the impetus for growth had been the weekly meetings at DawnToday.

Just as they were talking about how strong the impact of those meetings had been, who walks into the room? Dawn. It seemed as if the coincidence was almost planned.

The waiter had recently left the door ajar after visiting the room to replenish their appetizers and drinks.

Walking by the open door, Dawn saw them and stopped to say hi. They invited her to join them, which she did. They jumped right in, bringing her up to speed about the day's events, their new venture, and how they were just discussing some of the positive results they had each experienced as a result of participating in the meetings.

"It's amazing what is accomplished and how truly powerful clothing and personal packaging is. People underestimate it all the time, but I will say that I have never seen or been told about an outcome like the one I am hearing about right now," Dawn affirmed.

Something clicked, and Brandi, Charlotte, and Darby locked eyes for a moment. It was eerie—and at the same time comforting—to know that after such a short time of knowing each other, they were in sync like this.

When Dawn excused herself to the restroom, it was Charlotte who spoke first, saying, "I don't know about you two, but I just had the best idea."

"Yes, she has to be a part of this!" Brandi blurted out.

Darby laughed. "Absolutely!"

Charlotte leaned forward and whispered, "I *thought* you two were thinking the same thing. I saw it in your eyes!" As if in relief, she leaned back in her chair.

When Dawn returned to the table, she had that feeling you get when you know someone has been talking *about* you instead of *to* you, and the eyes of the other three women confirmed it. As soon as she sat down, the conversation commenced.

The three of them took turns sharing that they would want to contract with DawnToday if this new idea came to be, and at this rate, it was looking more and more like a reality.

They wanted to know that she and her team would be an integral part of whatever it was they decided to build because it had changed the course of their lives, the people they interacted with, and those whom they would interact with in the future. They understood the importance and impact and wanted *this* for all their employees.

Together, the four of them could brainstorm about how to integrate the program. It could be part of the onboarding process, an ongoing quarterly development program, or take on some other form of implementation. For now, the important thing was that they agreed to continue the conversation about a partnership.

Dawn told them her own life had changed as well. Saying yes to Quinn and working with the firm had already proved to be profitable, and not just financially.

The exposure her company received as a result of this contract with the firm put her on the map. The company's calendar had always been consistent, and they previously worked primarily through referrals.

Now, the phones rang off the hook with everything from requests for interviews in local and national outlets to contract requests, speaking engagements, and even some high-profile clients (who remained un-named, of course) who wanted to hire her for private sessions for themselves and/or their teams.

"Quinn's choice to connect with me has been a game-changer!" Dawn confided.

"Quinn! Yes, we have to recruit her, too!" Brandi interjected. "I have watched her navigate some sticky situations over the years. She is phenomenal at her job. She is also consistently undervalued and overlooked. I can't imagine she wouldn't *leap* at an opportunity like this. It would allow her to be in a setting where she can really shine! She'll be outstanding at recruitment—bringing on only the best of the best."

"And we know she's resourceful," Darby added, nodding her head toward Dawn.

"Absolutely, she's the one who connected all of us," Charlotte said. "But, I wonder, is it legal? We don't want to poach her from the firm, so how can we handle this?" She knew there had to be some protocol involved.

"You're both right, on all counts," Brandi answered, adding, "She would be an asset, for sure! And Charlotte, you're right about the timing. We can't approach or proposition her just yet. Right now, she is still legally bound to report anything that's going on outside the realm of 'business as usual,' which this is most definitely not.

"We can continue to plan while we wait for the right date to approach her. We have to have our deck fully stacked before showing our hands. As soon as our matters are in order—our ducks are in a row—and the timing is right, she can be our first stop!"

Hashing out the details with the broadest brush possible, they closed down Bellemore that night, and history was made. Their company, now named Twenty-Four (24), was born. 2 + 4 = 24! 2 (Power of Clothing and Personal Packaging) + 4 (4 women—Brandi, Charlotte, Darby, and Dawn) = 24! A powerful equation and combination!

Final Thoughts and Closing Session

QUINN

As we embarked upon our last session, Dawn and her team made a point to revisit some of the key components of the Power of Clothing and Personal Packaging. Placed at our tables were discussion points on heavy cardstock 5x7 cards.

A few of the highlights were:

- Remember to dress for your body type.
- Be keenly aware of the messages you are sending to yourself and to others with the clothes you choose every day.
- Dress for the role you will play today.
- Your personal package will evolve, and you will too.
- The confidence you gain on the inside will radiate to the outside and shine an undimmable, magnetic light.
- It's important to have a team who supports you. This will help you reach your goals and achieve quantifiable success.
- As a result of your work, watch for barriers to move, doors to open, and situations to change. The changes lead to transformation.
- Remove as many obstacles to success as you can.
- Remember to stack the odds in your favor.

After a final round of Questions and Answers, we took a quick break, and then as she had so many times before, Dawn stood before us in the center of the room to greet us for the very last time.

"It has been a great pleasure meeting each of you. I trust that because of your commitment and hard work, along with the things you have learned here, not only will your careers be enhanced but that your lives have been changed for the better. I believe true change has happened for some and transformation for others. Don't stop. Keep going.

"For our closing exercise, I would like to share a few of the transformation stories you submitted. You have been a diligent group. You have consistently submitted your homework, and this last assignment did not disappoint. My team and I thoroughly enjoyed reading each and every one of your submissions. Thank you for being transparent and honest.

"A quick note to reiterate what was shared in the notes section of that assignment. My team and I have compiled your submissions and created a document that will arrive in your inbox within twenty-four hours. You can use them as additional learning tool and source of encouragement.

"You may be surprised at how much you have in common with other participants, so don't hesitate to connect with them to offer encouragement or ask for support. Your group's private online group will remain open, and it is a good place to continue conversations, post suggestions, and ask questions.

"If you want to continue learning about how to stack the odds in your favor, don't forget about the resources, gifts, and discount codes that were included in your packets during your first week with us.

"As a congratulations for completing your work here, we are sharing a discounted option to join one of the paid groups and/or courses that we host. It's a platform like Facebook but with more privacy.

"I go more in-depth about various topics, and we go through a Q and A session where I address your most pressing pre-submitted questions. The meetings are live, but they are recorded so you can access them at your convenience. I also pop into the group from time to time to interact with you via the comments. We want to continue to support you as you develop your own personal package!

"Okay, business aside. Let's get started with these transformation stories!

"I will be reading a summary of the submissions the team and I selected. They have been paraphrased, and the original author approved these shortened versions." Dawn said this with a heartwarming smile, and then read the submissions of Brandi, Charlotte, and Darby. What a coincidence. (I am smiling here. Are you?)

Transformation Story: Brandi

"Ladies and gentlemen, I present to you, the transformation story of your fellow classmate, Brandi St. James.

"Growing up, things like investing, the stock market, real estate, and other financial matters weren't common conversations around her house. But after her first classes in accounting, business, and banking, she was bitten by the money-bug.

"The more she learned, the more her passion for the subject grew. She wanted to master the subject and then teach it. Sharing the information with families like hers who were financially illiterate when it came to wealth-building would be life-changing for them.

"Growing up just below the middle-class income line, her commitment to studying and getting good grades, applying herself in a variety of academic clubs, and all-around hard work helped her gain access and exposure she would not have otherwise had. But this did not come easy, she had to work hard for each and every step she took.

"As a senior in high school, when opportunities to participate in off-campus corporate events were presented, she was often overlooked. It wasn't until she finally got in and joined these groups and clubs that she was made aware of how this could impact her future. There were things taught and shared here that weren't talked about in any other area she was in. This is where her interest in the money-topic began.

"She didn't always know the right thing to wear or how to present herself to show her interest in participating. Even if she did know what to wear, she didn't have the resources to make it happen. Despite this, she created opportunities to shine, and it made a difference.

"Seeing and experiencing first-hand that people saw the outside long before they saw the inside, she learned a quick lesson: judgments were made and conclusions were drawn about a person's intelligence and abilities based on this.

"So, she made a subconscious note that once she started making enough money, she would never be overlooked because of something so seemingly superficial as an outfit.

"There were many times in high school and in college that she out-ranked other applicants on paper, but somehow the confidence and charisma of the other applicants seemed to enter the room long before they did.

"If selected, they were often placed in small groups with represent-atives from the company. This gave the students an opportunity to ex-perience a 'day in the life' while being observed under the watchful eye of decision-makers, who would offer internships or permanent positions as par for the course.

"When the well-dressed and well-equipped students entered a room of decision-makers, what the applicants wore always seemed to make heads turn. Their confidence was bolstered, no doubt, because they carried a popular and easily recognizable work tote, and an equally stylish outfit.

"She was convinced that what they wore had everything to do with how people were treating them. These students received constant compliments about their outfits, how amazing they looked, and how they were a 'complete package' that represented the industry well. Brandi found it repeatedly frustrating that they weren't introduced by something quantifiable that showed their intelligence. Her impressive test and competency scores would have easily done the trick!

"Sharing more about her early experiences, she mentioned how other students seemed to be impacted by what they saw on the out-side, too. She said that she would watch as their eyes would wander to logo-heaven when they looked at some of the outfits. They seemed to have difficulty hearing and focusing on what was being said during class or in a group project because they were fixated on the outside, and she saw how this put her at a disadvantage. Having access to high-end material things led to popularity, and popularity seemed to out-weigh intelligence, more times than not.

"Now, I don't normally interrupt a transformation story, but I am going to pause here and ask how many of you remember my story about shopping for a school uniform, or my experience when I dressed like a 'nerd,'" Dawn said, using air quotes with one hand and then con-tinuing.

"Can you see how this comes into play? Even at these early ages, opinions and norms are being formed.

"Okay, sorry for the interruption. Let's get back to Brandi!" she said enthusiastically.

"In college, there was more of the same. However, at this point she was able to lead with her grades and not her outfits. Candidates had to prove they belonged in the proverbial room and use their intelli-gence—not just their looks. This wasn't always the case, but when it was, she had a fighting chance.

"Unfortunately, there were still times she didn't even get the chance to overcome what was happening on the outside. The interviewers had already made a snap judgment and chosen others to interview based on outside appearance.

"She wanted to overcome the memories of those negative situations. All the smirks, the sneers, and the pointing. The interviewers who overlooked her for opportunities, the repeated exclusion, and the people who laughed at her outfits. She was done with it!

"She decided that by creating a wardrobe bold enough to make heads spin, she would solve a multitude of problems. She was going to self-appoint herself a member of this secret and unidentified 'club' of people who dressed well and made things happen.

"Fast-forward to several years later and her career took a sharp turn. She became a hedge fund manager and was introduced to billion-dollar venture capitalists. In these circles, she found herself in a world where money flowed like a river, and she was keenly aware of the fixed number that comprised the small and intimate group. She also noticed who *wasn't* represented among this elite group. She was making large sums of money while lining the pockets of some of the wealthiest people in the country, and she was taking copious notes.

"As her income increased, so did her ability to buy any designer brand's pieces she wanted (and she did). Over time, the attention she received increased, which made her feel like she was now an official member of the 'club.'

"Somewhere along the way, things changed again and now people stared, and there was no doubt in her mind she was enviable. She had no idea it was often pure entertainment, judgment, or even pity that caused the looks, the glares, and the stares. Admittedly, she'd gone from one extreme to the other—from no logos to a walking, life-size, billboard for the designer of choice on a given day. She did not know that there were oftentimes she really did look ridiculous and out of touch.

"Pride and greed had gotten the best of her. These unwanted characteristics had gone from renting space in her life to taking up permanent residence.

"Let's jump ahead now and learn about her moving from an elitist-thinking executive back to the driven yet compassionate person she was at the beginning of her career.

"She says she lost sight of her original plans and loved the attention she got when amassing large purchases and how others in the store would look at her with a sense of wonder and quizzical amazement.

"In her mind, her outfits said, 'I'm important,' 'Look at me,' or 'I belong.' But in reality, they said, 'I'm insecure but smart, and I need you to notice me; validate me.'

"After she learned about the transformative Power of Clothing and Personal Packaging, she realized she had become a victim and she didn't even know it!

"Frequently taken advantage of by the sales associates who could see her (and her money) coming a mile away, there seemed to be no limit to what she would buy or wear.

"As her career continued to advance, she had racked up a list of sales associates across the country and a few outside of it. Most were helpful and sincere, and a few became arms-length friends. Some would call to let her know of new items by a particular designer. Telling her she just HAD TO HAVE them before they were gone appealed to her insecurity and fear of missing out. Eight, or even nine times out of ten, she would take the bait and buy.

"Sadly, she came across a share of bad apples who were only concerned about their sales numbers and commission. They saw her as an easy way to reach their goals, and she got caught in the crossfire.

"Often when she would try pieces on in-person, they didn't tell her when items didn't fit her well and were unflattering to her figure. This is something that she learned because of her time at DawnToday. She wanted to believe that maybe, just maybe, they didn't know. Perhaps they had not had any training in this area but were thrust into a position and told to perform. It wouldn't be the first time that has happened to an employee.

"She now knows that some of these associates are nice people who simply lacked the skill set to adequately advise her. She still valued their time, appreciated their sincerity, and didn't want to give up the convenience of having a personal stylist dedicated to a particular store. It saved hours of time, so she decided that going forward she would take a quick look online and then provide them with a wish list of sorts with the proper sizing.

"With a greater understanding of her body type and how sizing works, she was able to do this with ease. She knew the size number on the tag didn't mean much because it could vary quite a bit, even within the same brand. With that in mind, if there was any vacillating about a size or fit, she would order two, or even three, of an item. This plan included her tailor being on speed dial so she was sure to get a perfect fit!

"She considered approaching the managers of some of the stores to suggest they hire DawnToday to educate their team, but with everything on her plate right now, this would have to take a backseat. Thank you for the consideration," Dawn said with a smile.

"Brandi has now curated a wardrobe that adequately represents her and the messages she *wants* to send. She understands which pieces fit her well and how to highlight the areas she is most proud of. She noted in her story that she's not going to let all those early morning workouts go to waste!" Dawn added, and the comment was met with understanding and supportive laughter.

This response was unlike the giggles she had grown accustomed to hearing when she walked by. These have stopped now, by the way. She receives several compliments a day about her outfit selection, people smile at her instead of averting their eyes, and things have just started to feel right.

"During the course of these six weeks, she was able to focus on all the ways to use the Power of Clothing to her advantage and show she is intelligent, powerful, diligent, and more than ready to be a decision-maker on a completely different level.

"She says she is done waiting to be chosen and she's betting on herself. She attributes this to what she has learned here but also to others who have entered her life because of the meetings. These people saw in her what she hadn't seen in herself.

"Always willing to take one for the team, she has grown tired of being overlooked. She says she lost count of the number of times she had done the heavy lifting on a deal and the credit was given to someone else. This really stung when it went to someone whose talent or skill set was clearly not on the same level.

"But with this new sense of confidence, she was taking ownership of how she was being treated. She was betting on Brandi, and she believed in herself.

"Her interaction and overall responses at work have started to change. The role she decided to play now was once again one of the empowered woman. She was ready to face things head-on. In the past, she had let things slide without challenging them; just letting things flow. She hadn't wanted to cause any waves—to be disagreeable. But all that was changing.

"The partners at her firm saw this new, no-nonsense side of her and realized that they wouldn't be able to control her for much longer. As a result, she was slighted for a position, again. Initially it felt like all the times before—as a high school student, college student, intern, and employee-hopeful—but this time, things were different.

"Naturally, there are other details, changes that led to the transformation, but with limited time we'll jump to the end of her story.

"As it turns out, she has collaborated with a few other participants in the room to work on something substantial that's bound to have a big impact. I won't be sharing any details, but suffice it to say, it's a game-changer!

"Brandi now has the opportunity to get back to her original ideas. She will be in an industry that has the power to change lives; to change destinies. Her own life has changed dramatically, and she wants to use her knowledge to help other people, too.

"She has chosen a role, dresses the part, and presents a powerful package to the world. She's sending the right messages to herself and to others, doing what she loves, while being compensated very, very well. Congratulations, Brandi!"

Dawn asked Brandi to stand up, and she did. The room cheered and actually gave Brandi a standing ovation. Shocked, she was moved to tears, which led others to tear up with joy as well.

No more hard-shell exterior, the real Brandi Michele had been uncovered and was present in the room, and quite frankly, she was pretty amazing!

Transformation Story: Charlotte

After everyone settled back into their seats. Dawn addressed the room again.

"Okay, let's move on to our next transformation story. Friends, I will now present to you the abridged version of the Charlotte Whitlock transformation story.

"Charlotte started out with ambitious goals and dreams but got sidelined by love. It was this love that led her to the exciting joy of becoming a mom, albeit a little earlier than planned. Willingly and lovingly, she put a pin in her career for what was supposed to be a few years and had now turned into ten.

"When it came to money, her mother's constant comments about the subject while she was growing up were about things like money not growing on trees, or the disingenuous demeanor or character of people who did have money. These were just a few of the thoughts that had settled into her psyche in ways she wasn't even aware.

"She bought her first designer suit as an act of celebration and to wear for her fast-approaching post-grad-school interview and acceptance into law school. After meeting her new in-laws and family-to-be, she discovered a world of kind people with money, and lots of it. They dressed well; very well, in fact. And she was sure that this was part of the reason she decided to buy her first Hugo Boss suit for women.

"Her mother had an absolute fit, and Charlotte knew she would likely never hear the end of her disapproval about the purchase.

"As she settled into married life, and soon after, mom life, she had the financial resources to buy what she wanted. But, because she had never been a clothes horse and because of the constant negative comments about money while growing up, she still bought the bare minimum.

"She would always keep things 'modest and appropriate,' which her mother had said was a requirement for a woman of her financial position—the wife of a prominent attorney, daughter-in-law of a sitting judge, and of course, a mom.

"What filled her closet was often referred to as 'soccer mom' attire.

"While some women in her social circle couldn't get enough of the logos or current trends, she was never one to get on board.

"She always looked nice and she had the occasional dresses for family gatherings—like the brunch where she had met her husband's family for the first time, and she also had a few things for the required formal dinners that came up throughout the year.

"Interestingly, the invitations extended to her to attend galas and fundraisers weren't as common toward the end of her ten-year marriage, and now she knew why.

"At first, she took it personally and considered looking into one of those personal sales associates or stylists she'd heard other ladies, including her mother-in-law, talk about but...Did you catch that?" Dawn said, asking this rhetorical question of the group with a knowing smile—bringing attention to Charlotte's comment about stylists.

"Her husband was having an affair, and she now knew that there had been more than one time he had crossed the line. She'd stopped the information source—who seemed to know far too much about the situation—from sharing any more of the details when she heard about instance number three."

Several people shifted in their seats—likely due to the uneasiness of identifying with Charlotte's circumstance as Dawn kept reading. It almost seemed as though Dawn was uncomfortable too because her pace increased while she shared that part of the story, but she continued nonetheless.

"Immediately after filing for a divorce, Charlotte made the decision to return to the workforce, but her confidence had been misplaced by timidity. The former high-achieving and competitive woman who entered law school a year ahead of schedule and landed a coveted internship that came with a high-ranking position upon graduation was nowhere to be found.

"The person who headed to the workforce was seemingly unsure of herself and the fact that she applied for a position well beneath her qualifications spoke to her insecurity.

"Now, after having consumed every word of these sessions, taking heed to the points raised in the POC Five Mistakes email, and embracing every opportunity for personal growth, she was a new person.

"The transformation was apparent, and people commented about it regularly. Where had this 'new' woman come from? The woman full of confidence, wit, and wisdom? She knew it was really just an improved version of the woman she was before she married her now ex-husband.

"Not only did she gain the confidence to apply for a position within the firm that was on par with her education, experience, and skill set, but much to her mother's chagrin, she had broken out the $1,500 Hugo Boss suit that hung at the back of the closet.

"She wore it with the confidence that said she believed in herself. But she didn't stop there. She has also been encouraged and supported by fellow participants to complete her last required class and to sit for the bar exam to complete what she started a decade ago. Based on her previous work ethic, grades, and intelligence, she is sure that she will pass the bar with flying colors!

"She is now in collaboration with some big-money folks and a proud partner and co-owner of a female-owned business. To add to this excitement, the company is projected to be among the top one hundred on *Forbes' Global 2000* list in the next five years.

"She attributes her personal transformation to the confidence she rediscovered along with the Power of Clothing and Personal Packaging."

When Dawn stopped reading, Charlotte was asked to stand, and with the confidence of an attorney approaching a jury to present closing arguments, she rose, waved, and smiled as we all cheered her on wildly!

Transformation Story: Darby

"For our final transformation story of the day, please join me in this short synopsis about your fellow classmate, Darby," Dawn said, interrupting the rumble of conversation and continuing on.

"Growing up in a culture where beauty and opulence were a regular occurrence, seeing beautiful things was never a shock for Darby. Dressing to stand out was part of her culture. It was something expected, especially for special occasions. There were no negative connotations, thoughts of self-indulgence, or judgments from others about being self-centered or too flashy.

"This being the norm, as a teenager and well into her adult life, Darby found this to be an area she could express her personal opinions about things she didn't agree with. To distance herself from the parts of her culture she found controlling, frustrating, unfair, and outdated (in her opinion), she showed her disapproval by dressing to blend in with mainstream American culture, instead of standing out. Where there was an inch to be taken when it came to getting dressed for an event you could be sure she was going to take a mile—and on the longest, slowest road she could find.

"She wasn't a clothes horse, for sure, but she was consistent in her approach to getting dressed. No frills, nothing out of the ordinary, just plain, simple, and easy.

"When her mother offered to take her shopping for her current job,

Darby insisted on inexpensive, trendy, fast fashion like she had all through college. They went to H&M and Zara, sticking with the neutrals—nothing flashy—and then concluded with pieces from Gap for a few basics. All the while, her mother repeatedly suggested they go to Nordstrom to create a 'fresh start' for her new career. Her mom didn't let up and she suggested Darby work with *her* personal shopper in the store who was sure to find some 'lovely things.'

"Darby was frustrated because she knew things could definitely move faster with the help of a personal shopper. She also knew that if she said yes to a trip to Nordstrom, her mom would suggest they walk by the formal dress department to 'take a quick peek.'

"If that wasn't the case, she would have her personal shopper gather dresses from that department in her size and have them waiting in the dressing room. Inevitably, this would lead to a conversation about her returning to meet the 'handsome Indian man' her father had chosen for her to marry once she finished her studies and got settled in her career.

It was beyond Darby as to why a woman would go through the arduous process of studying for good grades, landing a promising internship, and receiving a coveted, high-paying job—only to leave it all because her father had lined up a husband!

"The husband and his family would make the decision as to whether the new bride would continue to work. If she did, there was always the chance she would be told to quit. Of course, there were exceptions but this wasn't a chance she was willing to take. Thankfully, it wouldn't even be an issue to address because she had no intention of following this path—which is how she found herself here, at DawnToday.

"The company she works for has an internship program and she is proud to say she implemented the tools she learned here to secure a future there. But she wasn't sure if she wanted it.

"What she did know, without a doubt, was that her family didn't represent the whole of any culture. Every family is different. Unfortunately for her, she was born into one who didn't see the irony in this age-old process of finding a *suitable man* for every woman.

"She wouldn't be expected to move back to India. No, her parents would argue they were much more progressive than that.

"'Progressive' wasn't exactly the word Darby would use to describe them or their approach to life when it came to women, and specifically, where it pertained to marriage.

"Sure, her parents were both doctors and very successful in their own rights. They had embraced a lot of American culture, been recognized in a few medical journals, risen in their careers, and they seemed to live a comfortable life. But at the end of the day, they were tied to tradition and believed that an Indian woman should be married to a man of her father's choosing.

"In her parents' words, her marriage to this man would be 'equally beneficial for both families,' but Darby wanted nothing to do with it. She would much prefer both families find another way to *equally benefit*. Preferably one that didn't involve her signing her life away to a stranger and forfeiting everything she had worked for.

"So, with all this swirling in her head, she avoided Nordstrom with her mom and continued to push back against anything that reminded her in any way, shape, or form of what she was trying to get away from. The grandiose—and, in her opinion, unnecessary—adorning of women. That was a reminder she did not want.

"It wasn't until she attended the sessions here at DawnToday that she learned about the scientifically proven POC and PP. She became convinced that there is more to what a person chooses to wear than just the clothes themselves and that it has the power to impact a life. In this case, the life was hers!

"With a large number of science classes and research studies under her belt, data was something she had great respect for. It quantified a hypothesis—basically, supporting a claim with evidence.

"This information shared wasn't tied to tradition or emotion, just facts. What she was being shown about the topic proved to be undeniable. There was so much she had been missing out on simply because of the way she chose to dress and present herself in the world.

"Not one to waste time, she dove into the deep end of the pool, taking in every detail, rarely coming up for air. She was convinced that this was a way to take control of an outcome, and with that, she embraced all the meetings, assignments, extracurricular opportunities, and even social events.

"Not only did she experience changes as a result, these changes led to a personal transformation. She attributes that transformation to at least four major outcomes.

"The first is that she was accepted into the highly competitive career-boosting mentorship program at work. This news alone would be a game-changer, but there is more!

"Second, the changes and ultimately the transformation had spilled over into her personal life as well. She was now ready to have a potentially life-altering conversation with her parents. We are avoiding the finite details about how or when this will happen, but she outlines this in her story. Suffice it to say, she now has the confidence and resources—both emotionally and financially—to support her in making a decision that may have a ripple effect on generations that follow.

"Next, if all went well with that conversation, she thought it would be the perfect time to share that she is currently seeing someone. That someone is not only from a different race, he is someone with whom she has become quite serious and sees being in her life for the foreseeable future.

"She is prepared to go against the grain. Earning a favorable position, title, and income at a highly respected firm would be meaningful, for sure, but the news of her next announcement would definitely move the needle in her favor.

"This last and final piece of information, the fourth outcome of which she is most proud, would likely rock their world. She would be telling her parents she was part of a business venture backed by some of the country's most prominent figures in wealth management. Showing them the projections, the buy-in from some of the biggest venture capitalists on the scene, and upcoming articles in *Kiplinger, Baron's, and Investor's Business Daily* were the kinds of tangible evidence that they would want to see.

"At this point in her life, Darby has come to see that they want her to be safe and to be happy. They also wanted to be proud. Knowing they could go back to the family they had chosen her to marry into with this kind of announcement would be huge for them.

"Also knowing they could live their lives in harmony—her, her parents, her boyfriend, and his family would be the icing on the cake.

"She came full circle at the end of her story to share how the small changes were some of the biggest changes, and that she was excited to share with both families the concepts of the life-changing Power of Clothing and Personal Packaging.

"Darby is sure of something else. Just like the discussions she has had with her boyfriend about change and transformation, the two of them were going to do just that. They were going to make changes and transform lives by example. They would pave the way, and be trail-blazers for people in similar situations. She would be someone else's Indra Nooyi! A role model and an inspiration. They were making a real difference in the world—in more than one way!

At the time, Darby had wondered why Brandi teared up when Dawn asked her to stand. Now she understood.

When Dawn asked her to stand, the tears came. She stood and in-stinctively started waving with an undeniable grace and charm that seemed almost regal. This, along with her smile, made it obvious it was something inborn, and that there was still more to Darby we didn't know.

The room was electric! The more she waved, the more she cried. It was like weights were being lifted. We clapped and cheered some more, and she kept waving, in that princessy sort of way. I think she surprised herself! What was going on? She couldn't escape it, and now she no longer wanted to. Is she actually an Indian Princess? That is what we all want to know! After all, this wouldn't be the first time she kept a secret from us!

"Congratulations, Darby!"

After reading all three transformation stories, Dawn paused, clearly moved as she congratulated everyone in the room.

"Even if I didn't read your personal transformation story out loud," she said, "it doesn't make it any less valuable. All the submissions we read embodied tremendous growth and we are honored to have been part of it."

Dawn reminded us that even if our stories didn't *seem* to be as moving or to have huge outcomes *yet*, that we shouldn't despair—they were in the making!

"Every step you take moves you forward. You're not the same person you were when you started. If you are putting in the work then you are growing, every single day!" she said.

"As our time together officially comes to a close, I can't let you go without sharing a few more words of encouragement. These are a few of *my* personal confidence cards. Yep, I use them too! As a parting gift, we've had some made just for you. I hope you find them helpful. Let me read them to you.

- At first, they will ask you why, then they will ask you how.
- I will never beg someone to keep me on their team. I know my value and I know my worth.
- Go where you are loved.
- Know when to pivot.
- Never explain. Those who matter don't mind, and those who mind don't matter.

"You've got this!" Dawn told us with so much excitement and joy that it made it easy to believe it! "This may be the end of the meetings but at the same time, it is just the beginning!"

We saw a few tears, some high-fives, and a few quick hugs as this life-changing series came to a close as Dawn spoke the final words.

"Don't be a stranger, and remember that your brighter future begins when?!" And, as if on cue, we all yelled out, "TODAY! My Brighter Future Begins Today! DawnToday!"

For the last thirty years, Dawn has been the "secret weapon" brought in to help women in companies like Delta, Honeywell, and McDonald's, and she has been the "quiet force" behind the life changes experienced by tens of thousands of women across the US. What is her secret? She helps women to understand how to leverage what she calls "The Power of Clothing and Personal Packaging," and shows them how to get that little-known power working *for* them, instead of *against* them.

She and her husband of thirty-three years (and counting) share four adult children whom they love and adore. Their family number is twenty-four (24) and they currently reside in the Midwest.

Instagram: @mydawntoday

LinkedIn: www.linkedin.com/in/dawn-thibodeaux-746950192

Website: Dawntoday.org

Email: info@dawntoday.org

Podcast: Find DawnToday on Apple, Spotify or wherever you love to
    listen

Book Club Discussion Questions

1. What do you think about Darby's candor as she suggested that Charlotte and Brandi start their own wealth management company? Do you think she overstepped? What would your approach have been?

2. Have you ever been in a situation where you had to present uncomfortable information? What impact did it have on the relationship?

3. Is there a character you most closely resonate with? What is it about her that feels familiar?

4. Darby had mentors she never met but she used them as inspiration and motivation. Who are the people who fulfill this role for you? What are you doing that makes you this person for someone else?

5. When Charlotte was going through the transition from married to divorced, she took up running as a way to expend emotions and replenish her energy. How does having an outlet impact the progress and process of moving through life-altering circumstances? What are some tools you use?

6. When the Post-It note activity was in play, did you have any ideas about what each of the ladies may have received as feedback? Do you have any ideas about what people may say about the messages *you* are sending with your clothes and personal package?

7. Dan Kennedy's insight into the power of a personal package lets us see how he had a particular outfit for speaking, one for selling, and one for each region of the country. Do you have a wardrobe of costumes you rotate through? Is this a conscious choice or were you made aware of this subconscious behavior after reading about it in the book?

8. How do find that you react to a person who is wearing the "wrong" costume for the task at hand? What would your response be if you arrived at your next doctor appointment, and she walked in the room dressed as a sheet metal worker or circus clown?

9. While reading about body types, did you identify yours? Do your fellow book club members agree?

10. Have you ever used a stylist? What was the outcome? What referrals, if any, can you share with your fellow book club members?

11. As a result of Brandi's personal closet audit, she uncovered many pieces that weren't right for her. She ended up with several pieces that she later shared with Darby and Charlotte. What would happen if your group did a clothing and accessories swap? If that isn't feasible, which charity(ies) that specifically support women can you donate to as a group? Whether a clothing swap or donation drive, remember: no dented cans of pinto beans!

12. What is your previous experience and familiarity with the POC & PP?

13. What messages were you taught about how to dress, what to wear, etc.?

14. Share some of your biggest takeaways about the POC & PP with your fellow book club members.

15. How confident are you in your own personal package?

16. What message do you want to send to the world when you walk out of the door?

17. What limiting beliefs do you have about the power of clothing and personal packaging?

18. What is your plan to irradicate those limiting thoughts?

19. If you don't have any limiting thoughts about this, what is your plan to continue, increase, and enhance your confidence in this area? Who will support you and hold you accountable?

20. If you could ask Dawn, at DawnToday, a question, what would it be?

Thanks for reading and don't forget,
Your Brighter Future Begins Today!
DawnToday!

Acknowledgments

I have helped thousands of women find confidence and a new outlook on life through the little-known power of clothing and personal packaging. However, I knew I could help millions more by writing a book.

And while it's only the first of many, it's finally done.

So I wanted to say thank you to the important people in my life who helped to make publishing my first book a reality.

Thank you to my grandmother and great-aunt who were both living examples of The Power of Clothing.

Thank you to my mom and my Rudi—my biggest fans, wildest cheerleaders, and supporters extraordinaire. Without you, where would I be?

Thank you to my adult children—Kyle Rufus, Arielle Kapri, Parker Daniel, & Lexington Grace who make AAFNMW! And #24! Possible.

Thank you to my sister, Tiffane, my "person," whose unconditional support means the world.

And thank you to all those who consistently checked in and cheered me on. Your notes and surprise gifts are treasured in my heart forever.

Thank you to my editor, Susie—truly, an answer to prayer.

And last, but certainly not least, thank you to the more than 20,000 women who were my personal clients. By allowing me to win your trust I was able to learn from you while you learned from me.

Made in the USA
Las Vegas, NV
30 April 2023